GRIND

THE ALPHA ESCORT SERIES

SYBIL BARTEL

Copyright © 2017 by Sybil Bartel

ISBN-13: 978-1548285548

Cover art by: CT Cover Creations, www.ctcovercreations.com

Cover photo by: Adobe Stock Photos

Edited by: Hot Tree Editing, www.hottreeediting.com

Formatting by: Champagne Book Design

All rights reserved. No part of this publication may be reproduced, distributed, or transmitted in any form or by any means, including photocopying, recording, or other electronic or mechanical methods, without the prior written permission of the author, except in the case of brief quotations embodied in critical reviews and certain other noncommercial uses permitted by copyright law.

All characters in this book have no existence outside the imagination of the author and have no relation whatsoever to anyone bearing the same name or names. They are not even distantly inspired by any individual known or unknown to the author, and all incidents are pure invention.

Warning: This book contains offensive language, alpha males and sexual situations. Mature audiences only. 18+

Books by Sybil Bartel

The Alpha Escort Series
THRUST
ROUGH
GRIND

The Uncompromising Series
TALON
NEIL
ANDRÉ
BENNETT
CALLAN

The Alpha Bodyguard Series
SCANDALOUS
MERCILESS
RECKLESS
RUTHLESS
FEARLESS
CALLOUS
RELENTLESS

The Alpha Antihero Series
HARD LIMIT
HARD JUSTICE
HARD SIN

The Unchecked Series
IMPOSSIBLE PROMISE
IMPOSSIBLE CHOICE

IMPOSSIBLE END

The Rock Harder Series
NO APOLOGIES

Join Sybil Bartel's Mailing List to get the news first on her upcoming releases, giveaways and exclusive excerpts! You'll also get a FREE book for joining!

GRIND

Dane

I'm silent. I'm trained. I'm lethal.

My hand skimming down your thigh, my gaze a weapon—I know more ways to kill you than please you.

But you're not paying for my aim. You're paying for my control. Bringing you a breath away from ecstasy, watching you beg as I hold back your release, I'll show you exactly what you've been missing. Your hunger is my currency, and five thousand is my price. I only have one rule—no repeats, because I'm not for keeps. I'm for sale.

One slow grind and I'll give you exactly what you paid for.

DEDICATION

To my husband—
You should probably skip this one too.

ONE

Dane

I GRIPPED HER HAIR WITH MY GOOD ARM. "TAKE A BREATH."
She licked her lips and inhaled.
I shoved my dick into her mouth.
Naked, on her knees, she moaned as her fingers dug into my thighs.
"Suck," I demanded.
Her cheeks hollowed, and I ignored the burn of pain in my side. A stitched-up knife wound and a bullet graze were child's play compared to the number of times I'd been shot, stabbed, blown up or left for dead.
I tightened my hold on her hair. "You want to be fucked?"
Her hands moved to my ass and she groaned around my cock.
I knew what she wanted. It's what all my clients wanted. To be fucked until she came so many times, her legs gave out. "Get up."
Her lips slid off my dick and she stood without a word. She wasn't a talker, and neither was I, except to issue commands and bark out orders.
"On the coffee table." I wasn't going to stay long enough to fuck her on the bed.

She crawled on the table and got on her hands and knees. Too bad I didn't do repeats. She was submissive as hell, and my dick was rock-hard. Pulling a condom out of my pocket, I tore the corner with my teeth and had to roll it on one-handed thanks to the fucking mark I'd taken out two hours ago. I'd stupidly let my guard down for one second, and the prick had made his last move. I gave zero fucks about ending that asshole's life.

Concentrating on the brunette in front of me, I ran two fingers through her soaked cunt. "You ready?"

"Wait." It was the first time she'd spoken since I'd knocked on the hotel room door.

My fingers on her clit, I stilled. "What?"

She shivered, then looked over her shoulder at me. "Why only once?"

Brown hair, brown eyes, she could have been any woman when she opened the door. But on her knees, her ass out, looking over her shoulder like she couldn't wait to have a piece of me, she was everything I stayed away from.

"You know the rules. No repeats." I warned every client before I took their money.

She bit her bottom lip, and her voice turned quiet. "I'll pay you again."

I stepped back and pulled the condom off. "No." I didn't fuck for money because I needed the cash. I charged women for sex because that's how I liked it—no attachments.

Her gaze cut to my dick. "What are you doing?"

Not fucking her. "Get dressed."

Her eyebrows drew together as her face twisted with confusion. "Why?"

"You're going home."

She sat up. "Because I asked to see you again?"

"Yes." They usually waited until after I fucked them before they begged for a repeat. I yanked my zipper up.

She slid off the coffee table, dropped to her knees and reached for my cock.

Unspent adrenaline from tonight's kill coursing through my veins, I reacted. My hand was on her throat and my thumb under her jawbone quicker than she could gasp. Applying pressure, I dropped my voice to a lethal warning. "You suicidal?"

Fear widened her eyes and she swallowed. "What?"

"Did I say you could touch me?" I didn't wait for an answer. "Did I tell you to get on your knees?" I was wound so fucking tight, I had no business taking her money. I should've been paying her to take the goddamn edge off, but my text had been clear. *Hard cock, demanding orders, no repeats, five grand.* She'd agreed. She should've stuck to the fucking script.

"No," she whispered.

"Right answer." The line between my two jobs blurring, I dropped my hand. "Get out." I didn't deal with this kind of bullshit.

She glanced toward the windows. "But a storm's coming."

I didn't give a fuck what the weather was doing. "Then you stay." My hand itching to wrap around my gun, I walked the hell out, leaving her money behind.

Forty-five minutes later, I'd picked my dog up from the kennel and I was standing in my driveway, staring at lights I didn't leave on in my house.

I called the person responsible.

Alex Vega, a Marine I'd served with, had hit me up and asked to use my place when I was in the middle of my last job. Distracted, I'd agreed.

Vega picked up on the second ring. He didn't bother with a greeting. "Where are you?"

The wind kicked up and I scanned the tree line. "All the lights are on in my house."

"You said I could use it for three days," he reminded me. "What are you doing, standing outside?"

I was going to take another job right after the one today, but getting shot and stabbed threw me off schedule. "In the driveway." I couldn't see shit inside my house because all the storm shutters were down, but light filtered through the cracks at the edges. "Who is it?"

"Irina," he clipped.

Vega had turned to escorting after we'd gotten out of the Marines. For the past three years, he and Jared Brandt, another one of our Marine buddies he'd recruited into the business, had been making bank. So much so that they'd been giving me their overflow. Vega made the contacts, Brandt took the ones who wanted to play rough, and I handled the ones they were too busy to fit into their schedules. I used the women to unwind after my other jobs, and the money I charged let them know I wasn't for keeps. We all made out.

"The client," I confirmed what he'd said when he'd called earlier.

He hesitated, then gave me a clipped response. "I'm out."

I read between the lines. "You quit?"

"Yeah."

Damn. Alex Vega lived for the money he made escorting. "Because of the woman in my house?" I couldn't think of a reason he'd quit besides a woman or a legal problem.

"Unrelated."

The air snapped with the electricity of an impending

storm. "Another woman." It had to be. He was being cagey as fuck, and if it was a legal issue, he would've said first thing.

He didn't confirm or deny it. "I thought you were out of town for a few days."

I counted the different tire tracks leading up my driveway. "Plans changed."

"She's on the other line. What do you want me to tell her?"

I was over dealing with women clients today, and I sure as hell didn't want to deal with his fucking castoff. But the lights on in my house said I didn't have a choice if I wanted to sleep in my own bed. "She stable?" I didn't do crazy.

"Yeah. Just spoiled as fuck. You deal with this, I'll owe you."

"You already owe me." I didn't like women at my house. I didn't like anyone at my house except my dog. It was my fucking sanctuary.

"I'll tell her she has twenty-four hours."

I glanced at the sky. The storm would have passed by then and I could ignore anyone for twenty-four hours. Resigned, I agreed. "Copy." But I wanted to know what the hell I was walking in to. "Parameters?" Normally I didn't ask when I took the overflow clients from him or Brandt, because I could handle my own shit. But I was too damn tired to guess at what I was dealing with.

"None," Vega clipped.

"Tell her I'm coming in through the garage." I didn't want to get fucking shot twice today.

"Done. Thanks." Vega hung up.

With one last look around my property, I got back in my truck, and Hunter whined. "Yeah, I know." I scratched his ears. "We got company and a storm's coming. It's gonna be a long night." He put his head on my leg as I pulled into the garage and cut the engine. I took a few seconds to scan the security feeds of the surveillance system on my house from my cell phone app, but I didn't see anything other than Vega dropping her off earlier.

I glanced at Hunter as I shoved my cell in my pocket and gave him a warning. "Behave." Then I walked into my house with a German shepherd on my heels.

I didn't know what the fuck I was expecting, but it wasn't a stunning blonde.

With pale blue eyes and the face of an angel, she stood at the kitchen counter and did to me what no woman had done since I was eighteen—she made me pause.

She was fucking beautiful.

Hunter growled low and quiet, kicking my ass out of my stupor.

Mentally shaking myself, I did what I was trained to do. I cataloged. I scanned the room and her in under a second. No weapon, no bra, coffee had been made in the last hour, the door to the linen closet was open and she was fucking young. Memories of my past mistakes came at me like a goddamn blast wave.

Her phone to her ear, she glared at me. "Who are you?"

Accent, twenties, attitude, inherent fear—I guessed Russian.

My stare intent, I zeroed in on her. "Dane. Tell Vega all clear."

Her shoulders turned and she looked away. "Alex," she whined in a quiet panic.

"Hang up," I demanded.

Her eyes cut to Hunter, but she did as she was told, and ended the call. "Who is that?"

Hunter growled louder.

I snapped my fingers and issued a command. "Hunter, go lie down."

She tracked my hundred-and-twenty-pound canine as he obediently went to his bed against the far wall. "He looks like a hunter."

Fuck, she looked like my ex-wife. "He is. What are you doing here?" She had white-blonde hair, and ice-blue eyes that were almost colorless. She was too thin, but she was so damn beautiful she took my breath away. The sight of her standing in my house fucked with my head, and memories of a life I used to have surfaced.

She inhaled and fear crossed her features before she covered it with attitude. "Alex said I could be here."

I buried my past and studied her. "This is my house."

"So?" Her arms crossed. "You want me to ask nicely?" She bit the last word out with forced attitude.

She didn't look spoiled, she looked afraid. "Tell me why you're here." Expensive clothes, delicate features, she wasn't a woman who had nowhere to go.

"Because Alex decided to play house with someone else."

I looked for telltale signs of jealousy. "You in love with him?"

Her attitude morphed into defiance and her accent disappeared as she spat an explanation out. "He's a manwhore. I fucked him for three years because my husband paid for it. Only stupid women fall for unavailable men. Anything else you want to know?"

My dick pulsed at the thought of getting her under me,

but I shoved down the notion and picked up on the important part of her info dump. "You fuck your husband?" I'd ask what happened to her accent later.

 A faint blush hit her cheeks. "No."

 Calculated, slow, I moved toward the kitchen island separating us. Right-handed, I pulled my 9mm out of the holster at my back, set it on the counter and lowered my voice. "Why are you lying?"

 She eyed the gun, but she didn't back up. "I don't fuck him. His dick is useless."

 I didn't take my hand off my piece. "There's more than one way to fuck a woman."

 Her chest rose with an inhale, her face went blank and her accent showed back up. "I am tired with these questions. You want to shoot me? Shoot. You can't make this day any worse." She smirked. "Unless you want to fuck me."

 I dropped my gaze to her small, but perfect breasts. "I don't fuck for free."

 She snorted out a laugh. "Of course you don't."

 "I also don't fuck used merchandise." It was a lie. I didn't give a fuck, but I threw it out there hoping my brain would pick up on it and listen to reason, because my dick sure as hell wasn't.

 This time her cheeks went red. "You're an asshole. No wonder you're Alex's friend."

 "And you're his client."

 She scoffed. "Was. Past tense."

 "You still belong to someone." She hadn't used past tense when she'd mentioned her husband.

 She didn't deny it. "That's not a question."

 "How long has your husband owned you?" She was

cover-model gorgeous and she was all attitude. She was someone's toy.

"He doesn't own me."

Bullshit. "He paid for you." One way or another.

"No, he didn't."

He did, and she didn't look like property a man would easily part with. "He know where you are?"

"He kicked me out," she quickly rattled off the excuse. "He doesn't care where I am."

She was lying. I could see it in her eyes. "What's your name?" I asked, testing her.

"What's yours?" she countered.

"You know what it is." I shouldn't have engaged in conversation with her, let alone given a shit about her lying to me, but something was off and I wanted to know what it was.

"Dane what?"

I eyed her, wondering why she was being cagey. "You first."

Her shoulders squared, but not with pride. "Irina Tsarko Fedorov."

I stilled.

Fedorov.

Viktor Fedorov.

The Russian mafia's biggest arms dealer in the States. Viktor Fedorov, the gun runner who rumor had it was fucking impotent from a deranged sex slave who'd broken his dick as revenge.

That Viktor Fedorov.

And his wife was standing in my kitchen.

Jesus Christ.

I stared, but every sense I had went on high alert. I listened. I smelled her perfume. I cataloged everything in my peripheral vision as I went through a mental checklist. Exterior lights not tripped, outer perimeter breached twice, Vega's McLaren on the video feed both times, back property not breached, interior motion sensors deactivated, the access road's only recorded traffic was me and Vega.

I scanned the living room then I looked at her, really looked, because Fedorov had a reputation for being a sick fuck.

No bruising, no nervous glancing, no blood.

My gaze cut to the cell phone in her hand.

Fuck. *Fuck.*

"Give me your phone," I demanded.

She pulled it closer. "No."

"How long ago did you leave your husband?" How long had he been tracking her to my goddamn house?

"I told you, he kicked me out."

If I were him, I'd retrieve her before the worst of the storm hit. One, maybe two hours, then the roads wouldn't be passable. He'd have to wait until tomorrow. *Goddamn it.*

My jaw ticked and I fought to keep from ripping the cell from her hands. "Listen closely, because I'm only going to say this once." I leveled her with a deadly look. "If you're married to Viktor Fedorov, give me your phone right fucking now or walk out of my house."

She slid her phone across the counter.

I grabbed it, disabled the Wi-Fi and pulled the back off to look for a physical tracker. Nothing. I powered it down then pulled out the SIM card.

"What are you doing?" she snapped.

I ignored her question. "How long have you been here?" I could check the time stamp on the feeds on my phone, but asking was quicker.

She glanced at the clock on the oven, but she didn't answer.

"*How long?*" I barked.

She flinched. "A couple hours."

"Has he called?"

"No."

I threw her phone and SIM back on the counter. "Don't turn it on." Not that it mattered. He already knew where she was. "Have you ever run before?"

"I am done telling you that he wanted me to leave, not the other way around." The attitude in her tone started to falter under the weight of her bullshit.

Every word out of her mouth was lie, and Vega was a fucking idiot. "Three years?"

"What?" Her hands twisted.

"You fucked Vega for three years while being married to Viktor Fedorov?" And Vega never questioned who her husband was or why he paid for it?

She tried to glare at me. "I'm not repeating myself."

So she'd said, but I saw right fucking through her. "Did he ever make you come?" She was all show, no substance. I threw the question out to purposely take her off guard.

She didn't fall for it. "Let me guess, you're some kind of sick pervert who gets off on watching other people fuck?"

"I don't have to watch to know you never had a real orgasm." Too much adrenaline for one day, the storm kicking into high gear, I was out of patience. "I'm going to secure the house. You want to lie about why you're here, fine. But know this, anyone who steps foot on my property, I will fucking shoot." I holstered my gun and whistled for Hunter. He ran to the door and whined for me to open it. "Patrol." I issued the command and let him outside.

Panic finally laced the blonde's voice. "Wait! Where are you going? I closed the shutters."

I didn't spare her a glance. "I noticed." I walked out.

The wind blew bands of rain sideways as I walked across the yard to the barn. Hunter ran the perimeter like I'd trained him to do, then beat me to the barn door. "Good boy." I let us in then pulled the brace down across the heavy wood door. Not that it would stop an armed man, but it'd stop a spoiled blonde.

Kicking two pallets aside, I pulled on the trap door to my command center, and pain shot up my side. "Goddamn it," I grunted.

Hunter nervously paced.

"It's fine, come on. Downstairs." I bit out the command, and Hunter descended the steps in front of me. I gritted my teeth and shut the hundred-and-fifty pound hatch door with my good arm. Thirty seconds later, all my monitors were on. I scanned the security feeds and checked all the access point warnings. Thankfully nothing new had shown up since I'd checked my mobile security app.

I typed an encrypted e-mail one-handed, confirming today's assignment, then I waited two minutes to check the balance on the account number I'd provided. An eight-hundred-thousand dollar deposit appeared, and I diverted the funds to four different accounts.

I sat back in my chair and rubbed a hand over my face. "What do you think, Hunter?"

Hunter whined.

"Agree. She's fucking trouble."

He nudged my side and barked once.

I looked down. Blood soaked through my wet shirt.

TWO

Irina

H E WAS A THOUSAND TIMES SCARIER THAN VIKTOR. Huge shoulders, rippling muscles, perfectly cut features as if carved by an artist's hand, Dane was the most beautiful yet frightening man I'd ever seen. His intense gaze was ruthless. His cold detachment was that of a killer, but it was his commanding presence that had me terrified. He was so authoritative, he made me want to kneel at his feet, and that was a dangerous, slippery slope for someone like me.

Despite the comment he'd thrown out about fucking, I knew he wasn't an escort, not like the man my husband had sent me to for three years. Alex Vega lived for the money he made fucking women. But instinct told me Dane couldn't care less about the money. No, he wasn't an escort. Just like the bodyguards my husband hired to protect him, Dane had the markings of a killer. I'd stake my life on it. He had blood on his hands as sure as I had lies on my lips, and that threw me into a panic.

I didn't want to stay there another second.

But where was I going to go? Viktor had alienated me from all of my friends five years ago. My mother had more loyalty to Viktor than she did to me, and I didn't have two cents to my name.

I stared at the carnage of my phone, and defeat rose like bile in my throat. Before I could change my mind, I grabbed the pieces of my phone and put it back together. Dread crawled up my spine, and I did something I'd sworn I would never do again. I called my husband.

"You can't run." Viktor's sick laugh filled my head. "I know where you are, pet."

"Come get me." I tried to convince myself it was better to be with the enemy you know.

He spoke in Russian on purpose.

"You know I don't understand what you're saying."

His tone bled false patience. "How many times have I told you to learn the language of your heritage?"

He was in one of his moods. "I am American."

He snorted. "Because your mother made the mistake of coming here when she was pregnant does not change the fact you are Russian."

I glanced nervously at the door Dane had walked out of. "Come now."

He laughed. "What's the matter? Did your boyfriend throw you out?"

"Alex is not my boyfriend." He never was. He'd merely been the weekly appointment Viktor made me keep for three years because he got off on the control of making me fuck another man. And I'd stupidly kept going every week. Then I'd gone to Alex this morning when I'd run from Viktor, because I literally had nowhere else to go. But Alex told me he'd met someone then dumped me at his friend's house, saying I had three days to figure my life out before his friend came home.

Except Dane had come home early, there was a hurricane blowing in, and my life had gone from bad to worse.

"Do not pretend you did not like my gift," Viktor warned. "You like all my gifts."

My skin crawled. "If you don't want me to come home, then fine, I won't." I hung up.

Three seconds later, my phone rang and I answered without saying a thing because this was the game he expected.

"Are you trying to make me angry, petal?"

Hearing the nickname simultaneously made bile rise up my throat and moisture pool between my legs, because I'd been carefully conditioned. I swallowed down my hatred for him and threw out the one insult I knew would make him angrier. "You're not a man."

"Yet you always come back for more." There was no humor in his voice.

I ground my teeth. "Give me what you promised."

"Come and get it," he taunted.

My nostrils flared. "It's been five years. That was the deal. The clock has run out." He'd made me a promise when I'd agreed to marry him. It was the only reason I'd agreed to the marriage. We both knew that.

"I am perfectly aware of what the calendar says, but you haven't earned your keep."

I sucked in a breath and told myself not to fall into the trap. "I have a prenup. I can walk into any lawyer's office and get my five-hundred-thousand." I'd made sure I'd had that prenup before I married him. If we divorced before five years, I got nothing, but anything after five years, I got half a million. That was his promise.

"Then why haven't you?"

I hated him. I hated what he'd turned me into. And I hated myself for allowing it to happen. Exhaling, I dropped my voice to barely a whisper. "Please come get me."

"Are you on your knees?" he asked casually.

"No." Even now, I couldn't lie to him.

"On your knees," he barked. "Ask nicely."

I dropped to my knees in shame, as if he could see me. "Please, Viktor."

"Please what?" he snapped.

I gripped the phone tighter. "Please, sir."

"Please, sir, *what*?"

Damn it, damn it, damn it. "Please, sir, will you come get me?"

"And?"

Oh God. "And show me who I belong to?" My traitorous nipples pebbled as disgust crawled across my skin.

"Spread your knees."

My bare shins scraped across Dane's wooden floor, and I did what we both knew I would. "Yes, sir." Viktor had seen my weakness when he'd met me, and he'd carefully cultivated it for five years, turning me into a woman I no longer recognized.

"Lift your dress to your waist."

I glanced at the door again then took a risk. "Please, sir. Do not make me do this here." Anything I asked for could backfire horribly, but I was desperate. I wanted out of Dane's house. He was too handsome, too commanding and too much to think about. I didn't allow myself to think about other men, let alone a future. And I'd done nothing since I walked into his house except wonder what it'd be like to live there, and I couldn't do it another second. Especially now that I'd seen its owner. I didn't want to be there, and I didn't want Dane to see me like this. I knew nothing about the man, but the thought of him witnessing my weakness made my stomach crawl.

"Lift the dress above your breasts."

I pulled my lips into my mouth and made a choice. Viktor couldn't see me. He'd never know. "Okay," I whispered.

There was a pause, then barely veiled fury filled his voice. "Do you want to pay for that lie now or later?"

"Please, sir. He could come back at any moment." I bit my lip.

"Where is he?" he barked.

"He went outside. There's a barn on the property." The second I said it, I felt like I'd betrayed Dane.

"He is not watching you?"

Viktor always liked an audience. "No."

"Spread your legs wider."

I knew what was coming, yet I didn't say no. My mind and my body conditioned, I rocked back to my ass and dropped my knees all the way open. "Yes, sir." I bit my lip.

"Two fingers, *now*."

I shoved two fingers inside my own cunt and jammed my thumb against my clit. The exhaled moan was involuntary.

"Three strokes," Viktor demanded.

My eyes closed and I tried to drift like I always did. Making my core my sole existence, using my fingers as my only tether, I did exactly what he told me to do. I stroked three times, but I didn't drift. I didn't become a need and a relief. It wasn't a mindless act. My body wasn't taking over. I wasn't thinking about nothing except a physical release. I was thinking about a six-foot-four stranger with short dark hair and too many muscles.

"Petal," my husband purred.

In that moment, I wanted the orgasm more than I'd ever wanted anything. I wanted to come thinking about a man so fiercely handsome that all other men paled in comparison. I wanted to come on his kitchen floor, but for the first time in five years, I didn't want to come of my own accord. I wanted the stoic stranger to make me come. "*Oh God.*"

"If you come, I will make you bleed."

Fear mixed with shame and crawled across my skin as I pulled my fingers out. "I didn't, sir."

"Wipe those two fingers across your phone. Let me hear it."

My cunt constricting at the loss of contact, I rubbed my wet fingers across the speaker part of the phone, because that's what I had been trained to do. Obey.

Viktor growled low in his throat. "I am going to smell that phone when I get to you."

I wanted to cry. "Yes, sir." I hadn't cried in five years.

"In your mouth, clean yourself," he ordered. "Let me hear you suck."

I shoved my fingers in my mouth and sucked loudly. I swirled my tongue and hated every second of my body's quivering need.

"Cover my cunt."

I dropped my dress down and started to get up. "Yes, sir."

"No," he barked. "You stay on your knees until I come for you."

Chastised worse than any talking-to I'd ever suffered as a child, I nodded because a small part of me felt as if I deserved this. I'd brought my fucked-up life into a stranger's house, and now I was fantasizing about him on his kitchen floor as I had phone sex with my husband. "Yes, sir." I wasn't just a terrible person. I was pathetic.

The tone in his voice that said he controlled everything about me left and my husband's cadence returned to mild amusement. "Have you fucked the Marine?"

"You know I am not at Alex's." I dropped the *sir*.

"Your Mr. Marek is a marine," he said too casually.

"Marek?" That was his last name?

"Dane Marek," Viktor said with disgust.

"He is not mine." A man like that would never be mine.

"Alex Vega wasn't yours either."

My chest rose and fell with an exhale. I knew what was coming. "I know," I carefully answered.

"Should I kill him?"

My heart leapt against my ribs because it wasn't the first time Viktor had threatened this. I didn't love Alex. I was incapable of love because I carefully shut that part of myself off the second I became Viktor's. But Alex didn't deserve anything other than Viktor's money, so I recited the same speech I always gave Viktor when he got like this. "I am tired of Alex. He doesn't make me come. He is nothing. He can have his other clients."

Viktor chuckled. "That's right, only I tell you when to come. All right, I will give you your wish and leave Alex Vega alone this time. But if you change your mind...." He trailed off.

I pressed a hand to my chest and fake pouted. "Why aren't you coming for me?"

"There is a hurricane, pet. It was not my choice to have you go out in it."

And it wasn't *my choice* to have him drag me from bed and force me to crawl downstairs and kneel at his feet while he ate breakfast. "You made me lick your plate." He hadn't done that in years. Not since he'd broken me.

His voice turned to liquid charm. "Do you think I do not know what my wife needs? Did you think I did not see your willfulness? Your disrespect? You needed to be reminded who you belong to. *You asked for it.*"

"No, I didn't," I whispered, closing my eyes against the memory of the forced orgasms that came after. For five years my life had been brutal punishments followed by vibrator-induced orgasms. Viktor never touched me with his own hands in affection, only punishment. Still on my knees, I fought to keep from closing my legs and rubbing my thighs together because, despite the disgust in my mind, my body had wanted those orgasms. It'd been conditioned to want them.

"Where are you?" Viktor abruptly changed the subject.

"At his house?" The answer came out like a question.

"I know whose house you are in, pet. What room?"

Oh God. No. "The kitchen?" My voice faltered.

"Reach between your legs, petal," he quietly demanded.

"Please, sir," I begged. "Not here." I looked at the utensil canister on the counter by the stove. This time it wouldn't be a simple fingering.

He inhaled as if fighting for patience. "*Petal.*"

I said nothing. I waited like I'd learned to.

A string of Russian curses filled my ear, then he exhaled. "Fine, this once, I will come get you."

I remembered Dane's threat. "Mr. Marek said he will shoot anyone who comes on his property."

Viktor laughed for real. "Let him try." He hung up.

"Going somewhere?"

I jerked my head around.

Blood all over his shirt, soaked from head to toe, Dane stood there dripping on his kitchen floor.

THREE

Dane

I couldn't have been more wrong if I'd tried. She not only knew what it was like to come, she knew what it was like to fucking hurt for it.

I'd misread every single thing about her. "You're his sub," I accused.

Her nipples hard, her thighs shaking, she stared at me guiltily as she rushed to get up. "You're bleeding."

How long had she been on her knees? "How deep?"

"Wh-what?"

Goddamn it. "You want out?" I'd heard enough of her side of the conversation. I saw the look on her face. She was so fucking far past desperation, she wanted back in because she couldn't see a way out.

She averted her gaze. "My husband is coming to get me. Do not shoot him."

"I asked you a question." Something had happened. She was here for a reason.

She lifted her head only enough to look at my side. "You are hurt."

"Not like you." My wound was physical.

She reached for the towel hanging on the oven door. "You

are making a mess all over the floor." She dropped it at my feet. "Stand on that. I will help you before he gets here." She spun.

"If you don't tell me why you ran, he's not going to make it up the driveway." I didn't make idle threats.

"Men," she huffed in irritation as she walked down the hallway. Seconds later, a completely different woman than the one who'd been on her knees on my kitchen floor was in front of me. She dropped a larger towel at my feet and held on to another. "Tell your dog to come here and not bite me."

"Hunter, come. Sit." My German shepherd circled her then sat next to my feet. "He won't bite."

She bent and quickly towel dried his fur. Then she stood and eyed me. "Take your shirt off," she demanded.

Staring into her ice-blue eyes, I grasped her chin and she went dead still. I searched every inch of her face, but she didn't even blink. "You like giving orders?" I quietly asked. "Or taking them?"

She drew in a breath at my second question, but none of the defensiveness or attitude she had earlier returned. "Do you like bleeding all over your floor?"

I stared at her. I was no longer looking at another man's submissive on my floor. I was looking at a desperate, broken woman who was holding herself together. She wasn't just beautiful, she was fucking stunning. The instinct to protect kicked in and I wanted to kill Viktor Fedorov. "Tell me why you ran."

"What happened to your side?" she deflected.

I dropped my hand and pulled my shirt over my head one-handed. "I was stabbed."

Her gaze cut to my ribs then to my shoulder. She tried to hide her surprise. "And your shoulder?"

"Shot." She was no longer the inconvenience I'd encountered an hour ago. She was a fucking disaster about to detonate my life to hell. Every instinct I had said she was going to shred my careful existence worse than any fucking IED.

She scanned the other scars on my chest, then she pressed the kitchen towel to my ribs. "Your stitches aren't holding."

I lifted my arm to give her better access because I was a goddamn fool. "I broke through them in the barn." Her scent was pure woman and desire, but she smelled like fucking trouble.

Oblivious to my thoughts, she nodded once. "Do you have a first aid kit?"

I peered down at her, wondering how far I would let this go. "Would you know what to do with it if I did?"

"I guess you're about to find out. Where is it?" Her straight white-blonde hair covered her face as she pulled back the towel to see the wound.

Already pushing at the last boundary I had in my life, I brushed the strands behind her ear.

She flinched, then sucked in a breath and glanced up at me.

"You okay?" I quietly asked.

Her chest rose and fell, and she looked at me like she was seeing me for the first time. "Yes."

I didn't do affection. Affection was complication and complication was attachment, and I didn't get attached. Fucking ever. "Linen closet, top shelf." I brushed the back of my hand across her cheek.

Her small fingers closed over my wrist then she placed my hand on the towel. "Hold this." She walked to the closet a second time.

Every step she took, she transformed from a spoiled Goldilocks to a woman I wanted to fuck. Despite the pain in my side, despite the fact I shouldn't even be thinking about touching a woman as fucked-up as her, my dick took notice of her every movement as she set my kit on the counter.

"Wash your hands." I clipped out the order, then gave Hunter a hand command to do an interior patrol of the house.

The dog took off, and she did as I said without comment.

"There're gloves and peroxide in the kit. You good with a needle?" I hated staples, almost as much as I hated complications.

She put on a pair of gloves. "No." She opened the peroxide. "This is going to sting." Not waiting for a response, she pulled the towel back and poured the liquid all over my wound.

I inhaled through my nose. "Grab the skin stapler kit."

"You already have stitches." She took out one of the packaged sutures that was already pre-threaded with a needle.

"Stapling will be easier." I shouldn't have cared about wanting to make it easier on her. She wasn't going to make my life easy.

She shrugged and ripped open the preloaded single-use stapler. "Whatever."

"You need to—" I didn't get the rest of the sentence out.

She'd already pinched the sides of the wound and pressed the handle. "Staple. I got it." She put in another one.

I clenched my jaw. "You've done this before?"

Another. "No. But I sewed my mother's finger together when I was twelve." She put in one more, then leaned back to look at her work. "We grew up poor. I didn't have much choice. She'd cut it cooking dinner." She grabbed two sterile gauze pads and antibiotic ointment. "And I saw one of Viktor's bodyguards put staples in another bodyguard after a fight once."

Fuck. I needed to remember who she was. "Do you know why your husband needs personal security?" I looked down at my ribs. Two staples would've held the wound shut.

"He is Russian. Does he need a reason?" She smeared antibiotic ointment all over my stapled wound, then pressed the gauze over it. "Hold this." She put more of the ointment on the second gauze pad, and rested it on my shoulder. "Where is the dog?" She grabbed the tape from the kit.

"On guard." I whistled and Hunter came over. "Hunter, lie down." He lay down at my feet but kept his gaze on her. "Do you know what your husband does for a living?"

"He is in real estate." She put tape over both gauze pads. "There."

"That isn't how he makes his money." She had to know what he did.

She pulled her gloves off. "I learned a long time ago not to interfere."

"Why did you call him?" Her phone call made me angrier than my mark getting the jump on me earlier today, exponentially angrier. And that was a bad fucking sign.

Her back stiffened slightly as she looked around for the trash can. "He is my husband."

"Second cupboard under the sink. You said he kicked you out." I didn't know why I was asking, let alone talking to her. I should've stayed in my command center and let her husband come for her, but I wasn't stupid enough to think that would be the end of it with a man like Viktor Fedorov.

She threw the gloves away and ignored my statement. "He will be here soon."

"Give me one good reason to let him on my property." I'd closed the gate at the end of the driveway, but it wouldn't stop him or his men for long.

"So you can get rid of me, so he doesn't put more holes in your body, and so you can have your house back. There are three."

I didn't give a fuck about the second one. It was the first and third reasons that were pissing me off. "I'm going to change."

"Watch the bandages."

"They'll be fine." I walked to my bedroom, and Hunter followed. I couldn't reconcile the woman who'd put four staples in me with the woman on her knees on my kitchen floor. I threw on clean clothes and boots and switched out my holster for a dry one.

My instincts had already fucked me twice today, with the mark and with my first impression of the woman in my house. I wasn't taking any more goddamn chances. Grabbing my retrofitted AR15 out of my closet, I walked back into the kitchen with Hunter on my heels.

Alarm spread across the blonde's face when she saw the gun. "What are you doing?"

I pulled my phone out and set it on the counter, then I sat on one of the stools at the island. Hunter lay down at my feet and I eyed her. "Waiting."

She glanced at my dog then my rifle. "You are not going to shoot him."

"Not unless you tell me to." Or he fires first.

She exhaled, then tried to look unaffected. "Why do you have a gun like that?"

Who she was married to, why she'd landed on my

doorstep, what was about to happen—I made a calculated decision. "I kill people." I told her the truth.

Her gaze drifted to my arm and then my haircut. "You're in the military?"

"Former."

"Marines?" There was no surprise in her tone.

"He tell you that, or are you making a lucky guess?" I'd bet three of my bank accounts that Fedorov had run a background on me the second he'd realized where his wife was.

Heat hit her cheeks. "How do you know my husband?"

I checked the ammo clip. "Who says I know him?"

She watched my movements. "You know of him."

Who fucking didn't, besides Vega? "I know a lot of people." I slammed the magazine back into place.

She flinched. "In real estate?"

I stared at her for two breaths. "Gun trafficking."

The tint on her face turned red. "My husband is not into that."

"Isn't he?" My phone lit up with an alert. "Company." My rifle in one hand, I walked to the security panel on the wall by the front door just as the intercom buzzed. I pulled up the video feed on the panel and zoomed in to the front windshield of the car parked at my gate. It wasn't Fedorov. I glanced over my shoulder at her. "Who is this?"

She gracefully moved next to me and peered at the screen. "I can hardly see through the rain, but it looks like Peter."

I peered down at her. "Last chance," I warned. I wouldn't suffer one second of hesitation or guilt over killing Fedorov. "You don't have to do this."

She looked up at me with colorless blue eyes as her throat moved with a swallow. "Let them in."

I knew fear when I saw it. "Do you need me to make the decision for you?" I dropped my hand from the security panel.

"I already told you to let them in."

Her determination made her even more stunning. "I'm looking at a woman who thinks she doesn't have a choice."

"You're not my choice," she whispered.

"He is?"

She hesitated. "Yes."

Goddamn it. I tried another tactic. "Do you think I'm going to hurt you?"

"You live in the middle of nowhere. You have a trained attack dog. You're shot, stabbed and armed. I don't know who you are, and I don't know what you're capable of… except murder."

So she had taken me seriously. "You think you know Fedorov?"

This time she didn't hesitate. "Yes."

"How long you been married to him?"

"Five years."

"That doesn't sound like a marriage. It sounds like a sentence."

The intercom buzzed again as the driver pressed the gate button impatiently.

She crossed her arms. "Well, it's my sentence."

Realization dawned. "What are the terms of your arrangement?"

Her eyes cut to the screen and she shifted nervously. "What are you talking about? Let them in."

"What did he offer you to marry him?" Bribe or blackmail. It was one or the other. "Tell me," I demanded.

"Five years, five-hundred-thousand dollars," she snapped. "Okay? Now you know. Hurry up and open the gate or he'll be mad."

I opened the gate, but I made a decision.

She wasn't getting in that fucking car.

FOUR

Irina

His rifle in one hand, he calmly tapped on the touchscreen, and I saw the gate open on the video feed.

His intense gaze never left mine, and I realized his eyes weren't brown. They were the color of the storm raging outside. Forest green, charcoal gray and deep woods brown, the colors swirled together and confused me.

"You don't need his money." His deep voice wasn't just quieter than Viktor's, it was frighteningly more commanding.

"You don't know what I need. Viktor does." The lie didn't just taste like a bitter mistake, it filled my mouth and spread through my veins like poison.

He scanned my face. "No, he doesn't."

I watched with sick dread as the small security panel on the wall switched camera angles every few seconds, showing the big black SUV as Peter drove it up the driveway. "I need to get my suitcase." I turned.

He was so quick, I didn't expect it. With silent precision, he'd stepped in front of me and his gunshot arm rose as he gripped the side of my face. "Do you want to be his slave?"

Chills ran up my back and spread at the sound of his voice and the commanding precision of his touch.

I shuddered.

Not wife. Not submissive. Not property.

Slave.

Five letters. One syllable. One definition.

He knew.

This man had spent only minutes in my company, but he knew.

No one knew.

Not Peter, not my mother, not any of the other bodyguards. They took me shopping, they drove me to Alex's, they watched what Viktor did to me, but they saw a woman who appeared to be free to come and go. They didn't know. They didn't know the first month of my marriage was spent in a single room. They knew nothing except what Viktor told them, and he said I was his wife.

But this wounded marine knew.

I wanted to hate his touch, but oh God, I didn't. "Who shot you?"

As if he knew we were beyond lies, he answered truthfully. "A mark."

I knew Viktor wasn't only into real estate. I saw guns around the house. I knew women were sometimes kept in the carriage house for the bodyguards. I ignored all of it. But I wasn't going to ignore what this stranger who touched me with more gentleness than anyone else in five years was telling me.

"You're a hit man or an escort?" Because he'd given me more than one piece of information.

"I make people's problems go away. For a price."

"Because you like to kill?" I wasn't stupid. I knew why he was telling me this, and I knew the consequences of ever uttering a word about it to anyone. I would find myself on the other end of his rifle. Stupidly, that wasn't what alarmed me.

He kept up the honesty. "Because I have a skill set not many people have."

"And not fucking for free?" That's what alarmed me. Not what he did with his rifle, but my reaction the second he'd said he charged money for sex. I never got jealous. There was nothing in my life worth being jealous over. But the thought of him doing to other women what Alex had done for me made tight spasms churn in my gut.

"My release."

Two words and I wanted to clutch my arms against the riot in my stomach. "*Release*." I drew the ugly word out because releases in my world didn't come without strings.

His stormy gaze studied me like he could see every demented thought in my head, but he called me on none of it. "I charge women for sex, but I'm not Vega. I don't do repeat clients."

I didn't know which hurt worse, the thought of him with other women or that he would never be with me more than once. Not that either was based in reality, because I wasn't going to ever feel this man above me and I had no right to be jealous. Viktor was coming.

I glanced over his shoulder at the video feed on the wall as the black SUV pulled up in front of his house. I didn't remember Viktor having that vehicle, but the weather alone probably made him buy one.

I sucked in a breath and pulled away from the man who'd offered me more in an hour than my husband of five years had. "He is here."

Dane let me retreat. "You have a choice."

Choice wasn't in my vocabulary. "Do you know what happens when you hit bottom?"

"You taste defeat and lose all desire for hope."

I blinked. It wasn't his reply that scared me, it was the zero hesitation in answering. And I couldn't top that with anything except affirmation. "Yes."

"Bottom isn't an ex-Force Recon Marine standing in front of you offering a way out."

The dog jumped up with a growl and rushed to the front door a second before someone pounded on it.

"Hunter." Dane snapped his fingers without taking his gaze off mine.

The dog quietly whined but sat.

"You're too late," I admitted. "I hit bottom four years ago." I opened the door.

Peter stood in the doorway, soaking wet. "Let's go," he barked, his voice carrying over the roar of the storm. "I'm done cleaning up Viktor's messes, you stupid bitch. Get in the fucking car. You're going to regret you ever—" He stopped midsentence as his gaze cut to a growling Hunter then traveled over my head. He reached for his gun.

"*Irina.*"

Hearing Dane say my name for the first time made my heart jump. I turned, but I wasn't quick enough.

A thick arm went around my neck and Peter jammed his pistol into my temple. Pulling me back to his chest, he used me as a human shield.

Dane stood motionless with his rifle aimed at Peter's head. "Let her go."

Peter tightened his grip on my throat. "Who the fuck are you?"

Dane's lethal glare didn't waver from Peter's. "The last person you'll ever see if you don't let her go."

Hunter growled ferociously but stayed by Dane's side.

"You think I'm stupid?" Peter spit out.

"Where's Viktor?" I squeaked.

They both ignored me.

"I don't think," Dane quipped. "I know."

Peter scoffed. "You won't risk shooting her."

"You don't know me very well," Dane countered.

"She's Viktor Fedorov's wife."

"I know who she is." Calm, controlled, Dane said the words with absolute authority.

I sucked in a breath past Peter's punishing grip and tried to yell, "*Where is Viktor?*"

Peter's gun jammed harder into my skull as his arm crushed my neck. "You're stupider than you look if you thought he was going to play fetch."

I gasped for breath.

"Release her," Dane demanded.

"No." Peter smirked. "She's not your property."

"You think she's yours?"

"She's Fedorov's, and he'll kill you if you harm her."

My lungs fought for air, my vision tunneled and I clawed at Peter's arm.

For a split second, Dane's glare cut to Peter's arm. "I'm not the one choking her out."

Peter loosened his hold only marginally. "We're leaving. You shoot me, I shoot her."

"I'm not going to shoot you." Dane's aim and lethally calm tone never wavered.

I saw the look in his eyes and I heard the threat in his voice. It made me suck in as much air as I could and force words past my crushed throat. "Dane, stop. Not worth it."

Peter snickered. "Maybe you should listen to the little slut."

"I'm not going to shoot you." Eerily quiet, Dane's voice carried across his entryway and canceled out the storm. "I'm going to kill you."

Everything went slow motion.

Dane's nostrils flared. Hunter lunged. The gun against my temple shifted.

Air whipped past my cheek. Then hot spray covered my face.

The scent of copper filled my lungs. The gun against my temple dropped, and I was falling backward.

My ears rang, my heart pounded, and the muffled thud of a body hitting wood sounded right before I landed on top of Peter as his back hit the porch.

Stinging rain pelted my face and I turned my head.

Oh.

My God.

A bullet hole between his eyes, Peter's dead gaze sightlessly stared at me.

Dry heaving, I scrambled.

"*Stay down*," a voice barked out.

Oh my God.

Heavy boot steps and clicking of dog nails rushed across the porch. Car doors opened then slammed shut. The porch vibrated with footsteps again. "Clear. Get up."

I shook. My hands, my arms, my legs, everything shook. Driving rain simultaneously spread and washed away Peter's blood, and I shook harder. My knees spasming in time to the bile trying to leave my body, I couldn't stand.

He shot him.

I couldn't breathe.

He shot Peter.

Oh my fucking God.

An arm curled around my waist and lifted.

Panic set in and I kicked out. "Get off me!"

The dog gave a low, warning growl.

"Hunter, stand down." His voice softened. "I'm not on you. You're okay, sweetheart."

"Get off, get off, *get off!*"

A hand grabbed my chin and forced my face up. Stormy eyes zeroed in on me, and a killer did the one thing I understood. He issued a command. "Take a breath, right now."

Dominance blanketed my panic and I inhaled.

Dane gripped my chin tight. "Another."

My body listened and air filled my lungs.

Then he made a crucial mistake. He released me. "Go inside."

My tether broke.

Anger and fear rushed at me like water from a broken dam. I wasn't freefalling, I was spiraling. And that spiral landed on a dead Russian bodyguard at my feet.

A bodyguard who'd called me a slut.

Five years of abuse culminated into one single driving force, and I growled with rage at a corpse. "You called me a slut?"

I kicked a dead man.

"*I'm* a fucking slut?" I kicked again. "You watched me every second of my life for five years and you're CALLING ME A SLUT?" My heel drove into his stomach. "You know how many dicks I've come in contact with?" I stomped on his chest. "One, you motherfucker!" I stomped harder. "One goddamn dick because I'm not a slut. *You are!*" I kicked and kicked and stomped and stomped until I slipped in blood and fell to my knees.

My hands landed on still warm flesh, then my fists closed and I was pounding.

"You *asshole*!" Inhuman screams of anger and humiliation cut through hurricane-force winds and carried out into the night as I pummeled a dead body in rage. "I hate you! I hate you I hate you I hate you!"

Strong arms wrapped around me and lifted.

Rain hit my arms like needles and my bare feet slipped through hot, sticky blood. "*No*." I wanted to kill Peter.

"Calm down, you're getting blood everywhere." Dane set me down and shoved my back against the house.

With the same force I'd used to hit Peter, I hit him. "No! You killed him. You did this! *You shot him*." Both of my fists landed against his hard chest.

His fierce storm-colored gaze leveled me with a look, but he didn't touch me. "Irina."

The accusations started. "You could've killed me! He could've shot me! You didn't care what happened. You didn't care if he blew my brains out!"

The dog rushed at me with a snarling growl.

His impenetrable mask of control dropped and he roared out a command. "On your knees!"

The anger, the rage, the fear, it all instantly froze as if he'd pushed the pause button for my life. Stunned, I dropped to the porch.

"*Stay*."

The dog sat.

My head down, my arms at my sides, I kneeled in utter confusion as Dane searched Peter's pockets and came away with keys. Using the key fob, he opened the back door to the SUV, then he bent and lifted Peter's body with the strength and grace of a warrior.

As if he didn't have four staples in his side or a gunshot wound on his arm, he carried Peter over his shoulder to the SUV and threw him in. Locking the vehicle, he climbed the steps with his automatic rifle strapped to his back. Without breaking stride, he scooped me up like a child and strode into the house.

My shaking turned to shivering and my teeth started to chatter. Both of us soaked, Dane paused only long enough to kick the door shut, lock it, and swipe his finger across the security panel. Then we were moving again.

With the sound of canine steps following us, Dane walked down the hall.

I knew where he was going. I'd searched every inch of his house before he'd gotten here, and there wasn't anything at the end of the hallway except the master suite.

With a dead man's blood on my feet and the killer holding me in his arms, my mind bent. "He-he-he's going to kill me." Dane would fuck me and Viktor would kill me. "He'll f-f-find you and he'll k-k-kill you."

Dane said nothing.

I tried to force my chattering jaw to still. "I'm dead. You're d-d-dead." Everyone was dead.

He walked through his bedroom and into the master bathroom. He didn't pause, he didn't speak. He walked into a shower bigger than a closet.

"St-st-stop."

He didn't listen.

One swipe of his hand, and water was cascading down

on us from two sides and the ceiling. His huge hand gripped a handful of my hair and he set me on my feet as he put my face under the spray.

Forced to hold my breath or drown, I closed my eyes, but my hands went to cover my face.

"Stop," he commanded. "Wash his blood off."

Blood. The single word made my eyes open, and the realization of what the hot splatter on my face was sank in. Red-tinted water ran off my hands and down my arms as revulsion mixed with horror. My stomach lurched. Black spots crowded my vision, and ringing filled my ears.

Oh God.

My knees buckled.

Grabbing me around the waist, Dane shoved my head between my legs and barked out an order. "Breathe."

My stomach pressed against my thighs, I dry heaved as my lungs fought for air. "Blood," I cried. "*Everywhere.*" My legs, my arms, dripping down my hair, pooling at my feet. So much blood. I clawed at my stained dress. "Get it off!"

Impossibly warm hands whipped my dress up my back and over my bent body, yanking it off. A boot, then a pant-covered knee, then storm-colored eyes came into view. Water cascading down his face, my silk dress bunched in his hand like a rag, Dane gently brushed the material over my face. "We're washing it off."

I shook. "Pl-pl-please hurry."

"Sh," he murmured, wiping across my mouth, my cheeks. "You're okay."

"S-s-soap."

Dropping my dress, he reached behind him without taking his eyes off mine and grabbed a bar, but he didn't give it to me. "I'll clean you up in a minute. Take a deep breath. I don't want you to faint."

"N-n-not...." I fought to steady the chatter in my jaw. "Not going to pass out."

He searched my face, then finally nodded. With utter control and grace, he rose and took me with him. "Slow, deep breaths."

I panted shallowly, but the warm water pounding down on us eased the chattering. I didn't care that I was naked in front of him. I wanted Peter's blood off my body and the bitter taste of copper in my mouth to be gone. "Give me the soap."

His gaze never leaving mine, he didn't give it to me. He lathered his hands and issued another command. "Close your eyes."

I never considered not obeying. I closed my eyes, and rough, calloused hands soaped my face. His thumbs traced my cheekbones and his fingers gently scrubbed my forehead. The heat of his touch soaked into my bones as he scrubbed the blood away.

Tilting my head, he gave me a warning. "Rinsing."

Water cascaded down my face, but this time I embraced it. Angling my face into the direct spray, I held my breath until large hands gently turned me away.

Afraid to touch my dirty hands to my face, I blinked through the water on my eyelashes and looked up. The hard angles of his face morphed from killer into man, and his stare cut through five years of tempered emotion.

I swallowed. "Your gun."

Without a word, he slipped the strap over his head and set the riffle in the corner behind him. Reaching for a bottle on a shelf, he continued to stare at me as he poured shampoo into his palm. Slow, as if I would flinch, he raised his hands and spread the earthy-scented shampoo that smelled like him through my hair.

Hands that had pulled a trigger to take a man's life mere minutes ago massaged soap into my hair. Fingers that shouldn't feel good ran through my blood-soaked locks, and I closed my eyes. I wanted to feel his hands on me forever.

"He wasn't here for a retrieval." His deep voice broke the cocoon of avoidance I was floating in. "He was going to dispose of you."

"Viktor wouldn't let anything happen to me." The response was automatic. Viktor had fed me the lie for so many years, I was reciting it like a puppet even though his bodyguard had held me at gunpoint.

Dane picked up on the obvious. "Did Fedorov or any of his men ever pull a gun on you?"

"No."

At Dane's silence, I opened my eyes.

His stormy gaze didn't waver. "The guard was going to kill you."

Every minute of the past five years ran through my mind, painting a glaring picture, but I still stupidly questioned it. "You don't know that."

"He was a guard."

"So?" I knew what Peter had been.

"He left his charge." Dane paused for effect. "In a hurricane."

Peter had left Viktor's side many times over the years… hadn't he? "He's not with Viktor twenty-four seven."

"When he's not with him, he's not with you."

Despite the mounting evidence, my mind tried to deny the twisted sentence. "That doesn't mean anything." It meant everything. Peter had no loyalty to me.

"What does he usually drive?"

He always drove Viktor's Maserati sedan. "I don't know what kind of car he has."

Dane tilted my head under the water to rinse the shampoo. "When he's working, what does he drive?"

"Viktor's car."

"Which isn't a stolen SUV."

Stolen? "How do you know it was stolen?"

"Out-of-state plates, a tourist keychain and a stroller in the back."

"Maybe he borrowed it." He didn't. Peter didn't know anyone with small children. He knew Viktor and the other bodyguards.

Dane's hands slid down my hair like he was my lover. "You're not going back to him."

I knew I couldn't. Not now. Viktor would blame me for Peter's death, and I didn't want to know what that punishment would entail. "He will come for me." The mounting evidence, what I knew about Viktor, it should've terrified me. But with Dane's hands in my hair, I stupidly allowed the false sense of security he was offering to wrap around me like a blanket.

"Yes, he will."

I looked up at the marine who'd already saved my life once today. "What then?"

He didn't hesitate. "I'll kill him."

FIVE

Dane

I watched her for signs of shock, but all she did was breathe. Her colorless eyes stared, her chest rose and fell, and she simply breathed.

I didn't take my promise back.

She swallowed. "Are you going to call the police?"

We both knew the guard hadn't come to bring her home. He'd come to dispose of her and the weather was a perfect cover. "No."

"Why?"

I lied to everyone. Omission was my religion. But the second I saw her on her knees on my kitchen floor, fighting not to fall apart, I saw what I was when my wife left me. Broken and despondent, she didn't need any more shit. I wasn't going to lie to her. "I'm going to dispose of the body, wipe the vehicle then dump it." But I wasn't going to give Fedorov his wife back. No fucking way. "Are you legally married?"

"What?"

"To Fedorov. Did you sign any legal papers?"

She inhaled and reached for the soap. Small, delicate hands twisted around the bar. "I only signed a prenup," she admitted. "He said he took care of everything else."

The asshole probably hadn't even married her. "What's your legal last name?" I should've run a background check on her the second I'd had a chance.

"I didn't legally take his name."

One less complication. "Anything else he holds over you?"

Her head down, she didn't answer. She scrubbed the dead guard's blood off her arms.

I gave in to the temptation and stared at her hard nipples and her perfect fucking small breasts. She wasn't pretty, she was fuck-my-life-up beautiful. I fought to keep from touching her. "I asked you a question."

She scrubbed the same spot over and over. "I wasn't born in Russia. I was born here. I'm American."

The accent. "Okay." I knew where this was going. "And?" I'd forgotten to ask about it.

"I don't have an accent. I don't even speak Russian. My mother does. Her English is accented. I copied it."

"Why?" The fucking asshole had even controlled her damn speech.

"Viktor likes me to speak a certain way. He made me."

He'd done a lot more than that. "What else?" My jaw ticked.

She ignored the question. "He's going to punish me."

My nostrils flared. "He's not going to touch you ever again." Not him or any of his guards. Not as long as I was breathing.

"He'll find me." She didn't speak the words in fear, she stated them as simple fact.

"Good." Then I wouldn't have to find him to kill him.

She finally looked up at me. But instead of the panic or

fear I was expecting, she stared at me with zero emotion. "You want him to take me?"

She was steeling herself by cutting off feelings, and detaching. She was doing what she'd probably done for five years. It fucking killed me to see it, but it also told me how damn strong she was. "You don't have to worry about him anymore. I'm not going to let him do a goddamn thing to you. And yes, I want him coming for you. It will be the last thing he does. I promise."

"He owns me."

No, he fucking didn't. "Not anymore."

"Because you decided to own me now?" Zero intonation in her question, she could've been asking me about the weather.

"I don't own women." No real man did.

"Then why are you doing this?"

Because she'd dropped to her knees in my kitchen and spread her legs for an impotent arms dealer. I didn't need a goddamn reason beyond that. "You need help."

She held my gaze. "I didn't ask for it."

"You're getting it."

Something I couldn't decipher crossed her expression, then she inhaled and dropped her head. "Your clothes."

I didn't say shit.

She stared at my shirt. "They're soaked."

"I know." Goddamn, I wanted to fucking touch her.

"You should take them off."

I studied every nuance in her face, her voice, but there was nothing sexual about her comment. "You don't want me to do that."

"Why not?"

I told her the truth. "Because I haven't fucked in weeks."

Her head popped up and she looked at me with surprise. "But you said you take women as clients."

"On occasion." Most of the time I was too damn busy, but recently, none of the women had done it for me.

"Then what do you do the rest of the time?"

I stared at her. Then I said the last fucking thing I should. "Turn around."

She didn't question me, or even hesitate. She simply turned.

I reached around her and took the soap from her. Lathering my hands, I ran them over her back. Her soft skin, her submissive nature, her gorgeous fucking body, all I could think about was sinking inside her, but I wasn't going to. "Do you have family?"

"Why?"

"Because you're going to need somewhere to go after." If she stayed here, I'd fuck her for days.

She leaned back toward me. "After he's dead?"

I didn't repeat my intention. She'd heard me, but I fucking got it. Words were just words to her. She didn't know me enough yet to know I wasn't fucking around, but she would. "Parents?" I moved my hands slowly up the middle of her back.

She dropped her head forward. "My mother."

I rubbed circles on her neck with my thumbs. "She in state?"

A small moan escaped her lips. "Yes."

I pressed my fingers deep into the tight muscles below her shoulder blades. "Can you go there?"

She exhaled and suddenly her tone changed. "What do you care?" She stepped forward.

I spun her around and grasped her chin, then I did the first smart thing since she'd walked into my life. "I'm going to solve your problem. Then you're going to walk away from me."

Bitterness filtered into her voice. "Because you don't do repeat clients."

It wasn't a question, but I answered it anyway. "You're not my client."

She crossed her arms. "Good, because I'm not paying you."

I searched every inch of her face because, God help me, I was looking for a fucking in. One damn sign that she wanted me to touch her. Bitterness, defiance, it wasn't the opposite of indifference, I fucking knew that, but I wanted more than that small moan. "What do you want?"

She pulled out of my grasp. "Is that a joke?"

Her accent had all but disappeared. "Do I look like I'm joking?"

She gave me her back. "I want to finish showering, alone. Please leave."

I stepped out of my boots. Pulling my T-shirt over my head, I dropped it then unbuttoned my pants.

She turned back around. "I said…." Her gaze cut to my rock-hard dick, and she trailed off. "What are you doing?" Her throat moved with a swallow.

I kicked off my wet pants. "Leaving." I reached for the soap. "After I rinse off." I scrubbed my hands and arms. "Unless you want to fuck."

Her eyes on my junk, she didn't move.

"Step aside," I warned.

"You're even bigger than—" She stopped herself.

I locked down my expression. "Vega?" I didn't get attached to women. That was a luxury I couldn't afford in my line of work. And not getting attached meant not fucking attached, in any goddamn way. I told myself I didn't give a shit how many ways Vega had taken her. I told myself, if she could take a big dick, even better. But the thought of Vega grinding on her made my jaw clench and my muscles fucking twitch.

"Yes," she whispered.

Good. I wanted her to fucking look. I wanted her to see every goddamn inch of my cock and think about how I would feel inside her. "You going to move?" Because I was about to say fuck it and find out just how much of me she could take.

She bit her bottom lip.

Goddamn it.

I stepped up to her. My dick an inch from her small body, my chest close to those hard nipples, I reached around her petite frame and rinsed my arms. Low, controlled, I spoke. "You never answered my question."

Her gaze traveled up my body and stopped at my mouth. She licked her bottom lip. "What question?"

I braced my hands on the wall behind her. "Vega ever make you come?" I knew Alex Vega. He lived for money, not pleasing women. I also knew the rumors about Fedorov. He was a sick fuck. And I knew what I'd seen in my kitchen. This woman had been completely controlled. Fedorov had owned everything about her, including her pleasure.

She dropped her gaze to my chest, but not before I saw the faint blush to her cheeks.

"Answer me," I demanded.

Her voice turned quiet. "Why are you doing this? Do you think you could possibly humiliate me any more than him?"

I tipped her chin. "You think I'm trying to humiliate you?"

"Doesn't every man want to break a woman down?"

Fedorov was dead. So motherfucking dead. "No," I

answered. "Only the assholes." I fought for an even inhale. "I'm not trying to break you. I'm trying to gauge the mixed signals you're putting off, because I'm not some asshole who's going to force myself on you." I pushed off the wall. "You see my desire. You know where I stand." I stepped around her.

"Where are you going?"

I didn't look back. "To clean up."

I grabbed a towel and dry clothes, then my phone. I was so fucking pissed at what that asshole had done to her that I forgot to check the surveillance feeds before I called André Luna.

A sniper in the Marines, Luna now owned his own personal security firm. He answered on the first ring. "It's been a while, Marek."

I didn't deny it. "I need a pick up in thirty." I worked alone, always, but Luna had been there for me a couple times and I'd always repaid the favor.

"Last time you needed a pick up, you almost bled out on my front seat."

I pulled off my wet bandages then threw on a T-shirt. "And you upgraded to a new vehicle." Six of them, actually. I'd bought him the new SUVs because he'd needed them and didn't have the funds at the time. He'd been pissed as hell and tried to give five of them back, saying he didn't do handouts. I'd told him six vehicles didn't make up for saving my life.

"You injured?"

"I'm fine." I yanked my pants up. I was so fucking pissed at Fedorov, I barely felt my wounds. "I'll be under the new southern overpass to the port. Thirty minutes."

"You do know there's a hurricane making landfall?"

"It's still tropical force winds and it's only the outer bands."

"Regardless, I pulled all my men. Anyone not on a crucial assignment is here on lockdown till it passes."

I ran through a mental checklist of his employees. "Tyler still working for you?" No family yet, he'd do it.

"You're not hearing me, Marek. I'm not sending any of my men out in this. Can't it wait?"

"No." I needed the cover of the storm.

Luna muttered a curse in Spanish. "You know what my problem is?" He didn't wait for me to answer. "I'm too fucking curious. Every time you call, you make it sound like you need a pick up from some damn picnic in the park, but when I get there, something epically fucked has gone down. So yeah, I'm gonna bite. Where's the drop-off?"

"My house."

"That's it? There gonna be heat?"

"No." Not if I moved quick.

He chuckled. "Why don't I believe you?"

I didn't answer.

"All right, damn it. But hold up, let me check the radar."

I waited.

"*Mierda*," he swore low and quiet. "Thirty minutes out then twenty to your place and twenty, twenty-five back here. That puts us right in the middle of this thing."

"Weight the vehicle, make it twenty-five minutes and meet me at the southern overpass."

"Three tours in Afghanistan and I'm gonna get taken out by a fucking hurricane. Your ass is gonna owe me for this."

"If it gets rough, you can ride it out at my place." I was inland.

"I'm not locking myself up at your low-lying Fort Knox compound. You're in the middle of a fucking flood zone. The apocalypse? Yeah, I'm coming to you. But a hurricane? No fucking thanks. Now you have twenty-four minutes. Don't be late." He hung up.

I grabbed a tactical vest and two sidearms from the safe in my bedroom closet. Slipping the vest over my head, I adjusted the Velcro straps and holstered the weapons. I felt her presence before I heard her.

"I'm going out." I turned.

Holding the towel against her chest, she fought to not look alarmed. "There's a hurricane."

"The winds haven't reached category one yet." I loaded a few extra clips. "You're staying here. I have a safe room in the barn." Despite what Luna had said, it was safe as hell in a hurricane.

She bit her lip and averted her gaze.

Her body language gave me pause. "What's wrong?"

Her shoulders rose with an inhale, but she didn't look at me. "I told Viktor about the barn. If he shows up and I'm not in the house, he'll look there first."

Goddamn it. I pulled a jacket from my closet. "Put this on over your clothes and tie your hair back." I didn't need any of her fucking DNA in that SUV. "You're coming with me."

She glanced at Hunter as he lay at the end of the bed. "Is it safe to go out?"

"Safer than you being here alone and him knowing about the barn." I grabbed another jacket for myself. "Get dressed, then meet me in the garage." I walked out.

I grabbed a gallon of bleach and poured it over the front porch. With the rain already picking up, any visual evidence would be gone before we returned. Back in the garage, I opened the door, put on gloves, then jogged to the SUV and got behind the wheel. The wind gusting like fuck, I backed into the garage just far enough to cover the rear of the vehicle.

I was loading five-gallon gas cans in the back of the SUV next to the body when she came out of the house.

Swimming in my jacket, she was dressed in jeans and she'd pulled her hair back. She looked like a completely different woman than the one I'd found in my kitchen.

She glanced at the SUV. "We're going in that?"

I nodded once. "We're dumping it."

"Peter is in there."

I grabbed an extra pair of gloves and ignored her statement. "Put these on and get in the front passenger seat."

"How will we get back?"

"A friend of mine."

"Someone you trust?"

"We served together." I closed the back hatch. "Get in."

Pocketing my garage opener, I waited till she was in the SUV, then I got behind the wheel. "Buckle in but don't touch anything else." I checked the gas gauge to make sure we had fuel.

She reached for the seat belt with a gloved hand. "You sound like you've done this before."

"A few times." More than a few. But the two wounds on my body were evidence that I was losing my edge. I navigated my unpaved driveway. The SUV handled the wind gusts, but we were protected by the woods around us.

She was silent until we pulled onto the county road. "Why do you live out here?" Her eyes trained on the road, she stared straight ahead.

"I don't like cities." Four tours had cured me of ever wanting to live in an urban environment. Rain sheeted against the windshield and water filled the runoff ditches on either side of the road.

"You could live on the beach," she said absently.

I could live a lot of places. "Is that where you want to live?"

A gust of wind made the vehicle swerve, and she gasped.

"We're fine." I corrected and stepped on the gas as a huge gust threw a wall of water at the SUV.

She snapped. "We're in a stolen car with a dead body, enough gas to commit arson and we're driving through a hurricane. You have stitches and a gunshot wound, and I have an insane husband. *That isn't fine.*"

I navigated around a fallen branch in the road and pointed out the obvious. "If you never signed a marriage certificate, you're not legally married."

She gripped the shoulder strap of her seat belt. "I told you, he said he took care of that."

"By forging your name?"

She threw her hands up. "I don't know! Okay? I don't know what he did! I just want to live through this and not go to jail!"

"You're not going to jail." No one was out on the road, including cops. That's why I needed to dump the body now instead of later.

"This wasn't supposed to happen. I wouldn't be in this situation if Alex hadn't dumped me at your house!"

I gripped the fucking steering wheel and fought to keep my tone even. "And what situation is that? An abusive relationship with a manipulative arms dealer who loans you out to a male prostitute?" I gunned the SUV around another fallen branch. "Or almost getting killed in the back of a stolen SUV by a hired gun of your husband's?"

"He wasn't going to kill me. Viktor would never allow that!"

"Right. He was going to pay you half a million dollars and let you walk." She had no fucking clue who she'd gotten in bed with.

She turned in her seat. "You're a male prostitute. You said so yourself."

I threw her attitude right back on her. "Is that why you said no to me in the shower?"

She crossed her arms. "I didn't have to say no because you didn't ask a question."

Jesus Christ. "Let me spell it out for you, sweetheart. When a naked man with a hard-on asks you what you want, that's a fucking question." I pulled under the overpass. Construction on one side, stacked concrete barriers on the other, there were no security cameras and no direct rain. I cut the engine. "Get out."

SIX

Irina

I GOT OUT OF THE DISGUSTING SUV THAT SMELLED LIKE baby powder and death. I wanted to hate Dane for every single truth he threw in my face, but I had no one to blame for my life or my decisions except myself.

"Wait by the barricades," Dane ordered.

His command sounded no different than Viktor's, but nothing about it was anything like Viktor. I hated Viktor. He'd taken my virginity against my will, and everything since had been worse. So much worse that I'd become numb.

I stood watching Dane pour gasoline over every inch of the SUV, including Peter's body, and I didn't care. I only wished Peter was still alive to smell the stench and feel the agonizing pain of what was about to happen. The fact that my mind was even going down that road should've scared the hell out of me, but it didn't. All I kept thinking about was the way Dane had looked at me in the shower. My whole life I'd been waiting for a man to look at me like that, but when it'd finally happened, I'd turned my back. I was so screwed up, I didn't even know how to act around a man.

Dane stepped beside me and pulled a lighter out of his pocket.

"I want to do it." I wanted to be in control of something.

Careful not to set his glove on fire, Dane lit the lighter.

"No."

"Why not?"

"It makes you an accessory." He threw the lighter with exact precision.

Seconds later, flames licked up the inside walls of the vehicle and raced across the floor toward Peter's body. "Maybe I want to be an accessory."

"You don't." His arm landed on my shoulder and he pulled me face-first into his chest. "Don't watch."

"I want to see him burn." I didn't know if I did or didn't. In that moment, I just wanted to take back something of myself, but I couldn't even say what that was because I didn't know who I was anymore.

"I know." He didn't let go of me. "But I don't want you to."

He was protecting me. Again. Inhaling the scent of his soap and his musk mixed with gasoline, I regretted the shower all over again. "I'm sorry about the shower."

His other arm came around me. "It's okay. Let it go."

Careful of his staples, my hands went to his sides and I rested my head against his chest. "Is that what you do… when you kill someone?"

"Yes." He rubbed slow circles on my back.

"I don't feel anything," I admitted. "About Peter."

"Because it was justified."

"It was self-defense," I corrected. At least I thought that's what it was. But burning him? I didn't know what that was. Maybe karma. Maybe just efficient body disposal. I didn't know and Dane didn't respond.

The wind howling, the rain pelting, the flames roaring, I

didn't hear a vehicle pull up next to us until a door slammed shut.

A man stepped up beside us and took in the burning SUV. "*Dios mio.*"

Tall, muscular, close-cut brown hair, brown eyes, the man rested his right hand on a gun in a holster at his waist as if it were as natural to him as breathing. He was as handsome as Dane, but despite the position of his hand, he didn't have the edge of danger Dane carried.

He tipped his chin at the burning vehicle, then looked at Dane. "You said there wasn't going to be any heat." He glanced at me and smiled like an angel. "And you didn't mention company."

"André, this is Irina. Irina, André Luna. Let's go." Dane didn't give his friend my last name.

"Copy that." The man spun and got behind the wheel of a new black SUV with tinted-out windows.

Dane pulled his gloves off, then took mine off and stuffed both pairs in his back pocket. His gaze intent, he dropped his voice. "One down."

The acrid stench of the fire filled my nostrils, and I stole a glance at the burning vehicle. Flames hid anything that might have been left of Peter's body, but a horrible sense of dread still washed over me. I couldn't do this. I had to give Dane an out. This wasn't his fight. "You don't have to do this."

Dane didn't hesitate. "I'm already doing it." His hand landed on the small of my back and he led me to his friend's SUV, then opened the back door.

God, I wanted to get in and remain silent and let this man take care of all of my problems, but life didn't work like that. I closed the door and looked up at the striking angles of his face. This wasn't just about the shower. "I'm sorry. I'm sorry I called you a male prostitute. I'm sorry I brought my mess to your house, and I'm sorry you had to kill for me." I sucked in a breath and said what I should've said hours ago, "You can drop me off at my mother's and I'll leave you alone." If I was lucky, Viktor wouldn't have called her yet and told her I'd run, and she'd still let me in. If not, I could ride out the hurricane in the bathrooms her condo complex had by the pool, then figure out what to do next.

His gaze more intense than any man I'd ever met, Dane stared at me. Then he did what I was only beginning to understand was his superpower. He zeroed in on the truth. "You don't want me to let you go."

After everything he'd done for me, I couldn't lie to him. But I was also too embarrassed to tell him the truth. "I'm sorry," I whispered.

For a brief moment, his impenetrable mask fell away and he ran the back of his hand across my cheek. Then just as quick, the mask was back and he opened the door.

He was right, I didn't want to leave him. So I got in the back of the SUV and he got in the front passenger seat.

The ride back to his house was worse than the ride out. The wind gusted and threw the vehicle around, but Dane and André held a quiet conversation as if they did this all the time. My head spinning, I didn't listen to what they were saying. Before I could process what I was feeling, we were back at Dane's house.

André pulled into the garage, then Dane was out of the vehicle, and opening my door.

André acknowledged me with a polite nod. "Ma'am." He glanced at Dane. "Stay out of trouble."

Dane nodded, then André backed out of the garage. Without a word, Dane led me inside, and Hunter practically jumped all over us. Circling, whining, he didn't calm down until Dane scratched behind his ears. "Good boy." Dane pointed at his bed. "Go lie down."

I started to take off my borrowed jacket, but a large hand covered mine.

"You're quiet. You okay?" Dane slid the jacket off my shoulders.

His body heat at my back, I shivered. "Yes." I didn't know what I was.

Gentle hands threaded into my hair and he took my ponytail out. "Let your hair dry."

I swallowed past the sudden dryness in my throat. "Okay."

His fingers ran down my arm and he took my hand in his. His breath on my shoulder, his huge, muscular body at my back, he curved his tall frame around me and the room shrunk to just the two of us. "Hi," he said quietly.

My stomach fluttered, and I couldn't help myself. I leaned back into him. "Hi."

He took my palm and bent my fingers toward him, then his thumb ran across my fingernails. "You washed all the blood off."

His touch was so gentle but so commanding, I wanted to melt into him at the same time I wanted to run from him. "In the shower."

His other arm curled around my waist and his free hand threaded through mine. "You hungry?"

Not for food. "No." Wanting this moment to last forever, I closed my eyes to just breathe him in, but a loud creak followed by a horrible crash made me jump.

His arms tightened. "You're okay."

"What was that?" Both the storm and his hold on me made my heart race.

"A tree, or part of one." He squeezed my hands then released me. "I'll go check."

His heat left my back and I panicked. "Don't go out there." Wind rattled the shutters.

He looked over his shoulder at me. "I'm not. Just checking the security feeds. Be right back." He disappeared down the hall.

I made my way into the kitchen. My hands shaking slightly, I reached for the coffeepot and filled it with water.

"You drink too much caffeine."

Startled, I almost dropped the pot.

He walked past me to the couch and casually sat. The same finger that'd run down my arm swept across the screen.

I abandoned the coffeepot and walked up behind the couch. "What can you see?"

"Everything." The screen cycled through various camera angles of the house and property.

Already there were several trees down. "Will we lose power?" And would he lose his security feeds so we wouldn't see if Viktor was coming for me?

Dane inhaled deep and let it out slow, then he answered me as if he could read my mind. "I'll know if he comes for you."

Another crack sounded and I jumped. "What was that?"

The tablet in his lap, he looked up at me. "You're safe here, I promise."

The scent of rain mixed with his brand of soap, and all of a sudden I wasn't in a hurricane. I was in a Dane Marek storm.

His gaze a tether, it wasn't all the things I noticed about him every time I looked at him, it was all the things he wasn't that were suddenly obvious.

He wasn't cruel. He didn't treat me like a slave. He didn't intentionally put me on edge or lie to me. He didn't purposely ignore me or make me wait for his attention as if I were nothing. He was quiet, reserved, and disciplined. And he was risking his life for me. But he was also a trained killer, and now I knew enough about him to make me a liability.

Warm, strong fingers curled over my hand as I gripped the back of the couch, and awareness shot up my arm. I frowned.

"Talk to me." His thumb ran back and forth across my knuckles.

I stared at his hand over mine. "I'm a liability to you."

His fingers stilled. "How so?"

I didn't pull my hand away. "I know too much about you now."

He slowly nodded. "Do you know I have a sister?"

"No." I didn't look at him, but I could feel his gaze on me.

His thumb made a slow pass. "Did you know I was recruited by the CIA after the Marines?"

I wasn't surprised. I shook my head.

Without taking his hand off mine, he put the tablet on the coffee table. "I turned them down. Did you know I got a Dear John letter on my first deployment?"

"I'm sorry." His girlfriend must have been a fool.

"I'm not." He rubbed the back of my hand, all the way up to my wrist. "Did you know Hunter was trained to be a PTSD service animal?"

I looked up and met his gaze. "You have PTSD?" I was shocked. He was so strong and impenetrable.

He didn't answer my question. "Now you know more about me than Luna." He threaded his fingers through mine. "Does that feel like a liability?"

It felt worse because it felt like hope, but I wasn't going to be that naïve about any man ever again. I pulled my hand away. "I think I should get some sleep."

I made it one step.

"Irina."

I didn't turn, but I paused.

"I want to ask you for a favor."

My shoulders dropped and I closed my eyes. "What?"

"Sit with me."

Inhaling, not knowing what his agenda was, yet unable to walk away from him, I turned. "Why?"

His eyes were more turbulent than the storm outside as quiet command filtered into his voice. "I want you next to me right now."

Tingles spread across my skin, and I wanted to sit more than any command Viktor had ever given me, and that was terrifying. I knew Dane was aware of the effect he had on me when he barked out orders. I saw it in his eyes. But this wasn't that. He didn't command me to sit, he asked. Except his question came with a condition, and that condition had a time clock of two words. *Right now.* "Why are you doing this?"

"Sit down and I'll tell you."

Viktor had broken me and trained me. He'd used everything he'd ever learned about me against me. He used it for control. Alex Vega had also figured out I was submissive, but he had no idea what that truly meant. His orders had no depth. They were merely words. I only followed them because they were the easiest commands I'd gotten each week.

But Dane was different, so very different that I had no defense against him or the patient expression on his face.

Confused, I reverted to what I knew. My head down, my hands clasped in front of me, I sat.

"You're not a liability to me." His voice was all at once quiet and forceful. He tipped my chin. "I will never hurt you."

Yearning, so intense it hurt, spiked every nerve in my body, and I couldn't sit. I didn't understand what was happening, but I knew I didn't deserve this man's trust. I pulled away from his grasp and stood. "I'll leave once the storm passes."

He was on his feet faster than I could blink. But he didn't stop there. He grasped the back of my neck and his mouth crashed over mine.

Oh. *My God.*

Hot and needy, an instant heat crawled up my body and every nerve was on fire. He didn't kiss me. He drove his tongue into my mouth and took charge. Every stroke was an assault on my declaration to leave. His mouth possessing mine, his hips making a slow grind, he curled his huge arm around me and held me to him, not as if he wanted me, but as if he needed me. *Desperately.*

My head spun.

Viktor didn't kiss me, not ever.

But Dane was kissing me.

And my body responded.

SEVEN

Dane

Her arms wrapped around my neck and she melted into me.

I shouldn't have touched her, but I did.

She wasn't just vulnerable, she was a fucking mess. The right thing to do would've been to stay away. But the second my mouth was on hers, she turned into the submissive I'd seen on my kitchen floor, and I didn't give two fucks about right or wrong or Fedorov. I was going to take her from him, and I was going to show her how a real man fucked.

I didn't just kiss her. Every stroke of my tongue through her sweet mouth was a promise. I knew what she needed. I'd known it the second I saw her. Stunning, aloof, she was so goddamn beautiful, every move of her body was made for seduction, but it was all training. She didn't have an ounce of the confidence she should've had, but I was going to fucking change that.

Encircling her wrists, I pulled her arms off my neck. "Do you know what you're doing?"

Leaning into me, she drew in a ragged breath. "Kissing you."

"Kissing or fucking?" I pushed her upright. "Make a decision."

It took two seconds. Then the desire in her eyes turned to anger. "You kissed *me*."

I knew exactly what I'd done. "How many times in the past five years was it your choice to fuck?"

With a sharp intake of breath, she glared at me then turned and took a step.

I caught her arm. "I asked you a question."

She whipped around. "Let go of me!"

There it was. That was the woman I fucking wanted. "Almost." My dick got harder.

"*Almost?*" She bit the word out and her temper unleashed. "No, *now*. If you think I'm going to stand here and let you throw my past in face, then you're—"

I grabbed her around the back of the neck and fisted a handful of her hair. "I don't want to fuck Fedorov's submissive. I want to fuck the woman who put four staples in me." I stepped up against her body, but then I slowly let go of her and gave her a choice. "If you don't want me to touch you, walk away."

She didn't move. The anger in her eyes morphed back to desire, and her voice turned quiet. "You're insane."

My mouth an inch from hers, I gave her fair warning. "I'm going to taste you, touch you, and fuck you until you're so sore, you'll never forget my name. I'm going to grind against this sweet body of yours and make you feel like you've never felt before. But I don't want to fucking own you. I'm not going to take a damn thing from you, except your orgasms. Because those? Are mine."

Her gaze dropped, her breath rushed out on an exhale, and she shrunk in on herself. Then every muscle in her body froze.

Goddamn it. "What just happened?"

No response.

I fought from touching her. "Irina."

She stepped back. "I'm sorry," she whispered.

Realization dawned. "What was the trigger?"

"You're injured. You should—"

"*Tell me.*" Barking out the order, I wasn't any better than that piece of shit Fedorov. I knew what was going on, but I wanted her to say it. I wanted her to fucking acknowledge it.

She lifted her head and her colorless eyes bored into me. "I know what you're doing."

"Say it," I demanded.

The fire I'd glimpsed surfaced and the woman in her came out with a vengeance. "You think you can own my orgasms?" She laughed bitterly. "You won't even make me come. You can *grind* all you want. It won't change a thing." She spun.

I was on her before she could take a step. One hand between her legs, I wrapped my bad arm around her shoulders and brought my mouth to her ear. "You think I can't make you come?" She had no clue who she was dealing with.

Her back arched and she served me her ass on a silver fucking platter, but her voice told me everything I wanted to hear. "I know you can't." Bitter, angry, she spat the words out.

"Keep that up," I ordered. "I want that hatred for him to be the taste in your mouth when I make you fall apart harder than you ever have." I cupped her hard and dragged my teeth across her ear. "Unbutton those jeans."

She shoved her sweet cunt into my hand and bit back a moan. "I didn't give you permission."

I increased the pressure. "What are you waiting for?"

"You're a murderer." Her chest pushed against my arm, but her hips ground down on my hand.

"A cold-blooded and remorseless murderer," I corrected. "And the next man that holds a gun to your head will also die." I sucked the flesh under her ear then dragged my tongue across her jaw and pressed my hard dick into her lower back. "Unbutton those jeans, or tell me to stop."

She groaned and unbuttoned her jeans. "You're not going to make me come."

I walked her two strides to the kitchen island, then yanked her jeans down to midthigh. "Who you trying to convince?" I dragged two fingers down her ass to her cunt.

She gasped. "There's only two ways I come."

She was soaked. "How's that?" I thumbed her clit and rubbed my throbbing cock along her sweet ass.

"*Viktor.*" She cried out his name as she rotated her hips. "I only come if he makes me."

I shoved two fingers inside her. "And the other way?" Jesus fuck, she was tight.

An unintelligible sound emanated from her throat. "Me," she panted. "I make me come." She rode my hand like she was desperate.

I pulled my fingers out and grasped her jaw with my thumb and two smallest fingers. Then I shoved my pussy-wet fingers into her mouth. Covering her back with my chest, I leaned her down, flush with the counter. "See that faucet?"

She moaned around my fingers in her mouth.

"Grab it right fucking now."

She didn't hesitate. She reached for it and wrapped her hands around it like a lifeline.

"Suck." I shoved my fingers deeper.

Her tongue swirled, and her spit, just like her cunt, dripped down my hand. I pushed her shirt up. My dick straining to get out of my pants, I rubbed it against her thigh. Pinching her small tit through her bra, I gave her a warning. "Do not *ever* speak his name again while I'm inside you."

She moved her hips to try to get my dick between her legs.

I slid my fingers out of her mouth. "You want my cock?"

Gripping the faucet, spread out over the counter, she writhed like a cat in heat. "Fuck me, *now*."

I dropped to my knees. "No." I shoved my tongue into her cunt.

She didn't groan, she snarled.

I yanked her jeans all the way off and bit her clit.

Her whole body jerked.

"You let go of that faucet, you're not coming," I warned.

Lifting her legs, I put her shins on my shoulders. Her ass in my face, her sweet fucking cunt dripping down my chin, I drove my tongue into her.

Then I set out to prove her wrong.

EIGHT

Irina

O H MY GOD. *OH MY GOD.*
This wasn't happening.
Everything about this was wrong, but it felt so right. My head a mess, I couldn't think anymore. His tongue was driving into my pussy, and God help me, I wanted to come.

My legs on his shoulders, my ass in the air, I gripped the damn faucet so hard, I thought I would break it. "You're not even close," I lied.

His teeth raked over my clit, then he increased the pressure of his tongue.

Squeezing my inner walls, conditioned by years of abuse, I told myself not to come. Desperate, I said something I'd never said to Viktor or Alex. "Stop."

Dane's response was immediate.

His tongue left my cunt, his hand left my tit, and he gently lowered me to my feet.

My thighs shaking, my chest on the counter, my hands still holding on to the faucet, I didn't move.

I panicked.

Every horrific thing Viktor had told me he would do to

me if I cheated on him flooded my mind, and I started to shake.

I'd left. He'd sent Peter to kill me. We were done. I knew that. But I couldn't stop thinking about his threats.

A blanket wrapped around my body and the silent alpha who'd come home to a woman in his house gently pulled my hands off the faucet without a word.

Forced to hold the blanket or risk losing it, I pulled it up to my chest and pushed off the counter. "Thank you," I murmured.

He didn't speak, and I didn't look up.

But I saw him. He was right there. His hip leaning on the counter, he was facing me. And he was waiting. I didn't know a single thing about this man except that he was frighteningly beautiful in the most austere way possible and he was a cold-blooded killer.

But I'd lost my fear of what he was capable of doing with a weapon. I pulled the blanket tighter. "I'm tired."

He inhaled, and then his deep, hypnotic voice filled the space between us. "What did he threaten you with?"

I shouldn't have been surprised that he figured out Viktor had threatened me. Dane watched me for reactions. I knew he gauged my body language, and his questions were too poignant. He was an observer like Viktor, but the similarities ended there. "You're not much younger than him."

"Thirty-three," he answered.

I nodded. Viktor would be forty-three next month. Five years ago, I was flattered that such a well-dressed, thirty-eight-year-old successful businessman was paying attention to an eighteen-year-old innocent girl. Little did I know. "I was stupid… when I met him."

"He preyed on you."

"Maybe." Or maybe I'd just been desperate enough to let it happen. I didn't want to be that desperate for a man ever again, so I did what I never did with Viktor. I lifted my head and faced Dane head-on. "This is the first time I cheated on him."

His expression locked, he stated the obvious. "You slept with Vega."

"He made me. He said Alex was my gift." My anger toward Viktor grew by the second. "But he forbade me to enjoy it. He said he owned my pleasure. He said if I was going to come, it better be at his hands. He told me not to let my body fail him while I was with Alex, or he'd punish me. He convinced me he would be able to tell, and I believed him so I never let myself come." I didn't know why I was telling Dane this, except that I needed to tell someone, and I didn't have a someone. I didn't have anyone besides Viktor and Alex, but now Alex had found his someone and Dane was here and he'd killed Peter and he'd protected me, but more, he'd stopped. He'd stopped when I'd told him to stop, which was something Viktor had never done. I couldn't explain why that made Dane more dangerous to me than Viktor ever was, but it did.

I stared at a man who would ruin me worse than Viktor ever could, then I gave him the ammunition to do it. "That was my trigger. You said you would own my pleasure. But I walked away from that. I walked away from a man who owned every single thing about me for five long years, and I didn't think I would make it past the front door when I left, but I did. I made it, and I told myself no man would ever own me again." I pushed down the memories of five years of painful paddlings and endless hours of being tied naked to every piece of furniture and fixture in the house. I swallowed the shame of my body's response to every forced orgasm that came after every punishment, and I sucked in a breath for courage.

"But then you said my orgasms would be yours. And I wanted it." I desperately wanted to know the kind of pleasure he was offering. "I wanted it so bad, I was willing to forget everything I promised myself just to feel it… to feel *you*." My voice dropped to a whisper and I hung my head. "Because the second you walked into your house and I saw you, I wanted to be yours."

His huge arms caught me and pulled me in close. His body heat surrounded me as the scent of my desire mixed with his soap and gas and the scent of man. It filled my lungs as he did something no man had ever done.

He held me.

Silent and strong and no agenda, he simply held me.

My heart broke.

NINE

Dane

SHE FUCKING GUTTED ME.
With her small body in my arms, and her resilience tightening my chest, I fucking held her and plotted how I was going to kill Fedorov.

As if she knew the twisted shit going through my head, she pushed me away and started talking again like she'd never left off. "But this isn't going to happen." She gestured between us. "Because you don't do repeats, and I just had my turn and that turn is up."

Bullshit. "Try again."

She shook her head. "I don't need to try that again. I'm pretty sure you proved your point."

"That's not what I meant." I knew she was about to come when I had my mouth on her. I also knew it was why she'd retreated. "Your turn's not up."

She inhaled and looked away. "You don't own me."

"Never said I did."

She crossed her arms as if to protect herself. "Close enough."

Not touching her now was physically painful. Her scent marking me, her taste leaving me hanging, I wanted to fuck her until she was screaming my name. "Close will be when I'm inside you."

Her cheeks reddened. "We tried that."

"We're going to try it again." Beautiful, vulnerable, desperate, in danger—she had every marker for disaster I could think of. I didn't do repeats, let alone complications. But the second I got my mouth on her, I wanted more than one fuck from her. A lot more. The detrimental thought twisted in my head and mixed with my last few assignments. I didn't want to get shot at for six figures anymore because I'd contracted to fix some asshole's problem. I was fucking tired of an hour in a hotel room with a woman I'd never see again. My life plan was fucking shit, but I'd never stopped to think about it until I walked into my house and saw a gorgeous blonde in my kitchen.

She glanced at the counter where I'd had her laid out, and sucked in a breath. "I know what you are. I know what you do. I heard the words you said…." She shook her head, as if clearing her thoughts. "But we both know this isn't going to work." She started to walk away.

I let her get halfway down the hall. "He was your first, wasn't he?"

She spun and sexy anger spread across her face. "That's none of your business."

I was making it my business. "He took your innocence and you feel obligated to him."

"I don't owe him a thing."

"Then why give him your future?"

"I'm *not* giving it to him."

Bullshit. "You're walking away from me."

Anger colored her cheeks. "Because you killed a man in front of me and I'm practicing sanity!"

"He was going to hurt you." He was going to do a hell of a lot more than hurt her. I didn't regret pulling that trigger, not for one fucking second.

"*So are you,*" she accused.

I fought for patience. "I killed him because he had a gun to your head and I didn't like his hands on you. I have no intention of hurting you." I'd fucking told her that, repeatedly. "You know that."

"I don't know anything." She turned and took another step.

"You're afraid of me."

"What woman wouldn't be?" She didn't even look over her shoulder. She walked into my guest room and slammed the door.

I couldn't fucking help myself, I smiled, because goddamn, that was the woman who'd stapled my shit. I grabbed a water just as the phone she'd reassembled and left on my counter vibrated.

My smile dropped. I swiped to take the call then held it to my ear.

"Did you think I would not find out what you did to Peter, pet?"

My nostrils flared. "I'm not your fucking pet."

Pause. "Ah. It is like this, then."

"Yes."

"Cat and mouse. Tell me, do you enjoy the game?"

I didn't answer.

He laughed. "I suspect you enjoy it very much. You did such good work on Peter. The authorities will never identify him. Pity I am going to kill you. I could have used someone like you."

"You can't afford me."

"Ah, yes, well, you would be surprised what I can afford."

"You can't afford a bullet between your eyes." His money wouldn't save him from my aim.

He laughed again. "Who can, my friend?"

"I'm not your friend."

He dropped the fake affability. "You're right. Friends don't fuck your wife."

"I didn't fuck her." Yet. "And you're not legally married." I was only half guessing. He could have forged the paperwork, but with his track record, I was betting he never bothered. He was never going to keep her long-term.

"What can a piece of paper say that the heart doesn't?"

"That she's entitled to half of everything you own."

He snorted out a laugh. "I think I underestimated you, marine. Maybe you are just looking for a quick payout. Okay, I will humor you. How much do you want for her?"

He was so dead. "Come over and find out."

"After what you did to my bodyguard? Do you really think I'm that stupid?"

"Yes." He was egotistical enough to think I would hand her back to him.

"That's where you're wrong. We're going to meet in a public place and you're going to bring my wife with you."

"Or?" He was too confident. He had something for leverage.

"Or I'll give the police the GPS coordinates of the embedded tracking device my late employee had and they'll see his last location at your residence before his unfortunate incineration."

"There are a dozen ways you could get my address, not the least of which is tracking her phone when she called you."

"I'm glad the military taught you to be skeptical." He smirked. "There… believe me now?"

My current work phone, a prepaid toss-away with a number I gave out to no one, vibrated in my pocket. I pulled it out as it lit up with a new text. I clicked the text then tapped the picture. A map with a tracked route leading from Key Biscayne to my place ended at the location of the overpass.

Goddamn it. I'd been so fucking caught up in her, I'd never thought to look for a tracking device.

Stalling to buy time as I strode to my guest room, I played it out. "Looks bogus." I pushed her door open and put my finger to my lips as she looked up.

Still wrapped in the blanket I'd put around her, she sat with her knees to her chest as her gaze cut to her phone. Her face fell.

"I assure you, marine, there is nothing *bogus* about the precautions I take to ensure the safety and well-being of my employees."

I quickly typed a note on my phone and showed it to her. She shook her head.

I nodded. "Precautions you don't apparently take with your wife."

"Her safety is of my utmost concern."

Right. Fucking asshole. "Is that why you sent your guard to kill her?" I held the phone away from my ear and put it on speaker so she could hear the asshole's response.

Fedorov laughed. "I assure you my bodyguard was only going to teach her a lesson. If she chose to fight him on that, then her fate was in his hands. I am not responsible for that."

"I don't call rape a lesson."

He chuckled. "Then you are too soft. She is young and she

needs to be kept in line. Something you would know nothing about."

Anger contorted her features and she opened her mouth.

I shook my head once in warning. "Women aren't animals you give obedience training to."

"Ah, yes, your dog. Hunter, is it? Quite the pedigree he has. You would know about obedience training, wouldn't you?"

My expression locked, I didn't let her see an ounce of the alarm churning in my gut. "Come over and I'll introduce you to him."

He laughed. "Maybe another time. Tomorrow afternoon we will meet at the rooftop restaurant Indigo. Bring my wife and I'll lose the computer file with my bodyguard's GPS tracking information for the last twenty-four hours before his death. If you are not there by two p.m., I will hand the information over to the police and report him missing."

Irina started shaking her head.

I held a finger to my lips again. "She's not coming. She's done with you."

"Oh, she will come. I know you have her listening right now, and I know my wife. Something you didn't factor in when you decided to try to keep her, marine. She is my wife. Not yours. I know what she needs." He chuckled. "And she'll be begging for it by tomorrow afternoon."

"Outside patio, me only. You give me the file and we'll discuss you seeing her again." He was never going to lay eyes on her again.

"Inside, Irina comes. I am not negotiating with you further."

Shit. "You afraid to sit outside?"

"And be taken out by your sniper rifle?"

"I'll be sitting across the table from you. How am I going to manage that?"

"With your reputation, marine, I have no doubt you will at least try. Enjoy the rest of the night with my wife. It's the last you'll get to spend with her." Fedorov hung up.

"Dane—"

I held a finger up and dialed on my prepaid.

Luna answered on the first ring with a chuckle. "I knew a pickup wouldn't be the last of it."

"My prepaid was hacked. My security's been compromised."

He instantly sobered. "On it. Don't say another word. Protocol."

"Copy."

He hung up.

Pissed as hell, I spared Irina a single glance and held my hand up before stalking to my bedroom. I cut the modem and the Internet, turned off all security cameras, and powered down both cell phones. I used my laptop in my bedroom to first make a copy to a zip drive of the security footage from the front porch earlier, then I wiped all the security backups from the past week and shut the machine down. Pulling a scanner out of my gun safe, I did a quick and dirty sweep of the house for bugs but found none.

On my heels the whole time, Hunter quietly whined as he followed me back to my bedroom. The house was clear, but I gave him a command to occupy him. "Patrol."

"You can't go meet him."

I turned. Her jeans were back on and she'd put her hair

up. The bone structure of her face stood out even more. "Do you know how to shoot?"

She looked more than alarmed. "I'm not using a sniper rifle."

"Handguns." But I liked where her mind went.

"I don't like guns. What's going on?"

"I have to go out to the barn. You're going to stay here with Hunter."

"What? No. I don't want to stay here alone."

"You won't be alone. Hunter will be with you." I put the scanner back in my safe and locked it.

"And what's he going to do?"

I turned to her. "Kill. If you command it."

She looked down the hall as Hunter walked the inside perimeter of the house. "What's the command?"

"Attack. Say his name, then say the word."

She hugged her arms to her chest. "You can't go meet Viktor. He'll give the police the information no matter what."

"I know."

She looked back up at me with determination. "Then I'll go with you to meet him. I'll talk to him."

"Not an option." I handed her my smallest weapon. "It's a Beretta PX4 Storm Compact Carry. It has a smooth trigger pull and minimal recoil."

She took the gun, released the magazine, and checked the ammo.

Fuck, she was sexy. "Fifteen plus one." I told her the ammo count. "The magazine's fully loaded."

"I see." She put the magazine back in. "What am I supposed to do with this?"

"Shoot anyone who isn't me or Hunter."

She set the gun on my dresser. "What makes you think I know how to use that?"

"Anyone who checks to see if the gun is loaded knows how to shoot." The wind gusted and rattled the storm shutters. "I'll be back in thirty minutes."

She glanced at the shuttered windows in the bedroom. "You can't go out there. It's too dangerous."

It was more dangerous not to find out how Fedorov had gotten to me. "Thirty minutes, max. I'll be fine." I walked to the door to the garage and she followed.

"What if a tree falls on the barn?"

"I'll be underground." I opened the door.

"*Dane.*"

The panic in her voice made me pause, but the look on her face made me want to kill Fedorov a thousand times over. I gripped her chin and left a kiss on her cheek, because if I touched her mouth with mine, I wouldn't walk out that door. "You'll be fine, promise."

"Hurry," she whispered.

I nodded once and closed the door behind me. Fighting the wind and rain to the barn made me confident Fedorov wouldn't attempt to drive in this shit. If he was willing to send a guard to teach her a lesson, he didn't fucking love her. She was merely a possession.

Cognizant of my staples, I carefully opened and closed the hatch behind me, but I didn't turn on any of my equipment. I called Luna first.

He answered immediately. "*Dios mio.*" He typed on a keyboard. "Your shit is hacked to hell."

"How did it happen?" He'd set up my security.

"One tricky motherfucker is how. Hold up." He typed

some more. "Damn, amigo. Whoever it is, they were attempting to download the footage from your security camera feeds."

I rubbed a hand over my face. "How much did they get?"

"Hold on… okay, I stopped the breach. Scanning now… *shit*. The download was stopped before the footage showed you pulling the trigger, but what they did get is pretty damning. Who's after you?"

"Could Viktor Fedorov have done this?"

Pause. Then, "*Jesucristo*. You have got to be kidding me. Fedorov? What the hell are you into?"

"I have his wife."

Luna exhaled, low and quiet. "*Holy mother of God.*"

"She needs an exit strategy."

"Are you fucking suicidal?" He was incredulous. "Because there's only one way Fedorov will give up his property."

I didn't reply.

"Do I want to know who was in the vehicle you torched?"

"His guard."

"Which one? He has a dozen of them."

"She called him Peter."

"*Shit*, Marek. That was his cousin."

"Now he's his dead cousin." I glanced at my watch. I'd only been gone four minutes but I wanted to get the fuck back to her. "He wants to meet at Indigo tomorrow at two. He's expecting me to bring his wife. I need backup."

Luna let loose with a stream of cuss words in Spanish. "Fuck, that rooftop restaurant? All right, all right. Let me pull up the Google Street View and see what we're dealing with. You meeting him inside or on the patio?"

"He specified inside, but I plan on getting there first and being outside."

Luna typed some more. "You still have the penthouse at Mira Vista?"

"Yeah."

"Roof access?"

"Yes."

"Hmm…. There's a possibility of a clean shot from there if you're on the southwest side of the patio."

"Options if it's not clean?"

"If he uses valet, there'll be a small window, otherwise, a car bomb, breach his residence, poison his food? Shit, bro, I don't know. This is your specialty."

And I was losing my touch. "Did he personally hack my security?"

"I'm still trying to trace it, but my guess is yes. He has a reputation for knowing his shit."

"What do you know about his residence?"

"Besides it being surrounded by water on three sides and having a twelve-foot wall on the other side? Nothing. But you can guarantee his security will be better than yours. You have his wife, ask her about it."

I will. "You set up my security," I reminded him.

"And he hacked it."

"I've got another issue." I exhaled. "He had a GPS tracker embedded in the guard I killed. He's going to the police with the guard's last tracking before he died if I don't hand over his wife."

"*Mierda*. Does his wife have a tracker?"

"She said she doesn't have one."

"Thank God for small favors."

No fucking kidding. I needed to get back to the house. "I'm not asking you for a favor tomorrow." He would get what I meant.

"Copy that, but I'm offering."

"Your business." This could jeopardize everything he had, and I knew he supported his parents and two of his sisters.

Luna didn't hesitate. "My business will be fine."

I wasn't going to let him take that kind of risk, but I would use him another way. "You take the meet." We were similar height and built, enough that it would give Fedorov pause, and that's all I needed. A three-second window. "I'll take the shot."

"Take it or make it?" Luna asked. "We both know who the better shot is between us."

"I'll make it. Dress like me and be there by one-thirty. Is he going to recognize you?"

Luna paused. "Possibly. I keep my distance, but we know of each other. My men had a run-in with his last year."

Fuck. "Just keep your head down."

"Always," he reassured. "What are you doing about the wife?"

Not bringing her. "I'll handle that."

Luna muttered a curse in Spanish. "You're just as cagey as Christensen, you know that?"

We'd both served with Neil Christensen, and no one was in the same damn orbit as him, let alone as cagey. "The less I tell you, the better."

"You expecting this to blow up?"

I didn't know what to expect with Fedorov. "No idea. But he gave me proof already of the tracking file. Who knows who else has it."

"What are you going to do?" Luna scoffed. "Take out as many as you can?"

Tempting, but a public hit was risky enough, let alone one with multiple casualties. I'd done it before, but it wasn't something I wanted to repeat. "I'll start with Immigration." If I was lucky, none of them were here legally.

Luna half snorted, half laughed. "Not a bad idea. In the meantime, I'll work it from my end and see if I can get into his system and wipe it."

Which wouldn't do me any good if he'd made a copy of the information. "It could already be too late."

"True, but that doesn't mean I'm not going to enjoy the fuck outta trying." Luna chuckled. "Besides, I have friends on the force, and trust me, they and the Feds would love to bury Fedorov. They've been after him for years."

I scrubbed my hand over my face. "Anything you can do about my security system? I want to catch a few hours sleep."

"Yeah, you're all set for now. I fixed the breach and remotely powered you back up. I rerouted your feeds so I can see what you see, and I'm filtering you through my system to prevent any other hacker attempts. Get some sleep. We'll monitor it here and I'll alert you on this line if anything comes up."

"Thanks."

"*De nada.* Hey, how'd you wind up with his wife?"

"She was Vega's client."

Luna burst out laughing. "You have got to be shitting me."

I didn't respond.

"All right, all right, I get it. So what, you, Vega and Brandt trade off clients?"

"Now you're pissing me off."

He chuckled. "Come on, I'm only kidding. Okay, half kidding."

Tired as fuck, I exhaled. "Vega didn't have a clue who she was, and no, we don't switch clients. Vega asked for a favor. Said he had a former client who needed a place to land. I wasn't home at the time. I let him use the house."

"Bro," he drew the word out. "That's rule number one. Never let anyone fuck with your casa."

I know. "That was my first mistake."

"*Cristo.* And your second?"

I sighed. "She looks like my ex-wife." Except she was a hundred times more beautiful and a thousand times more dangerous.

Luna laughed his ass off. "Oh how the mighty have fallen."

I refrained from telling him to fuck off. "Don't wear your company logo shirt tomorrow."

He laughed harder. "That's all you got?"

"Be on time and watch your back tomorrow."

Luna sobered. "Copy that. I always make sure me and the guys—"

No way. "I don't want anyone else on this," I warned. I wasn't going to be responsible for any of his men if this thing went south.

Luna exhaled. "Listen, I know you work alone, but I don't. I trust my men. Most of them you know from when we were downrange. The others go through a six-month vetting process. I trust all of them with my life and they trust me."

"That's not the issue."

"I'm not going to assign anyone to this if that's what you're worried about. I'll ask them."

Asking would require background or an explanation. "This doesn't go beyond you and me."

Silence.

"You and me, or I go solo." The second you had to give someone an ultimatum, you'd lost control of the situation. But there was no way I was letting anyone else get involved in this. I knew my best resource for tomorrow would've been Jared Brandt. When Vega and I had served with him, he was a fucking ghost. He could get in or out of any situation without being seen and his aim was almost as accurate as Luna's. But I wasn't getting him involved either. If I hadn't had my security hacked, I wouldn't even be talking to Luna right now.

"All right, I hear you. But this is a mistake. Fedorov will have his bodyguards with him and who knows how spread out they'll be."

If Fedorov was smart, he'd have his guards positioned over a two-block radius and he'd take me out before I got to the restaurant. But gunrunners weren't usually that smart. They favored standoffs because they thought their weapons made them invincible. "Just make sure you have a clean exit before you go in."

"I know what I'm doing, *amigo*."

"Good."

"Hey, I'm serious about his wife. Don't leave her at your house. He'll send men there. It's what I'd do."

I decided to tell him. If something happened to me, he could look out for her. "I'll take her to the penthouse."

"Bring her to Luna and Associates. The men here will keep an eye on her."

That was exactly what I didn't want. "I got it covered. See you tomorrow." I hung up.

TEN

Irina

I HELD THE GUN BECAUSE THE WEIGHT IN MY HANDS GAVE me a false sense of security. I knew I would never shoot Viktor, not even if he came crashing through the front door and dragged me out by my hair.

A four-year-old memory surfaced and I shivered. I'd told Viktor one night I was too tired to play. At first, he'd just smiled at me and I'd stupidly thought I was off the hook. Night after night of being assaulted with sex toys for hours on end, I'd wanted an evening off. It wasn't as if I was turning him down for sex, because Viktor had never had actual sex with me. I'd never even seen his cock. He'd told me on our first date that he didn't fuck. He'd said he'd had an injury and he *played games* instead. I was young and naïve, and I never could've imagined the depths of his depravity at eighteen.

But the night I'd said no, I got a lesson in it. He'd dragged me naked through four downstairs rooms by my hair then tied me to the front staircase by his office door for six hours where all his guards could walk by and see my shame. The next night, he'd played his games for twice as long, twice as hard. I'd never told him no again.

The door from the garage burst open with a gust of wind

and Dane's height crowded the frame before he walked in soaking wet.

His eyes trained on me, he strode across his hardwood floors. "You okay?"

The entire space changed in a nanosecond and my cheeks burned with the memory of his tongue on me. "Yes."

"Then why are you pointing your gun at me?"

I looked down. "It's not mine. It's yours." I lowered the small 9mm and set it on the coffee table.

"Keep it."

"I don't want it." I tried to tell myself I didn't want anything from him.

Water dripped off his close-cropped hair and landed on his huge shoulders. "You need it."

"A gun isn't the answer to my problems." With his hair wet, he looked even more austere.

"No, but a hired gun is."

"I don't have any money to pay you." He knew I didn't, but I wasn't saying it just to remind him.

"I don't want you to pay me."

No, he wanted something more than money. Much more. "Then you aren't a hired gun."

"I'm many things you wish me not to be." He held his hand out. "Come on."

My heart raced and the whisper of his scent through the rainwater drenching his body filled my head. I ached to touch him. "Where?"

"To bed."

The convoluted thoughts that had been circling through my screwed-up head spilled out of my mouth. "I'm not a cheater, you know."

"You already left him, and I never thought you were."

"I can't... with you." I had reasons, but I was rapidly forgetting them.

His hand never wavered. "I need sleep. You need sleep. I'll rest better if I know where you are. Come."

Of everything Viktor had ever done to me, including tying me to the front stairs naked, none of it had made me feel as vulnerable as I felt right this second. I reached for an excuse, but what I wanted more than anything was to lie in the arms that had wrapped around me in comfort earlier. "You said no repeats."

"We already discussed this. Give me your hand, Irina."

Knowing I shouldn't, knowing I was crossing an invisible line I would never return from, I gave him my hand.

He didn't hesitate. He pulled me to my feet and took a step.

I panicked. "Wait." Oh God, *don't say it, don't say it*. "I can't do this. This will mean something to me that it doesn't to you."

Cool gray-brown eyes stared down at me without mercy. "Do not speak for me."

"I just meant—"

"I know what you meant."

I gave him the truth because it was all I had left. "You're taking what I don't have to give."

His shoulders dropped, his frame leaned toward me, and he lowered his voice to a barely audible whisper. "Trust me." Rain dripped from his cheek and landed on my arm. "This is what I ask of you, only this. Nothing else."

If you could fall in love in a single moment with a perfect stranger, I fell in love. "You will break me, Dane Marek," I whispered.

"You are already broken, Irina Tsarko."

ELEVEN

Dane

Her vulnerability caught in her throat. "Then what are you doing with me?"

"Solving your problems." I tightened my hold on her. "One by one."

"Dane—"

"Come with me. If you need to talk, do it in bed." I was done talking, and she didn't need to hear any words from me. She needed actions. I led her into the bedroom and dropped her hand only long enough to set my cell and 9mm on the nightstand, then strip out of my soaked clothes.

As if she were too afraid to look up at my eyes or down at my dick, she stared religiously at the scars on my chest. "What are you doing?"

I heard the anxiety in her voice, I saw the tension in her expression, but I ignored them and grabbed the hem of her shirt. "Undressing. Same as you."

"I wasn't undressing." She lifted her arms.

"Now you are." No bra, her nipples hard as fuck, she sucked in a breath as I pulled the shirt over her head. Fuck, she was gorgeous. I reached for her jeans.

Her hand shot to mine.

My dick pulsed, but I stilled. I could've given her words. I didn't. I leaned down and kissed her forehead once. It said more than anything I could've told her.

Her breathing sped up, but she dropped her hand.

My gaze locked on hers, I dropped to a squat and dragged her jeans down her legs. She gracefully pointed her toes and stepped out of them. Resisting the urge to touch every inch of her naked body as I stood back up, I allowed myself one indulgence. I took her chin. "Were you a dancer?"

Heat hit her cheeks. "I practiced ballet when I was younger."

I searched her face for any other goddamn triggers that asshole had given her, but it was her posture that was telling. Her back straight, she didn't lean toward me. "I'm not going to fuck you."

She exhaled.

"Unless you want me to."

She pulled away from my grip and dropped her gaze. "I know what you're doing."

It was what I wasn't doing that she should've taken notice of. Not taking her nipples in my mouth, not shoving my dick in her tight cunt, not claiming her moans with my mouth. My dick hard as fuck for her, she had no clue what I wasn't doing. "No, you really don't." Impatient, tired, fuck—testing her, I put force into my tone. "Get in bed."

She flinched, but then she scrambled on the bed and got under the comforter. "Just because you know what my triggers are doesn't mean you get to use that against me."

I lost patience. Yanking the covers back, I crawled on top of her. My hands on either side of her head, my knees straddling her hips, I hovered above her sweet body and forced her truth on her. "Why do you think he chose you?"

She turned her head and crossed her arms.

Quick, precise, I grabbed her wrists and held them over her head. "He chose you because you were naturally submissive."

She bucked, but she didn't even attempt to pull her wrists out of my loose grasp. "I was not."

Smelling her desire, seeing her hard nipples, I knew she was fucking turned on. "You like this." Calculated and slow, I brushed the head of my cock across her thigh.

Her knees fell open and her voice dropped to a whisper. "No, I don't."

My dick settled against her pussy. "You like a man telling you what to do. Your cunt's wet. Your legs are spread. You want me to fucking take you." I lowered my voice and fought to keep from thrusting into her. "You're a submissive, sweetheart. He did not give that to you."

She pretended to struggle against my hold. "Yes, he did."

"No," I corrected. "He didn't."

"Get off me." There was zero force in her tone.

"Say it like you mean it and I will."

She stopped struggling and looked up at me with the burden of his abuse etched across her face. "You don't know what he did."

I switched her wrists to one hand and cupped her face. "I don't need to." It would fucking enrage me. "You were a natural submissive, and he preyed on you. That wasn't your fault."

"You think I'm weak."

"No. I don't." The fucking opposite.

"You're lying."

"Watch it," I warned.

"Or what? You'll hit me?"

Flippant and offhand, I knew it was a knee-jerk response. I knew what abuse did to a person, but I answered her anyway. "I will never hit you."

"No, you'll just pin me down."

"Ask." She needed to fucking ask. She needed to know I would stop if she said the word, but she also needed to know I liked her submission. I fucking wanted it. I was going to push her and dominate her and take her every damn way I wanted, but we needed her boundaries out in the open. I'd respect her fucking triggers, but not if she wasn't honest with me.

"You think that makes you a man? Holding a woman down?"

Ignoring the venom in her tone, I answered her calmly. "You're not asking to be let go. Know why?"

Her chest heaving, looking like she was going to spit in my face, she didn't say shit.

I answered the question for her. "Because you don't want that power exchange. You want me in charge. You want me making the decision." I leaned closer and drove it home. "You wanted him making the decisions."

She crushed her thighs against my ribs and bucked against my hold. "He did this! He turned me into this! He made me into a freak who begs for it!"

My stab wound ripped with pain and my nostrils flared. "Spread your goddamn legs."

She tried to head-butt me.

"*Right fucking now*," I yelled.

Her thighs eased off my waist and she fell back to pillow to glare at me. "Go ahead," she taunted. "Fuck me."

I breathed past the fucking burn in my side and leveled her with a look. "You want to beg, you fucking beg. You want me to let go, ask. You want to walk out that door, then walk. But if you want to be fucked like the submissive you are, know your triggers and set your fucking boundaries. I will respect every goddamn one. But know this—when you're in my bed? There is no ambiguity. I call the goddamn shots because that's how I fucking like it."

"You're not calling any shots. You're yelling at me. You can kill a man, but you can't fuck a woman?"

"Ask." I wasn't fucking yelling, and I wasn't playing her goddamn game.

"With a pretty please and sugar on top?" she mocked. "You're naked and on top of me with a hard-on. Don't you know how to use it?"

I didn't fucking work to get a woman. I didn't put up with bullshit, and I sure as fuck didn't play immature games. I lowered my voice to a deadly calm and gave her one last chance. "You want to fuck, you ask. You want to be dead to me? Mouth off one more time." I let go of her and sat up.

Her arms above her head, her chest heaving, she didn't move.

Not one inch.

Then slow and deliberate, her knees fell open, exposing her wet pussy.

It was all the invitation I needed.

I grabbed her waist and shoved into her tight cunt. Sinking to the hilt, my cock hit her fucking cervix and she gasped.

"Take a breath," I commanded.

Her eyes wide, she drew in air as her small hands grasped at my forearms.

Goddamn, she was tight. Unbelievably, lose-my-fucking-mind *tight*. "You need me to pull out?"

Soft and breathless and pure submission, she whispered, "No, please."

My cock throbbing, I almost lost it. "You know what you're gonna give me?"

She bit her bottom lip. "Trust?"

Jesus, she was fucking with my head. "An orgasm." My thumb on her clit, my palm pressing into her lower abdomen, I thrust into her. Tight and slow, I ground my hips against hers, and fought to keep from shooting my load.

Her back arched and her fingernails dug into my arms. "Oh my God, what are you doing?"

"Making you come." I gave her another slow grind.

Her inner muscles clenched around my dick. "This… oh God. I've never felt…."

I pulled halfway out and fisted myself. Pressing my cock up as my other hand pressed down on her abdomen, I shoved halfway in and stroked her G-spot. "Felt what?" I watched as my dick sank into her small body.

"*Oh God*," she moaned, moving her hips with mine. "No condom."

My gaze shot to hers. "You on the pill?"

Her chest rose and fell, and guilt spread across her face. "Please, don't stop."

Goddamn it. "Answer me."

"No," she whispered.

My dick pulsed, my chest rose with an inhale and I cataloged. Seven knife wounds, five gunshot wounds, two IED explosions, three concussions, four bounties on my head, two hundred and thirty-seven confirmed kills, and at least a dozen other assholes who wanted me dead.

That wasn't father material. No attachments, no family.

That's how this worked. I didn't get to take advantage of her. I didn't get to think about a future.

I stared at her then I told her the truth. "I could be dead tomorrow." I never told anyone the truth.

She didn't blink. "So could I."

"I won't let that happen." I hadn't fucked without a condom since my ex-wife.

Her hands moved up my arms. "You can't control everything."

I wanted to fucking claim her. I hadn't wanted to claim anyone since I was eighteen. Slow and measured, I eased out then rocked back into her. "I'm going to control your orgasms."

She bit her bottom lip, but her gaze drifted. "I don't know what you want me to say."

"I don't want you to say a thing. I want your tight cunt to pulse around my dick, and I want you to fucking know what consensual sex feels like."

"I've had consensual sex," she whispered.

Because she fucking whispered it, because she was conditioned by Fedorov, because she was so goddamn beautiful but she didn't have a single ounce of self-confidence not related to sex, I knew she was lying. "Whose idea was Vega?"

She didn't answer.

"Who drove you to him? Who told you not to come? Who picked you up afterward?"

She shivered.

I didn't let jealousy or anger rule me. Ever. But I was balls deep in a woman who deserved more than Fedorov's abuse. She deserved more that what Vega had ever fucking given her, and she deserved a hell of a lot more than me. But

I wanted her, and I was pissed the fuck off. "Who paid Vega to fuck you?" I demanded.

She closed her eyes. "I don't want to talk about this."

"We're not fucking talking about it." She wasn't saying a goddamn word. I pulled out. "Make a choice."

She sucked in a sharp breath and her eyes popped open. "I already made a choice."

One way or another, she was going to tell me to fuck her before I let her come. "Did you tell me to fuck you?"

Silence.

"Do you know what you're not doing?"

She stared at me. Then without an ounce of ambiguity in her voice, she answered, "I'm not saying no." Her voice dropped to a whisper. "Fuck me. Please."

I shoved back into her.

Her head fell back and she cried out.

I circled my thumb over her clit. "That was a choice, sweetheart."

"Please," she panted. "Make me come."

I grasped her jaw. "This, right here, is who I want to fuck." I kissed her.

TWELVE

Irina

HE KISSED ME.
My thoughts upside down, the wall around my heart shattering, his giant cock stretched me past my limit and *he kissed me*.

Urgent and hard, his tongue stroked through my mouth like he needed me so bad he couldn't breathe. But then he swirled his tongue in a soft caress and I lost my mind.

Tears dripped down my face.

His giant hands cupped my face and his body stilled. "What's wrong?"

No one had ever kissed me like that.

"Irina?"

I shook my head because I couldn't speak. I wasn't afraid of him. I was terrified. I wanted him so bad, it hurt.

His arms wrapped around my back. "Come on." He rolled with me securely in his embrace and sat back against the headboard. Buried deep inside me, his cock pulsed as I sat astride his huge, muscular thighs. "You cried when I kissed you. Why?"

Horrified by my tears, more slid down my cheeks.

He made no move to wipe them. "Am I hurting you?"

So, so much. I shook my head.

He gently brushed my hair from my face, then his hands encircled my waist. "Move with me, sweetheart."

I choked back a sob at the term of endearment.

His hips thrust up and he lifted me a few inches. Intently watching me, he brought me gently back down. His lips still wet from our kiss, he was no longer just striking to me. He was the most beautiful man I'd ever seen, and I couldn't look at him anymore.

My forehead fell to his chest and I gripped his giant biceps. "Please," I begged. "Make me come." I needed to know, just once, what it felt like to come from a man inside me.

He ground his hips. My aching clit rubbed against his hard body, but he didn't pick up the pace. Naked of clamps, my nipples ached for attention. I tried to buck my hips to speed up the rhythm, but his hands held me steady.

"No," I cried. "I need more."

His thumb slid to my clit. "Look at me."

I groaned and thrust against his hand to capture more pressure. "Yes," I panted. "Like that."

"*Look at me.*"

I lifted my head.

His eyes fierce, his jaw set, he gave me a slow grind deep inside my core. "Give me the reason for the tears."

The tight circle of pleasure his thumb kept unleashing on my clit went from desperate need to painful pressure, and my mind did what it did every time I wanted to escape from Viktor. It shut down.

As if reading my thoughts, Dane shook his head. "No. Don't you shut down on me." His giant hands grasped the sides of my face. "This doesn't work like that."

My fears bled out. "It doesn't work anyway. This is all I get." My voice faltered. "One time."

"I'm not going to be done with you after one time." He thrust into me so hard, my breasts bounced.

I groaned and forced myself not to believe what he was saying. "Don't lie to me." I gripped his arms harder.

"No lie, sweetheart." He dropped his hand back between us and pounded into me, over and over.

His thumb working my clit, his sheer size making my G-spot sing, I told myself two times with him would be enough. He felt so incredible, I almost believed the lie. "You're going to break me."

"I'm going to make you come." He thrust hard, then ground his hips. "Right now."

He didn't even get the last word out before the sound crawled up my throat and burst between us like a caged animal screaming for freedom. My back arched, my body bowed, and every nerve ending exploded at once.

I didn't come. I violently burst through the orgasm he owned.

Tendrils of ecstasy crawled up my spine, over my shoulders and spread across my nipples. Pulsing spasms shocked my core, and my hips thrust like I was riding my first rodeo, but there was something missing.

"Oh my God, *oh my God*, come inside me!" I didn't know what I was saying, I didn't understand what I was feeling, I didn't even know my own name, but I knew one thing for certain. I needed his release inside me. "Please," I begged. I never wanted this feeling to end. "Don't stop." I gripped the short hair on his head and growled at him, "Don't stop, don't stop, *don't stop*." I was on a trajectory, and he was my orbit.

He didn't even let me touch the sky.

His tongue thrust past my lips and the sweetest taste of dominance spilled into my mouth. He swept through my heat and rocked against my G-spot as he cupped my breasts. "That's one, sweetheart." He pinched my nipples hard. "You're gonna give me another."

His cock grew inside me, and I gasped in pleasure-pain. I didn't know it could feel like this. I didn't know I could fly and soar. I didn't know I could reach past the sky and never touch the earth. This wasn't holding back an orgasm. This wasn't my own finger rubbing my clit. This wasn't a vibrator wand pressed so hard against me it hurt. This was everything I'd been missing, and it simultaneously made me ecstatic and enraged.

But I didn't get to process a single emotion.

Stormy green-brown eyes sucked me into their vortex as impossibly rough hands worked me into a frenzy. Pinching my nipples, rubbing my clit with finesse, dominating my body with a hand on my nape and another on my hip, Dane kissed me.

I never stood a chance.

The second orgasm didn't build on a slow recovery. It reared up and stole every last molecule of air I had. I fought to keep from drowning at the same time I wanted to sink into this world of impossibility.

I'd barely grasped the thought when his cock grew unbelievably big and violently pulsed. My entire body shook and the first burst of his orgasm hit my core.

I flew apart.

If my body had not been conditioned for five years for multiple orgasms, my heart would have stopped. "*Dane.*"

He gripped my hips and slammed me down on his pulsating cock. "That's it, sweetheart." His hot seed pumped into my body. "Feel me."

The clutches of my orgasm wrapped around my heart and constricted my chest as my body exploded with ecstasy.

Dane Marek wasn't a problem solver.

He was my savior.

A six-foot-four, muscled-like-a-god savior who took my heart and crushed it into oblivion as he branded my body with a taste of heaven I'd never get again.

THIRTEEN

Dane

I FUCKING CAME INSIDE HER.
Her tight cunt constricting all around me, she milked every last ounce of my orgasm.
I didn't think.
I didn't catalog.
I didn't look for a way out.
I wrapped my arms around her and sank my tongue into her mouth. Stroking through her heat, feeling my cum spread inside her cunt, it was everything I never knew I was missing. And it fucking took hold in one singular driving force.
More.
I needed more. I needed to dominate her.
Holding her slight body tight against my chest, I rolled and shoved her thigh with my knee. My hips between her legs, my dick buried deep, my mouth on hers, I thrust once then pulled back to see her. "You with me?"
Her hands were curled possessively around the back of my head, but it was the look in her eyes that drew me in. "Yes."
"You ready to go again?"
"Is this my second time?"
I stared at her because I was missing something. Stroking

slow, I rode her a few moments, studying every inch of her face. She felt so fucking incredible, I never wanted to pull out. "By my count, it would be three." Goddamn, she looked beautiful under me.

She turned her head. "You came inside me."

I caught her chin and brought her back to me. "You told me to."

"You're not the type of man who does what a woman tells him."

I stilled. "You're right."

"Then why did you?"

"Is that an accusation or a question?" My dick already pulsing again, I was ready to come a second time.

"How can you joke about this?"

I wasn't fucking joking. "You don't want children?"

Alarm spread across her face. "This isn't funny."

"I'm not laughing, sweetheart." I brushed her hair from her face.

She sucked in a deep breath and let it out slow. The panic in her eyes dissipated. "Do you ever laugh?"

"Yes." I just couldn't remember when.

"Is this my second time?"

I finally put the pieces together. "I'm not going to be done with you after two fucks. And if you're carrying my child, I'm never going to be done with you."

She stared at me a moment, then resignation clouded her expression. "You tell me you don't do repeats, but you'll risk getting a woman pregnant and break all your rules for her? Why? Out of a sense of obligation because she'll be carrying your child? Or do you just like the idea of knocking women up?"

"Not women, woman. One. You. And you would be the first woman who ever carried my child." I didn't point out again that she'd asked for this. This wasn't one hundred percent on her. I could've pulled out, but I didn't.

"That you know of."

"Only one other woman I ever fucked without a condom, and trust me, sweetheart, my ex-wife wanted nothing to do with kids."

Her eyes went wide. "You were married?"

"You look shocked."

"I am."

Fuck, I wanted to move inside her. "Because of what I do." It wasn't a question. I knew what she was thinking.

"What do you do?"

Besides have the longest conversation I'd had with any woman since my divorce? "Solve problems no one else can."

"And I'm just another problem to fix." She pushed at my chest.

I reluctantly eased out of her. "No. You have a problem. I can solve it."

"You said I was broken."

I rolled to my side and dragged my palm over her gorgeous tits. "You are." Her nipples pebbled under my touch.

She tried to push away from me.

I threaded my hand through her soft hair. "You're beautiful and broken and the strongest woman I know. If you're carrying my child, I will take care of both of you for the rest of your lives."

Her eyes welled with unshed tears. "And if I'm not."

I could only give her the facts. "You're in my bed." The rest was up to her.

"For how long?"

I resisted what I wanted to say and said what I should. "You can do better than me."

"You push me away in one breath then drag me under in the next."

I breathed through two heartbeats before I replied. "Having my child is a death sentence?"

"I don't know. Is it?"

She was pissing me off, but I'd promised myself I wouldn't lie to her. "Probably."

She pushed at my chest and sat up. "You call me broken, but you're the one acting insane. You can't treat a woman like this. You don't get to speak in contradictory sentences and kill someone in front of her then sleep with her without a condom and call it a death sentence!"

I forced myself to keep my tone even. "You were the one who said I was dragging you under. I haven't lied to you about anything."

"But you don't tell the truth either! You withhold half of what you mean and talk in cryptic sentences for the other half."

Thirty-six hours without sleep, adrenaline spent, I lost my fucking patience. "Which truth is that? That Viktor is going to kill you if I don't kill him first? That you look like my ex-wife? That my future is a gamble even I won't bet on? That I want your body full with my child? Or that I want to fuck you until you're so goddamn sore you don't remember a fucking thing Fedorov did you."

Her lips parted with a shocked expression.

"Is that too much truth for you to handle?" I challenged.

She blinked. "I look like her?"

Jesus Christ. "Similar."

Her eyebrows drew together in suspicion. "I either do or I don't."

I didn't have time for this bullshit. "Her blonde was fake, but her blue eyes and attitude were as real as yours, and no, I don't have a fucking complex for blondes. Sleep, fuck or eat—pick one." I was done talking.

"What happened?"

Fuck. "I already told you. I got a Dear John letter. She left me while I was on my first deployment. You hungry?"

Understanding descended over her features and her anger bled into caustic sympathy. "Ah. I get it."

Goddamn it. "There's nothing to get."

"Sure there isn't." Sarcasm laced her tone.

My nostrils flared and I held back from pushing her down on the bed and fucking this out. "Do you know what kind of psychological evaluations you go through when the CIA decides they want to recruit you and turn you into a killing machine?"

She crossed her arms over her tits. "No."

"Then know this. I passed." I got up.

"Where are you going?"

"You lost the right to ask when you didn't choose fucking." I walked to the kitchen.

FOURTEEN

Irina

HE WALKED OUT STARK NAKED AND I MOMENTARILY froze.

The tattoo was huge. Dark, sinister, giant wings spanned across his shoulders with the detailed feathers covering every inch of skin all the way to his waist. It was beautiful and intricate, and I couldn't believe I'd slept with him without even knowing something so massive was tattooed on his body.

I didn't just sleep with him, I'd told him to come inside me.

Then he'd walked out.

My jealous anger over the comment about his ex-wife returned and ramped up to destructive. I was off the bed, grabbing his 9mm from the nightstand and running after him like a pathetic scorned lover before I could think about what I was doing.

"Forget something?" I held the gun up and the stupid dog appeared out of nowhere. His low growl made the hair on the back of my neck stand up, but it was his bared teeth that scared the shit out of me. "Call him off," I demanded.

Dane barely spared the dog a glance before his gaze

dragged the length of my naked body. "You're holding a gun. You're lucky he isn't already on you."

"I am not threatening you with it!"

"Doesn't make a difference to him. He's trained to protect me."

"Call him off!"

He turned his back on me and opened the fridge. "Put the gun down."

I stared at the tattoo. "I could shoot him." The lower left of his back looked inflamed and red, like he'd had fresh ink done.

"You won't."

Egotistical, arrogant jerk. "You don't get to walk out after coming inside me."

He took something out of the fridge. "Is that what this is about?"

Yes. "No." What the hell did he think this was about?

"You always this temperamental?"

The more I wanted a reaction out of him, the more I realized I wouldn't get one. But it didn't stop the misplaced rage that was brewing in my head like the hurricane outside. "Turn around and face me." I put all the warning in my voice I had, but truth be told, I didn't know what I would say to him if he turned around, because I wasn't angry. I was hurt.

As if the bastard knew me and my thoughts, he casually set a damn pan on the stove. "You don't want me to face you."

The dog growled, the gun in my hand got heavier by the second, and his sexy fucking rock-hard, muscled body stood there naked as hell.

I lost it. "You fucking asshole, turn around!"

He turned.

His gaze zeroed in on mine, his body conditioned for

war, he didn't walk toward me, he stalked. Every measured step was a warning I foolishly ignored as he came right at me.

The dog's growling got louder and the gun in my hand shook. "What are you doing?"

His face impenetrable, he snapped his fingers at the dog then reached for the 9mm. Flipping the weapon in my hand, he pointed the gun at his chest. "Put your finger on the trigger," he commanded.

"No." My voice shook.

He moved my finger into position then wrapped his hand over mine to steady it. "You take the safety off and you pull the trigger." He moved the aim of the barrel to just right of center on his chest. "Aim for the heart." He lifted my hand holding the heavy gun and pressed it to his forehead, dead center. "Or between the eyes."

Fear licked up my spine and settled in my heart. I pushed words out through my suddenly dry mouth. "What are you doing?"

"You want to kill a man, don't hesitate." Lightning fast, he ripped the gun from my hand, spun it, and in less than a second, it was aimed at my temple. "Otherwise, you lose." Before I could blink, he reached behind him and set the gun on the kitchen island.

My heart in my throat, I fought for a steady breath. For the first time since he'd walked into his house, I was truly afraid of what he was capable of. "You're insane."

"And dominating and controlling and ruthless." He gripped a handful of my hair, walked me back two steps, then grabbed the back of my left thigh. "You want to fuck?" He lifted my ass to the back of the couch then rubbed his hard cock through my wet heat. "You say so."

Desire, sharp and painful, clenched in my core and raced to my nipples. "Asshole."

He shoved in to the hilt.

"*Ahhh.*" I grabbed his arms as he pushed my thigh to my chest.

He thrust three times, hard and merciless. "You want to know how many times I'm going to fuck you, ask." He pushed in deep and ground his hips, slow and controlled.

My mouth open, my eyes fluttered shut.

He yanked on my hair. "Look at me."

My eyes popped open at the command.

"You want to freak out about me coming inside you?" He pulled back then thrust deep. "Get the fuck over it. It's done, and I'm going to do it again. Know why?"

Oh my God. "No."

"Because you feel like a goddamn dream."

It wasn't a profession of love. It wasn't even a confession. But for this hardened killer who'd decided to save me from myself? His words felt like a Shakespearean love sonnet. "You feel good too."

"Good, because I'm going to fuck you until I'm the only goddamn man in your head."

A smile, as rare as the scarred man fucking me, spread across my face as everything fell into place. "You're jealous."

"I don't get jealous." He leaned down and bit my nipple just hard enough. "I get even." His tongue swirled across his sting. "And, sweetheart?"

My pussy clenched around his cock, and I bit my lower lip. "Hmm?" Oh my God, he felt good.

"I'm going to get so goddamn even, that asshole won't know what hit him."

I didn't have time to respond.

Dane Marek reared back and slammed into me. His hands caught my hips, both thumbs went to my clit and he started pounding.

Rough and hard and so mind-numbingly incredible, his body worked mine. Every thrust hit my G-spot, and I was coming before I could even wrap my legs around his hips.

A half cry, half scream erupted from my chest and I was flying.

Heat and the exquisite pain of his big cock bottoming out on every thrust mingled with the shock of an orgasm not self-induced or stolen, but given with such heart-melting determination that I wasn't just flying, I was breaking free.

FIFTEEN

Dane

HER CUNT CLENCHED AROUND MY DICK, AND I PICKED her up. Holding her ass, pushing her into me as I thrust, she came like a fucking IED blast wave. Her whole body shook as I let go and pumped inside her.

For ten seconds, my head went straight.

Then I realized what the fuck I was doing.

Holding another man's wife as my dick impaled her and my seed dripped out of her cunt.

Four tours, two hundred and thirty-eight kills, and I was brought down by the hundred-and-twenty-pound wife of a Russian mafia arms dealer.

Jesus fuck.

Her thin arms tightened around my neck. "I'm not jumping into another relationship."

I mentally shook my head and switched gears. "You weren't in a relationship." Fuck, she kept me guessing.

"Well, I'm not jumping into a relationship with you."

The fuck she wasn't. "If you're carrying my kid you are." God help her if she was. What we were doing was irresponsible at best and fucking suicidal at worst. The second anyone found out I was attached, let alone a father, my kid and her would be bigger targets than me. Leaving the business would no longer be a thought, it'd be necessary if I wanted to keep us all alive.

"Put me down. I'm making a mess all over your hardwood floors."

"I don't give a damn about the floor." Part of me wanted Fedorov to show the fuck up right then so he could see my cum dripping out of her before I put a bullet between his eyes.

"What do you give a damn about?"

I eased out of her and lowered her to her feet, but I didn't let go of her. "Making Fedorov dead." I studied her face for a reaction. She hadn't said shit any of the times I'd warned her about what I was going to do to him. She either had the best poker face of any woman I'd ever met or she wanted him dead.

Her small hands on my biceps, she looked up at me, but she didn't say a word.

I tucked a strand of her hair behind her ear. Jesus, I could get used to this. "You got a problem with that?"

"What's the right answer?"

"There's no wrong answer."

"I don't care about him."

That was the right answer, but I called her on it anyway. "A few hours ago, you were on my kitchen floor with the phone to your ear doing exactly what he told you."

Her fingers traced the muscles in my arms. "I thought you were the worse option."

I digested that for a moment. "And now?" Did I give a fuck if I was an option or a choice?

She traced the outline of my graze wound. "Now I know you're the worse option."

I fucking smiled.

As beautiful as the first time, she graced me with another smile. "I see you have a sense of humor."

"On occasion." Seeing her smile, I didn't give a fuck if I was an option or choice. I just wanted her. "Let's go to bed." I was fucking tired and I wanted her in my arms.

Her smile dropped and her expression shut down. "Excuse me." Without an explanation, she turned and walked her sexy-as-fuck naked body down the hall and into the guest room. She shut the door.

I should've gone to bed.

But I didn't. I grabbed boxers from my bedroom then walked into the guest room without knocking.

Her back to the door, her suitcase open on the bed, she was slipping something over her head. A dress, a nightgown, I didn't know what the fuck it was, but it was torture. Similar to what she'd been wearing when I first saw her, the thin material showed every curve and her lack of underwear.

I knew she'd heard me come in, but she didn't turn. She didn't even react. I cataloged the information to analyze later.

"You're sleeping in my bed," I reminded her.

She turned. "What happens after?"

Every time I looked at her, she was more beautiful. Her hair shining in the dim light from the nightstand lamp, her complexion free of makeup, you could've told me she was royalty and I wouldn't have questioned it.

I forced my thoughts back to her question and what was going down tomorrow. "We lie low." I didn't have any other jobs scheduled.

"We?" She crossed her arms.

"Yes."

"What about your other clients?"

I knew she was asking about the women clients. "I don't have any."

"But you said you didn't fuck for free."

Every time she said *fuck*, I noticed the dichotomy of her speech patterns. She could converse like a princess or speak like a street whore. I hadn't decided which pattern was hers and which one was from Fedorov. Her accent had all but disappeared except for a few slight nuances that I would attribute to being raised by a non-English-speaking parent.

I studied her face for telltale signs of jealousy, but I couldn't find any. "I didn't. Not for three years. Now I have."

"That's not really an answer."

I held her gaze and purposely paused before answering to see if she would react. When she didn't, I gave her the information she wanted. "I never do repeat clients, escorting nor mercenary. I don't have any other escort clients because I don't preschedule them. When I decide to take a woman client, I contact a name off the list and arrange a meet that day. All of my clients knew it was a one-time deal."

"Where do you get the list?"

"From Vega or another escort, Jared Brandt. We all served together, we all fuck for money. Them more than me."

"Why?"

"They're in it for the money. I'm not."

"Clearly. Because cutting off a paying client is bad business."

I ignored the jab. "The sex is a release. The terms of the arrangement let them know I'm not for keeps."

"How often do you call a woman off the list?"

"Usually after one of my other jobs."

She glanced at my ribs then my shoulder. "When was your last job?"

"Earlier."

"Today?"

Yesterday, last night, today. I'd dragged it out because the fucker had pissed me off. I nodded.

"So did you call a client off the list?"

Fuck. "Yes."

Her arms tightened around her middle. "You said you hadn't had sex in weeks."

"I haven't. I didn't fuck the client earlier today."

She inhaled then let it out slow, but her expression didn't change. Pissed, resigned, about to let loose, I didn't know what the hell she was thinking until she spoke.

"Lucky me." Her voice was dead flat.

She was pissed.

I reminded her of my promise. "Did I tell you I would take care of you?"

"No, you said, not asked, that I would be in a relationship with you if you knocked me up."

I ignored the asking part. "That's not taking care of you?"

"Not even close."

Shit, she was frustrating. "As long as you're with me, you don't have anything to worry about."

"Nothing?" Skepticism in her tone, she frowned.

I couldn't blame her, but it was pissing me off that she didn't trust me. And that was a dangerous slope. I didn't have room for emotion in my life. "Except pissing Hunter off."

"I'm sure he's just waiting to have me for a snack."

I told her more than I should. "He won't touch you unless I give the command."

"How reassuring." She crossed her arms and stared at the floor.

I waited, but she said nothing else. "Any other questions?" I was fucking tired, and I needed to check the security feeds. I hadn't gotten any alerts, but I wanted to see what the fuck was going on outside with the storm.

She toed an invisible spot on the floor. "There's more than the risk of pregnancy with unprotected sex."

"I'm clean." And I figured she was too. Vega wasn't an idiot, and Fedorov was a nonissue unless he'd farmed her out, which she hadn't mentioned.

She nodded on an inhale, then looked up at me. The vulnerability in her expression was back tenfold. "Am I with you?"

I took a step toward her. "You're standing right in front of me." I needed to shut the fuck up. "You're in my house." I had no right to give her hope. "And you're going to sleep in my bed." I gave it to her anyway, because for the first time in more years than I could count, I wanted more from a woman.

"Past tonight, that doesn't mean anything."

She had no fucking clue. It meant more than anything else had in my life in a long damn time. I gave her the truth. "You're the first woman to stand where you're standing."

"You were standing next to another woman hours ago."

"You were standing next to Vega." I'd seen them on the security feeds on my front fucking porch.

"That was different. I'd made a choice to leave. I had nowhere to go, but I was going. You didn't know who was in your house when you came home."

"Nothing is chance." Life was circumstances, and she was here.

She threw her arms up. "You know who says things like that? People who aren't desperate. People who can financially handle the obstacles life throws at them. Yes, I'm here for a reason and *everything* has a reason, but I'm not just some stupid, pretty package all wrapped up for you to play house with for a night!"

The sight of her pitching a fit shouldn't have made me want to smile, but it did. My expression locked, I didn't react. "You ready for bed?"

"No, I'm not ready for bed. I don't even have a bed because I have nothing. No car, no place to live, no money." She ticked the list off on her fingers, then her hands went to her hips. "I don't even have a job because I haven't worked since I met Viktor. He didn't *allow* me to work, let alone have my own bank account. Do you know how hard it is to hide a stupid bank account? One single checking account with no money and I wasn't even allowed that. No, he had to pay for everything and I had to ask if I wanted anything. But asking was a whole other game to him." She laughed bitterly. "You wouldn't believe what it cost to get a bottle of shampoo just so I could wash my hair."

I couldn't erase her past, but this shit right now? This I could fix. "Do you still have the account?"

"Of course I have the account. And not you, nor your stupid growling dog or anyone else is going to make me close it. I don't care how little money is in it. It's *my* money."

"What bank?" I had multiple accounts.

She named one I had an account at. "Why? Are you going to try and take that from me too?"

I gave her a pass on the insult comparing me to that piece of shit, Fedorov. "Do you know the account number?"

"I'm not telling you."

I put just enough force into my tone to get her attention.

"This is where you trust me." I walked out, grabbed my phone from my bedroom, then went back into guest room as I logged into my account at that bank. "Account number?"

She crossed her arms again. "You can't buy me."

I decided I hated it when she crossed her arms. "I'm going to ignore that insult. What's the account number?"

She glared at me. Then understanding kicked in and she briefly closed her eyes. "I don't need your charity."

She had resilience and determination, and I admired the fuck out of her for both. If she'd put up with half the shit I suspected Fedorov of dishing out, she was more than a fucking survivor. With the back of my fingers, I stroked her cheek. "I know."

"I'm not using you," she insisted.

She looked so fucking vulnerable standing there, telling me she didn't need a goddamn thing from anyone, it made both my chest constrict and rage boil in my veins. "I wouldn't let you." I'd give her anything she wanted, including the fucking shampoo.

Her cheeks reddened and she exhaled. "I know I'm in your house, that's not what I mean."

"I know exactly what you meant. This isn't charity. This isn't me buying you. This isn't a damn thing except a gift." I shamelessly put the kind of force into my tone I knew she would react to. "Give me your account number."

She gave me the number.

I transferred the funds. "Now you can buy whatever shampoo you want without having to ask." I cupped the back of her neck and brought my forehead to hers. "I'm tired and I want you to sleep next to me." Dropping my voice, I did something I never do. I fucking asked. Nicely. "Can we go to bed?"

She pulled her bottom lip into her mouth and bit it like she was fighting tears. "How much?"

Not even close to what she was worth. "It doesn't matter. You can walk away at any time and the money is still yours."

She dropped her gaze and stepped into me. Her arms at her sides, her cheek against my chest, she didn't say a word. She didn't need too.

I wrapped my arms around her.

My lungs filled with her scent, and more than coming inside her, my fucking world righted.

SIXTEEN

Irina

I FOUGHT TEARS.
He didn't have to do that.
He didn't have to do any of it.
And he especially didn't have to hold me. But he did. For the third time in as many hours, he simply, inexplicably, held me.
No one held me.
Not even my mother.
But Dane Marek held me and fucked me and made me come and gave me money and did things to my heart I shouldn't let any man do.

His huge hand stroked over my hair and his lips touched my head. "Come on, sweetheart, I know you're tired. Let's go to bed."

I nodded because I couldn't speak. I was going to bed with a killer who treated me better than anyone I'd ever met.

I didn't want tomorrow to come. I wanted this moment to last forever, because for the first time in my life, I felt like I belonged.

His arm slipped to my shoulders, and with the grace of a warrior, he led me to his room with a canine trotting behind us. As if it were the most normal thing in the world, he tossed his cell on the nightstand, then he dragged my nightgown over my head. Stepping out of his boxers, he pulled the covers back for me to crawl in, then followed. His chest hit my back and a hundred-pound attack dog jumped on the bed and lay at my feet.

"I didn't make you dinner," he murmured, gently brushing my hair from my shoulder.

It wasn't the first time I'd been sent to bed without a meal. "I'll survive."

His lips touched my shoulder. "I know you're a survivor, sweetheart."

Every time he said *sweetheart*, an unfamiliar feeling spread through my chest. "I'm just a problem taking up space in your life."

"A beautiful, sexy-as-hell problem that I don't want to get rid of."

"Like I said, you're crazy."

His hand traveled down my side and over my hip then flattened against my lower abdomen. He pulled me back into his hips and huge erection, then let out a slow exhale. "I like this brand of crazy."

His sexy voice rumbled in my ear and made goose bumps race up my neck and down my arms.

He skimmed a hand down the bumps on my arm. "What caused this?"

"Your voice." And his scent, and his arms, and his desire pressing into my back—all of it.

He chuckled. The deep and melodic sound was as rich as it was unexpected.

A smile broke out across my face. "I like your laugh," I whispered.

His lips touched my shoulder. "I'd like to hear yours."

My smile disappeared. "Maybe." One day. If we had any days beyond this one.

"Why does that make you sad?"

"Who says I'm sad?"

"I heard it in your voice just now." He laced his fingers with mine.

"You know this isn't going to last." I had to keep saying it to remind myself.

He lifted our combined hands and brought them to my chest as he trailed slow kisses across my neck until he reached my ear. "Right now, there's only one reason."

I could think of a dozen. None of them good. "Only one?"

"Yes."

Curiosity got the better of me. "What?"

"If you walk away."

"You don't do repeats. By definition of your life, this is already over."

"We already talked about this." With a slow grind, he pressed his hips into mine. "This is just beginning, sweetheart." He lifted my thigh and the head of his cock slid through my wetness, then he sank inside me.

The moan crawled up my throat and filled the quiet of his bedroom.

"Hunter, down." The dog jumped off the bed as he thrust and hit my G-spot. "You like that?" he murmured, his lips against my ear.

I didn't just like it. "Yes." I bit my tongue to keep from letting any more traitorous words spill out of my mouth.

He moved our intertwined hands to my nipple and used

my palm to tease one then the other to an aching hardness as his shallow strokes teased my pussy. "Arch back into me, love. Let me in."

Oh God. "Please, don't," I begged. I didn't want him calling me *love*.

The storm shutters rattled as his hands wrapped around my hips. "Don't what?" With agonizing slowness, he stroked deep into me.

"Call me that." I gripped a handful of the sheets and grunted. "Harder." I pushed back into him.

Controlling my hips, he gave me a slow grind. "Tell me why." His mouth closed over my neck and sucked.

My eyes fluttered shut. Gaining purchase against the mattress with my feet, I pushed against him.

He rolled to his back.

I landed on his chest and shoved down on his cock. "I said *harder*."

He lifted me off him and tossed me on my back. Before I could blink, he was on top of me. "What are you doing?" he demanded.

My heart beat frantically. "Fucking you." This was fucking, not love. He didn't get to call me that.

His body went perfectly still. His intense stare relentless, his expression gave nothing away. "That wasn't fucking."

"Yes it was." I raised my hips to meet his.

He shoved them back down. "I can't make love to you?"

"I don't make love." Thick and bitter, the words stuck in my throat.

His mouth landed on mine. Slower than the torturous ecstasy of his cock sliding in and out of my body, he stroked his tongue through the heat of my mouth. Alpha, dominant, he didn't just kiss me. He slipped his hands into my hair and showed me what I'd always been missing.

He wasn't ruthless.

He was cruel.

Kissing me passionately, consuming my mouth like he was touching my soul, he stole more from me than Viktor ever had.

My arms at my sides, I fought not to kiss him back. I fought so hard, even though I wanted to give in to him. I wanted nothing more than to do what he'd said we'd been doing, but I was terrified of jumping off that cliff.

As if he knew my thoughts, as if he knew exactly what I needed, he pushed me to the edge. His hands gripped tighter, his hips ground harder, but his kiss turned heartbreakingly gentle as he moaned into my mouth.

My resistance flew away like a bird taking flight. My traitorous body bowed off the bed, and I gave in to play with my demons. I kissed him back.

His cock slid back into my body.

The tremor started in my core and radiated. My pussy clenched, my legs shook, and every inch of my body convulsed in orgasm.

He pumped hot cum inside me.

SEVENTEEN

Dane

I MADE LOVE TO HER.

EIGHTEEN

Irina

HIS SCENT ALL OVER ME, HIS LIPS RAINING KISSES ON my mouth, my throat, my neck, he rocked deep inside me, spreading his seed. "That"—his voice washed over me like a drug—"was making love."

I didn't have words. I had nothing. I untangled my arms from his neck.

He pulled out.

An emptiness, so profound it hurt, settled in my chest. I turned my head.

His arms slipped around me, and he whispered, "I'm not letting you go." He pulled my back to his chest and snaked an arm under my head. "Sleep."

Sleep? Sleep wouldn't fix this. I'd lost. Everything.

"Stop," he quietly commanded.

"I'm not doing anything." It hurt to speak.

"You're fighting against this."

It hurt to breathe. "I have no fight left." I had nothing. Except yearning.

Thick fingers stroked through his seed as it leaked out of me. "You don't need it with me."

It hurt to feel his gentle caress. "Don't."

He drew his fingers through the mess on my thighs then pressed his release back inside me. "Don't what?"

He was crushing my heart. "Give me false hope."

"Don't doubt me." He sunk two fingers inside me and stroked. "Are you sore?"

"A little." Incredibly, amazingly sore, but I didn't care. I wanted every orgasm he was willing to give me. He didn't torture my body to coax out my pleasure. He stroked and caressed and hit every spot as if he simply wanted to make me feel good.

"Do you want to come again?"

My pussy contracted around his fingers. Viktor had never wanted to give me pleasure. I knew that now. He wanted control.

Dane nipped the flesh on my neck just under my ear. "It's a simple question, love."

My body tensed at the term of endearment.

His fingers in my pussy and his thumb on my clit stilled. "Is it the word or the idea?"

I didn't pretend to not know what he was talking about. I was quickly learning he had a sixth sense. "You don't know me." It was the simplest way I knew how to answer without giving myself away. Viktor had never said that word to me. Not once. I didn't believe in love. I couldn't. Love was a luxury for little girls and fairy tales, not ruthless killers and abusive gun traffickers.

His lips touched my temple. "How many men have you been with?"

I weighed the embarrassment and vulnerability against the risk of not telling the truth. In the end, I was a fool for wanting more with this man. "Three... including you," I whispered.

His fingers began to stroke in a slow pace. "Do you know why I want to make you come?" Every gentle thrust hit my G-spot as his thumb rubbed sweet circles around my clit.

My hips moved with his strokes. "No," I breathed.

"Because every orgasm is a step further away from him and closer to me." He pressed down hard with his thumb.

I cried out in desperate need.

"And you're beautiful when you let go." He stroked against my G-spot. "Come."

I fell apart.

A thousand points of pressure erupted from my core and spread across my body like an electrical current. Tingling, shaking, pleasure-pain, I didn't have words for the feeling of simultaneously soaring and plummeting.

One arm across my chest, the other slowly stroking through my aftershocks, he wrecked me further. "That's what it feels like, beautiful." He kissed my neck, my cheek. "That's how a man should make you feel."

I turned my head away as a tear slid down my face, but nothing escaped him.

Tender kisses fell on my head. "I'll take those too, love." He gently pulled his fingers out of me then cupped me with a soft caress. "Now sleep."

I didn't want to sleep. I didn't want to waste a minute of the time I had with him. Despite what he said, tomorrow was coming and Viktor wasn't going to let either of us walk away.

He brushed my hair from my face. "You're safe. Close your eyes."

He was everything Viktor wasn't. "We should talk about tomorrow."

"I'll deal with it."

"He's going to do something." And it would be bad. "You don't know him. He won't show up without backup."

"I'm aware," he replied calmly.

"You can't go alone." It would be suicide.

"I'm not."

"Who's going with you?" I didn't expect him to tell me, but I asked anyway.

He changed the subject. "Tell me about his house."

I stiffened. If that was his plan, he was screwed. "It's a fortress. You won't get close to him there."

He stroked my arm. "What kind of security does he have?"

"Every kind you can think of."

His fingers sifted through my hair. "Yet you walked away."

Even the minimalist of touch from him felt incredible. "He was distracted by the storm. He and Peter were discussing a shipment and how they couldn't afford the storm to delay it, and I called a cab."

"How did the cab get in through the front gate?"

My cheeks heated. "I promised the front guard a favor." I never intended to keep it, but he didn't know that. "I said I needed to get supplies before the power went out."

"There aren't backup generators?"

"Of course there are."

He was silent a beat. "It seems unlikely that you were able to bribe one guard and walk out."

I exhaled. "It was a… rough morning." They'd all seen what he did to me at breakfast. They'd all heard what happened after. Viktor had made sure of it. He'd told me to scream. After that, none of the guards would make eye contact. "No one wanted to deal with me."

He rolled me to my back and looked down at me. His expression was tightly controlled, but his jaw ticked. "What did he do?"

I wanted to feel the soft skin of his full lips under my fingers and trace the hard edge of his jaw, but I didn't touch him. "Nothing he hadn't done before."

His nostrils flared. "Tell me."

I never told anyone what Viktor did to me. I didn't have friends anymore. I barely even spoke with my mother, not that she would've believed me or wanted to hear it if I did tell her. She thought the sun set and rose with Viktor and she hung on his every word. So I'd been putting in my time with Viktor until my five years was up, then I'd planned on starting a new life. But that time had come and gone last week.

I pushed what had happened this morning down deep. "It's not important. I'm fine."

"You're underweight, you have fading bruises on the inside of your thighs, one of your knees is skinned and the dark circles under your eyes say you sleep less than me."

I touched his ribs by his knife wound then traced the outer edge of the burn mark on his shoulder that he'd said was a bullet graze. There were three other scars on his chest and two on his shoulder that looked like they were from bullet wounds. Two thin lines of scars on the other side of his ribs looked similar to the smattering of thin scars on his thigh. "You are not unscathed."

"No one beat me."

"Viktor didn't beat me." Not exactly.

"Tell me what he did," he demanded.

I couldn't explain it, but his dominance made me feel secure. I relented. "He dragged me out of bed." By my hair.

Naked. "And made me sit at his feet while he ate breakfast." In front of his guards.

Dane inhaled sharply. "Clothed?"

Silence my only defense against my shame, I stared at him without answering. I didn't have to.

Rage cracked his carefully controlled mask. "What did the guards do?" he bit out.

Leered at me and made crude gestures while Viktor wasn't looking. "Nothing."

Every muscle in his body tensed. "That's when you called the cab and bribed the front gate guard?"

"No, that's when I pulled my suitcase out of the hiding spot I'd found in one of the tunnels and took it to the west exit beyond the front gate and stashed it in the bushes. Then I went back, showered, dressed and called a cab. By the time I walked to the guardhouse, the cab was waiting and I told the gate guard I was going shopping. He said I wasn't scheduled to go out. I told him he wasn't scheduled to meet me after dinner in the pool house. He opened the gate and I got in the taxi."

His chest rose and fell twice. "Tunnels?" he ground out.

Tension I didn't know I was holding on to released when he didn't question me about the pool house promise I'd made the gate guard. "They're all over the property. Viktor told me he had them built to escape if the house ever caught fire, but I know they're for an escape route if we get raided by the police. He even has one that leads out to the docks. He took me through them when I moved in but forbade me from ever entering them alone. He said they weren't safe, but they're reinforced concrete." They were safer than anything in the house.

"Where does the one you used let out?"

"West of the front gate, there's what looks like a sprinkler pump housing. Underneath it is a grate. The grate leads to the tunnel."

"It's not locked?"

"There's a combination lock, but Viktor stupidly used his birthday for the combination." It'd taken me all of two tries to get it open five years ago, after the first time he'd *taught me a lesson*. I stupidly didn't leave. I sat on top of the fake sprinkler housing and smoked a pack of cigarettes then went back. When he'd smelled my hair the next day, the first lesson had seemed like child's play.

Dane cupped my face. "This will be over tomorrow."

"You can't promise me that." He had no idea who he was dealing with. "Even if you could, then what? I don't have a life to walk into."

"Is that what you want?"

I evaded any real answer. "Isn't that what everyone wants?"

"You're not everyone." He pulled me back into his arms as if that settled it, as if everything about what was happening was normal.

"Neither are you," I stupidly countered.

The breath of his tired exhale feathered across my shoulder. "No, I'm not."

A thousand questions about him, about what he was going to do, about what would happen tomorrow tumbled through my mind. The worst of them being what would happen to me if Viktor got to Dane first. Guilt would destroy me, if Viktor didn't. I knew this, but something had been in the back of my mind since I'd seen him standing naked in the kitchen.

"Ask your question." The deep and quiet timbre of his voice interrupted my thoughts.

I could listen to his voice for the rest of my life and never get tired of it. "How did you know I wasn't asleep?"

"Besides your breathing, I'm not sure you're ready to hear the answer to that. Ask."

I briefly wondered what I wouldn't want to hear, but I had a more pressing question. "What is the tattoo on your back?"

NINETEEN

Dane

My jaw tensed, but I kept my breathing even.
"Wings."
"What does it mean?"

I'd killed in front of her. I'd covered up evidence. I'd committed a dozen crimes she could sink me with. I'd come inside her. Not once had I hesitated with any of those decisions.

But now I was hesitating.

No one asked me what the ink meant. Not even the tattoo artist.

I could lie. I could withhold information like she'd withheld what all the fuck Fedorov had done to her. I didn't owe her shit, but I stupidly wanted to tell her.

Goddamn it.

"They're kills."

She turned in my arms and looked up at me with disbelief. "What?"

I wanted to remember this moment. I wanted to remember the scent of her body, filled with my seed, as she lay in my arms. I wanted to remember the look on her face before it turned to fear. I wanted to remember the trust in her body language as she lay in my bed with her head resting on my arm and her white-blond hair floating around me like innocence.

I wanted to remember all of it because I was about to lose it.

"They're all my kills." I held her colorless gaze that made me feel like there was still purity in the world and I threw away the tenuous trust I'd built with her. "Every feather represents a life I've taken."

She didn't blink. "There are hundreds of feathers on your back."

I inclined my head once. "Two hundred and thirty-seven."

"You've killed two hundred and thirty-seven people?"

"No." Fuck. "Two hundred and thirty-eight."

She stared at me. "How many of those were when you were in the military?"

"Does it matter?" She knew the truth of me now.

"I could be carrying your child. I think I deserve to know."

Every muscle tensed, my expression locked down, my heart rate betraying me, I studied her for a reaction she should've had but didn't. "One hundred and ninety-six," I admitted.

"How long have you been out of the military?"

"Three years." Four months, twenty-seven days. I didn't know why I counted.

Her eyes drifted for a few seconds then came back to me. "That's a kill a month."

More. "Yes."

"Do you enjoy it?"

"I get paid for it." But I didn't need the money. I had enough for five lifetimes.

"What kinds of people do you… kill?"

"Bad ones." Not that I was in any position to judge, but I had my parameters.

She stared at me a moment. "Why?"

Because I was on watch when a sniper in Afghanistan took out three of the men in my unit, because I never got the fucks who blew up our Humvee, because the first leave after my Dear John letter, I didn't even punch the asshole who'd fucked my ex-wife. Take your fucking pick. I didn't have one reason, I had too goddamn many. The world was a shit place full of evil, and I only knew how to do two things after the Marines. Kill and fucking survive.

"Call it exacting a balance." A balance that would never bring back my fallen brothers, but one I kept trying to fucking compensate for.

"Are you going to keep doing it?"

"Yes." Fedorov and any of his guards who got in my way were fucking dead. After that, I didn't know what the fuck I was going to do. I'd never thought about it. I'd never had to. But now she was making me wonder just who the fuck I was doing this for, because the dead didn't need balance.

"I didn't mean Viktor."

I studied her, but she wasn't reacting at all how I'd thought she would. "I have no other contracted jobs."

"If you did?"

If I did, and she asked me not to, I wouldn't. "I deal in absolutes, not speculation."

"That's not what I asked."

"Rephrase the question if you want a different answer."

Her eyebrows drew together. "Do you do it for money?"

I smoothed the skin between her eyes with my thumb. "I

used to." I didn't know why the fuck I did it anymore. I was losing my edge, and that would get me killed.

"Who are some of the people you've killed?"

I fingered a strand of her hair. It was the softest thing I'd ever felt, next to her pussy. If someone had told me a week ago that I would be talking about this shit to a woman in my bed, I would've shot them on principle alone. I stared at my downfall and gave her the truth. "Drug dealers, murderers, kidnappers." I didn't hold back. She already had enough information to get me the chair.

"What's going to make you quit?" her voice casual, she slid the question in like a pro.

"Your stomach swollen with my son." I was only half kidding.

A faint smile touched her lips. "Not a daughter?"

I took my first full breath since she'd asked about the ink. "That might make me kill more."

Ethereal and soft, she laughed. "Very funny."

For the first time since I'd gotten that fucking Dear John letter on my first deployment, I saw a future. "You think I'm joking." I smiled.

Her face turned serious and she hesitantly touched the corner of my mouth with the tip of her finger. "I like your smile more than I should."

"I like you more than I should." But I needed to tell her the truth. "Irina… there is nothing safe about being with me."

She dropped her hand. "Don't you think it's a little late to be warning me off?"

I added practical to the list of her traits I admired. "I'm being realistic."

"Which means what?"

"I'm hunted. You will be too."

"Are we talking beyond tomorrow?"

I didn't hesitate. "Yes."

She inhaled then breathed out slow. Her gaze drifted over my shoulder to the shuttered windows. "I think you need to decide what side you're on."

"There are multiple ways I can interpret that statement."

"You say you don't do repeats then you knowingly have unprotected sex. You tell me about your… occupation, as if you trust me, then you warn me off." She turned and gave me her colorless stare. "You can't afford a casual relationship, and I never wanted one."

Loving the fuck out of her honesty, I stroked her cheek. "What did you want?" Touching her was my new favorite drug.

Her face softened. "Summer nights and porch swings and little feet running through a house with a screen door."

It sounded perfect. Too fucking perfect. "You're missing something." I ran my fingers through her hair then gripped the back of her neck.

"You're right."

She was so unyielding, the corner of my mouth tipped up. "You wanna tell me what that is?"

"Fine." She sighed like she was put out. "But you've surpassed crazy."

I grinned. "Still waiting."

"An arrogant, alpha hit man who knows how to fuck might be on the list. As long as he isn't off killing people the second I have my back turned."

I sobered. "I wouldn't do that."

Her hands drifted to my chest. "I don't know what you would or wouldn't do because we don't know each other."

"I wouldn't put you at risk, and you know more about me than anyone living."

She traced the scar from an old bullet wound. "You know this isn't normal, right? Most people don't have the relationship conversation until they've been dating awhile, and they definitely don't talk about killing."

This conversation was already more real than anything I'd ever discussed with my ex-wife. "I dated my ex for years before we had this conversation. Time didn't help." She never would've let me fuck her like I'd fucked Irina in the kitchen. "And just to make the distinction, I'm not a hit man. Clients hire me when they're out of options. Retrievals, hostage situations, imprisoned in foreign countries, security—I've had a range of assignments. I'm successful because I'm not afraid to get my hands dirty."

"Or get shot." She traced the bullet wound on my shoulder.

"Work hazard."

Her fingers skimmed over the burn scars on my right arm and side. Her voice dropped. "What happened to you?"

"IED in Afghanistan." I turned her, pulled her against my chest and wrapped an arm around her waist.

"Your body is a road map of scars."

My head was worse. "Go to sleep."

"It's just the two of us here. Viktor has a lot of guards. He could send someone else."

"My security system will pick up anyone approaching the property." I glanced at the security panel on the wall by the door. The three green lights told me everything was up and running.

"What if the power goes out?"

"It already did." An hour ago. "The house generator kicked in." Seamlessly, like it was supposed to. It was the Wi-Fi I was concerned about.

"You've thought of everything." She yawned.

Except her. I never fucking considered having a woman here. But this one had somehow crawled under my skin in a matter of hours, and I didn't want to let her go. I kissed the top of her head. "Sleep, beautiful."

"Fine." She drew her legs up and snaked her hands around the arm I had under her head. Holding on to me, she settled in. "But stop calling me pet names."

For the third time tonight, she made me smile. "Good night, sweetheart."

"I hate you." She snuggled closer.

I chuckled. "I'll try and remember that."

She didn't answer, and within two minutes, her breathing evened out.

Hunter jumped on the bed and lay at her feet. Panting, he eyed me.

"Traitor," I whispered.

He gave me a look that said he didn't give a fuck.

I smiled. Then, for the first time since I was eighteen years old, I fell asleep with a woman in my arms.

TWENTY

Irina

I WOKE WITH A HUNDRED-POUND MUTT ON MY LEGS.
I glanced behind me, but I already knew he was gone because I'd felt his absence before I opened my eyes. I looked down at the dog.

Big, brown, sad eyes stared at me.

"Are you going to bite me?"

He put his head on my leg.

"What do you want?"

He nudged me with his muzzle.

"Now you're talking to me?"

His tail thumped.

Stupid dog. "You're supposed to be an attack dog, not a tail wagger."

"I told you he won't attack unless he's given the command." Dane's deep voice rumbled through the quiet bedroom.

My heart leapt and a shiver ran up my spine. I looked over my shoulder. Standing in the doorway, leaning on the frame, he held a coffee mug. Sharp jawline, perfectly cut features, more muscles than three of Viktor's guards, he didn't look like a man who'd pulled me into his arms and held me until I fell asleep. He looked like a formidable warrior.

"Good morning." He winked then took a sip of coffee.

Suddenly self-conscious, I pulled the covers up. "Good morning."

His biceps straining the sleeves of his T-shirt, his cargo pants bulging with his huge cock, he pushed off the frame with his good arm. "Sleep okay?"

Better than okay. Better than I had in five years. "Yes, thank you." He looked even more beautiful than last night. I reached for something to change the subject. "It's quiet."

"The storm passed." His lazy stride toward the bed didn't fool me. Every move he made was calculated.

"Why is your dog on top of me?"

"He wouldn't leave you when I got up."

I didn't even hear him get up. I never slept through the night, let alone any movement in Viktor's house. Every little noise always woke me. But last night, this warrior of a man had pulled me into his arms and I hadn't been able to keep my eyes open. I didn't even want to.

I smoothed a hand over my hair. "What time is it?"

"Almost noon." He stood over me. "Don't be self-conscious. You look beautiful."

Drawing my lips into my mouth, I closed my eyes and inhaled. "Dane—"

"Coffee?"

I looked up at him and my stomach fluttered. "Viktor is going to—"

"Be my problem." He stroked my cheek with the back of his fingers. "How do you feel? You sore?"

My instinct was to pull away from Dane's touch. Viktor was never nice to me without there being an ulterior motive. I forced myself to be still as I glanced at Dane's ribs. I couldn't see an outline of any kind of bandage. "I should be asking you that." Putting staples in him had made my stomach turn.

"I'm fine."

He was more than fine. I nodded and pulled the sheet with me as I stood. "I'm going to shower." Used to a different kind of man, my tone came out more abrasive than I intended.

Dane caught my arm. "You don't have to be defensive with me."

"I'm not." I was.

With his impenetrable stare, he studied me, but he didn't say anything.

I pulled the sheet tighter. "What?"

"Which part bothered you, when I touched you or asked how you were?"

I turned away. "Neither," I lied, wanting to find a way to be okay.

"You're pulling away."

I ignored him. I may never be okay. "I need to shower." I didn't want to face today.

"You're scared."

It wasn't a question, but even if it was, I couldn't answer it. I wasn't scared. I was resigned and sad and confused, and all of it was masking anger I'd pushed so deep for so long, it was a part of my every breath. But I wasn't scared. Scared would mean I had something to lose, and Dane wasn't mine to lose. One night didn't mean I owned a right to him.

I pulled out of his grasp. "What am I doing while you confront Viktor?"

I heard his deep inhale. I felt the tension in the air coil around us. I smelled the clean, sharp scent of his soap and shampoo, but I didn't move. Not one inch. Viktor had taught me more than resilience, he'd taught me the art of not showing emotion.

But those lessons were no match for Dane.

He cupped my face as his stormy gaze held me captive, then he let me know he saw right through me. "I will never touch you in anger. I will never force you to do anything. When I hold you, it's because I want to. When I ask after you, it's because I want to know how you are. Everything is going to be fine today, and you're going to be a safe distance away."

I stopped pretending to hide my fears. "Don't leave me here."

"I won't. I have a condo in Miami Beach. You're going to wait there."

"Do I have a choice?" Viktor would know about any places Dane owned. That's who he was. He looked into people and found their weaknesses.

"If you prefer, you can wait at Luna's office. It's secure and his men will protect you."

My stomach knotted. "What does he do?"

"He owns a personal security firm."

A bunch of men who wouldn't let me leave even if I wanted to. I fought to keep from recoiling and letting my body language give me away. "The condo."

He nodded. "We'll leave in thirty minutes."

"Okay."

He didn't let go of me. His eyes intent on mine, his thumb brushed across my lower lip and he lowered his voice "You never answered my question."

Viktor didn't condition only my psyche. I wasn't sore. I was aching and needy, and if Dane so much as breathed on my clit, I would come. As if all of my sexual training and conditioning by Viktor just switched to another vice, I wanted Dane. I wanted him like I'd never wanted another man, but I didn't give him that truth. "I'm not sore."

His thumb stroking my lip like I wanted him to stroke my clit, his eyes darkened and he issued a quiet command. "Turn around."

Desire raced up my spine and spread across my body like liquid fire. I didn't just turn. I dropped the sheet and crawled on the bed on all fours.

If this was going to be my last taste of Dane Marek, I wanted it to count.

TWENTY-ONE

Dane

Sexy as fuck, submissive as hell and right for all the wrong reasons, she crawled on my bed.

Ass up, head down, her cunt was wet with need.

My dick throbbed, but I knew what she was doing.

I leaned over her back and brought my lips to her neck. "This isn't the last time you're going to have me inside you."

She rocked against my dick and let out a small groan.

I rubbed a firm hand over her ass. "You like offering yourself up to me?" I ran my thumb through her wet pussy.

"Yes," she hissed.

"Good." I unbuckled my belt and unzipped my pants. "Because I'm going to want a hell of lot more of this." Fisting myself, I dragged the head of my cock through her heat. "You want my cum inside you, sweetheart?"

"Don't—" She pushed back into me with a grunt. "—call me that."

Holding her hip firm, I gripped a handful of her hair. "What would you rather I call you, love?"

"Stop it." She rocked against my hold. "Just fuck me."

I sank into her. One torturous inch at a time. When I bottomed out, I leaned over her. "I'm going to fuck you." I nipped her ear. "And I'm going to come inside you so hard, you feel me all day." I sucked her neck then I grasped her chin. "But later tonight, I'm going to make love to you for hours." I thrust my tongue into her mouth.

Moaning around my kiss, her cunt slicked with desire, she rocked against me.

Fuck yes. I stroked my tongue through her sweet mouth once more then spoke against her lips. "That's it, baby. Show me how good it feels."

"*Dane*," she cried as I hit the wall of her womb on a thrust.

"Goddamn, I love how you take all of me." *Fuck*, I loved it.

"Don't stop." Her pussy already starting to clench around me, she grasped two handfuls of the sheets.

I leaned back, took her hips and ground into her. "Never."

"Oh my God, I'm coming." She slammed her hips back into me. Her tight cunt constricted and she started to pulse.

I maintained control. Always. I could fuck for hours. But seeing her drop the sheet and crawl on my bed, her ass in the air as she offered it up to me, her willing submission, and now her cunt milking my dick like it was made for me—*fuck*.

I couldn't hold back.

I let go and pumped inside her.

My legs locked as I held her hips against mine. I came so fucking deep, visions of her knocked up fucked with my head.

A small sound escaped her throat and aftershocks shook her body.

Jesus fuck, she would be so goddamn beautiful swollen with my kid. I ran my hand down her narrow back. "You okay?" She was so fucking small.

"Yeah." She didn't move.

My cell vibrated in my pocket. Goddamn it, I didn't want to pull out yet. "Hold on." Still buried deep, I pulled my phone out and answered without saying shit. Years ago I'd made a crucial mistake assuming it was a client when I'd answered a call from their number. I'd given out information, but it'd turned out to be the mark on the other end of the line. I never made that mistake again.

"You there?" Luna asked.

I ran my hand over her perfect ass. "Yeah."

"I've got movement. Two SUVs left Fedorov's two minutes ago."

Damn it. My hand stilled. "You're doing surveillance?" He'd spot Luna's man.

"I know what you're thinking. My guy wasn't made. He's in a cable truck a block over."

The tremors in her legs stopped, and I eased out an inch. "Direction?"

"Not north."

The restaurant was north of Fedorov's place. Where the fuck was he going? "Copy. Intel?" I eased all the way out and she flinched.

"None. I gave the order not to follow, so I don't know what he's up to." He paused. "Something's up, amigo. You should bring her here. I've got seven men on site right now."

"Negative." She'd been scared as fuck when I'd offered it.

"Where are you keeping her?"

"Penthouse." My seed dripped down her leg.

"I'll put Tyler on her."

Running two fingers up her thigh, and through my cum, I shoved my seed back into her.

She softly moaned.

"Negative." I didn't want Tyler or any other fucking asshole around her.

Luna exhaled. "I think that's a mistake, bro."

Everything I'd done since I'd walked into my house last night was a mistake. "Noted." I just didn't give a fuck anymore. I wanted her, and I wanted her all for myself. I didn't have a fucking explanation why. "We good?"

"Yeah." Luna didn't sound happy. "I'll see you at quarter of. I know you work solo, but I've got two men on standby that I think should be on perimeter. We could use the extra eyes."

"No." I knew how Fedorov worked. Extra men were potentially extra collateral damage. I didn't know how green Luna's men were, and I didn't want to find out.

"Fine, but for the record, you're stubborn as fuck. I'll leave coms at your penthouse before I head to the restaurant. Anything else you need?"

"Two clean cell phones and a rental. Park it in the garage and leave the keys with the phones in the penthouse." I didn't have time to get new phones, and she'd need a vehicle if I didn't come back.

"Done. Anything else?"

She dropped her chest and her head to the bed and looked over her shoulder at me as I absently stroked two fingers in and out of her. "Don't wear the uniform or use a company vehicle."

Luna smirked. "Okay, boss. You wanna hold my dick while I piss too?"

"Negative." But I wanted to fuck her again. "Don't be late."

"Don't *you* be late. I hear what the fuck you're doing, amigo." Luna laughed and hung up.

TWENTY-TWO

Irina

He answered the phone while he was still buried deep inside me. I didn't even care. I never wanted him to pull out, but one slow inch at a time, he slid his huge cock out of me, and his release dripped down my leg.

God help me, all I felt was loss. I wanted to carry his child. I wanted to be tethered to this man who was a killer so bad, I could taste it. As if he were having the same thoughts, his fingers ran up my thigh and slowly drove into me, pushing his seed back inside.

I was more fucked than I ever was with Viktor.

Dane hung up, but his fingers didn't leave my body. "I want to see you come again."

"Do you?" I rocked back on his hand. I didn't care what he did to my body. It was my heart he was stealing.

He didn't answer. His thumb circled my clit, and then he gently pulled his fingers out. Grasping my hips, he rolled me to my back.

I sucked in a breath at the sight of him standing over me. His expression fierce, his pants unzipped, his giant cock wet from my pussy, he stole my breath and my reason. I foolishly opened my mouth. "I don't want you to do this."

His hands on my knees, he pushed my legs wide and leaned over me. Gentle and slow, he sank his still hard cock inside me and cupped my face. "Nothing is going to happen to me."

"I want us to leave," I blurted.

He stroked my cheek. "I will never hide in fear."

I exhaled as he seated himself all the way inside me. The invasion was all at once too much and not enough. He was so big and consuming, he could make me come just by being inside of me. I grasped for reason. "Running isn't hiding."

"There's no difference." He pulled back an inch and slowly stroked.

I grasped his rock-hard biceps and closed my eyes for a moment. "Stop." I couldn't think while I was looking into his stormy eyes.

"Look at me, beautiful."

No willpower, I opened my eyes.

He touched his lips to mine once. "I'm not going to let you hide in fear either. Understand?"

I nodded but then bit my lower lip as he pulled halfway out. "How are you still hard?" I arched my back to get him to sink back inside me.

He grasped my hips and stayed only halfway in. Making short, quick, hard strokes, he thrust against my G-spot. "I'm always hard around you, love."

I wrapped my legs around his waist and fought from coming. "Stop calling me that."

His hips froze and he caught the side of my face. "Why do you think you don't deserve to be loved?"

My breath fast, my heart rate faster, a lump formed in my throat.

"Answer me, damn it."

I'd told myself for five years that love didn't exist. I lived it. Men didn't love, they used. Women were toys and men used them up. Viktor used me. Over and over, he said I had to earn his love. But I couldn't tell Dane that.

His chest heaving, veiled anger tightening his jaw, Dane still looked down at me like I was the most important woman ever to him. "Do you know why I'm inside you?"

I didn't move.

His thumb stroked my cheek and his voice dropped even lower. "Do you know why I told you who I am?"

I didn't blink.

"Do you know why I'm not letting you go back to him?"

Dane wasn't making me earn anything. He would never do that. Traitorous tears welled in my eyes and one slid down my cheek, because I knew right then how damaged I was. "I'm sorry," I whispered.

"No," he barked. "Don't fucking cry."

I squeezed my eyes shut and fought like hell to keep from bursting into tears as I blurted out the ugly answer to his question. "He said love was earned and I—"

"Open your goddamn eyes!"

No matter how much I wanted to ignore him, I couldn't. I was trained. I did what I was told. I opened my eyes, but I didn't look at him. I couldn't.

He grasped my chin and forced me to face him then he lowered his voice. "You want to cry over any other goddamn thing, you do it. But don't you *ever* cry over what that piece of shit said or did again. You fucking hear me? He doesn't deserve it. He doesn't deserve a goddamn thing from you." He abruptly pulled out.

Tears slid down my cheeks and I curled into a ball.

"*Irina.*"

He barked my name like Viktor barked my name, and I flinched.

"Goddamn it," he cursed. "I am not yelling at you, sweetheart. I am *not* yelling."

His voice only slightly raised this time, he was right. He wasn't technically yelling, but it hurt nonetheless. God, it hurt. "You said I was broken." I never denied it. What did he expect? I didn't know what I was supposed to do. I didn't know how I was supposed to act, or what I was supposed to say.

Huge arms scooped me up then he sat on the bed. Cradling me to his chest like a child, he dropped his voice to a quiet baritone. "You were abused, Irina. I can't undo that. Only you have the power to heal… if you want to."

Oh God. Tears of humiliation and regret dripped down my cheeks.

"I'm here. I'm fucking here, but you have to let me in."

I wrapped my arms around the neck of a man who gave me more than anyone ever had, and the words, they just started pouring out.

"I can't let you in, don't you see that? I can't let you hurt me. You could hurt me so much worse than he ever did, and I don't know what I'm supposed to do. I don't know what to say. I don't know how to act. I don't know who to be without someone telling me how to be it. I can't be your love or your sweetheart. I'm no one. I have nothing, not a name, not an opinion, not even a wardrobe I picked for myself. Everything, *everything* you see is him. It's all him. I am nothing…." I choked on a sob. "I have nothing."

Strong hands held my face and firm lips kissed my forehead. "You have me."

I forced myself to look up at him. "Why?" He had to know this wasn't normal. He had to know no sane person would be saying that. "Because I'm a problem you can solve then move on from?"

"No."

"Don't you see? You can't say those things to me. You can't throw away words and not consider that they'll stick. You can't tell me you'll take care of me if I'm carrying your baby."

His chest rose with an inhale and his expression turned fiercely protective. "I am not careless."

I wanted to scream in frustration, but at the same time I wanted to throw my arms around him and never let go. He *was* careless. More careless than any man had ever been with me. And I knew that meant that he was dealing with feelings himself, but how could he not see how careless he was being? "Your release is dripping out of me."

"That wasn't careless." He stared into my eyes and reached for my soul. "That was intentional."

As if the world stopped spinning, everything froze.

Me. Him. The chaos in my head. The insecurity. The questions. The anger and hurt and self-hatred and the regret. All of it went silent.

That was intentional.

He *intentionally* wanted me.

He *intentionally* tried to tether us together.

He *intentionally* came inside me.

"Dane," I whispered.

He kissed me once. "You don't need to question my intent."

"We don't even know each other."

"I knew when I saw you on my kitchen floor that you were the first woman I've wanted since I was eighteen years old."

I bit back hope. "Because I was submissive?"

"No, because you were beautiful and resilient and I was looking at a survivor."

I didn't deserve it. I didn't deserve any of his words. "I sold myself for five hundred thousand dollars." There was nothing poetic about that.

"The weak don't have a price."

"Don't romanticize who I am. You'll only be disappointed."

"You think I didn't sell myself?"

"You sold a service. It's different." Killer, escort, it didn't matter, it was still a service he was selling, not his soul.

"When I got out of the Marines, do you know what I knew how to do?" He didn't wait for an answer. "Wreak havoc. I know more ways to kill you than fuck you. Causing the most amount of pain with the least amount of effort wasn't a service, it was an addiction, and I was weak."

Stunned, I stared at him. "I'm sorry." No words could undo what he'd been through.

"Channeling four tours worth of rage into a desk job was never an option. I was unhinged."

I didn't know what to say, so I said nothing.

"I was you." He sounded like he was admitting defeat.

I couldn't even be angry at the comparison because I knew who I was. It'd taken me five years and three days to walk away.

"I saw you on my kitchen floor and I knew who you

were. I knew what was going on inside your head." He stoked my hair, my back. "You were thinking survival."

I didn't deny it. "Better the enemy you know."

"I wasn't the enemy." His quiet determination filled the space between us.

"I didn't know that." Not at the time.

"I know." He easily lifted me and set me on the bed next to him. "I purposely didn't tell you either." He stood and picked up my suitcase from where it sat by his dresser. Realizing he'd moved it into his bedroom while I'd slept made my stomach flutter. Placing it on the bed, he opened it without asking and quickly, but systematically, looked through the clothes.

His movements were precise, almost as if he'd choreographed them. "Why?"

"You didn't need to hear who I was."

I didn't understand. "But you told me anyway."

"Later." His gaze caught mine as he handed me clothes. "After you saw what I was capable of. After you realized I would protect you. Put these on."

I took the leggings I worked out in and a blouse I would have paired with dress pants or a skirt. "Why did you tell me?" I didn't question his choice of clothes for me. If I stopped to think about it, I'd have had to admit to myself that I liked him making the decision for me.

"Because you had nothing to lose."

He was right. I didn't have anything left to lose. It was why I'd chosen that exact moment to leave Viktor, but hearing Dane say it made me feel ashamed, and that made me angry.

Dane immediately picked up on it. "You're angry."

I stood. "I'm not. I'm going to shower."

Dane caught my arm. "You don't need to run from me."

He paused. "But if you want to, then after this is done, I'll take you wherever you want to go. No questions asked."

I stared at his hand on my arm. Huge fingers, bruised knuckles, a cut across the back of his hand. My first thought was rejection. It spread through my mind before I could fight the emotion and back it down. He wasn't getting rid of me. He was offering me a way out. He was offering me what no one had ever offered me. And I had to question it. "Why?"

"A caged bird never flies."

I looked up at storm-colored eyes and war-hardened features, and I thought of every reason why I should take him up on his offer. "Thank you for the offer."

His hand dropped. "You're welcome."

TWENTY-THREE

Dane

GODDAMN IT. SHE WAS GOING TO RUN. I SAW IT IN HER eyes.
I locked down my expression. "Shower. I'll meet you in the kitchen." As I turned toward the door, Hunter went to her side.

"Dane?" Desperation filled her voice.

The mission, I reminded myself, the fucking mission was still the same. Fedorov was dead. I turned. "What?"

Her hair fell over her face as she looked down. "I wouldn't know where to go," she quietly admitted.

I didn't give her an in. I fucking wanted to. I wanted to tell her to stay, but I'd meant what I said. I wasn't going to cage her in. "Whole world out there." And I hated most of it.

"I don't need to see the whole world." She held the clothes that fucking tool bought her in front of her naked body.

I didn't want her to dress in them any more than I wanted her to think about him, but she was so damn small, I couldn't put her in anything of mine. "You need to get ready." I didn't want to fucking talk to her about where she was gonna go.

She sucked in a breath and nodded. "Give me a few minutes."

Taking only a few minutes was an accommodation for me, but I didn't care. Somewhere I'd lost the battle. Maybe I'd never won. Maybe I'd never gotten through to her. I didn't fucking know. But now I was going to have to deal with the fact that there was a woman walking around who could be carrying my kid.

Pissed at myself for not seeing how this could play out, I snapped my fingers at Hunter. Instead of coming, he lay down at her feet.

God-fucking-damn it.

Now she'd stolen my fucking dog too.

I stalked to the kitchen and put on the tactical vest I'd retrieved from the barn this morning. I disassembled my McMillan CS5 sniper rifle and packed it into a backpack. I checked the magazines on two of my untraceable handguns and holstered them. I was scrambling eggs when she walked into the kitchen with Hunter on her heels.

She paused when she saw me at the stove. "You're cooking."

I plated the eggs. "You're eating."

She stared at the food.

I put a fork on the plate and shoved it across the island to her. "Eat."

She didn't move.

I poured a cup of coffee, put cream in it and set it in front of her. "We don't have much time."

"You made this for me?"

If I wasn't so fucking pissed off, I would've taken her mouth. She looked fucking gorgeous standing there with no makeup and her hair down. "Yes."

"Thank you." She reached for the mug.

"Food first," I warned. "You didn't eat last night." Nothing in my fridge had been touched, and I knew from the security feeds what time she'd gotten to my house.

She picked up the fork. "You're bossy this morning."

"I'm bossy every morning."

She glanced at Hunter. "Your dog is following me."

"I noticed."

"Why is he doing that?"

"He likes you." He was protecting her. From me.

She looked down at him and he wagged his tail. "Last night he wanted to bite me."

"Now he doesn't."

She didn't look convinced. "What will he do if I pet him?"

Give up his last ounce of loyalty to me. "Lick your hand."

She didn't pet him. She took a small bite and slowly chewed like she hated it.

I stared at her. "Something wrong?"

She set the fork down. "I'm not sure what's right."

She was. For me. "Eat. Then we'll discuss it."

She looked at me over the rim of the coffee mug. "Why are you angry?"

I picked the least inflammatory reason from my growing list. "You're in his clothes."

Slowly, as if she understood something I didn't say, she set the mug down and nodded. "Thank you for making me breakfast." She picked the fork back up.

I wasn't going to watch her eat. It'd make me want to fuck her again. Everything she did made me want to fuck her. Like her cunt was my own personal redemption. "I'll be in the garage when you're ready." I didn't wait for a reply. I gave Hunter a hand command to stay before I walked out, but I didn't know why I bothered. The traitor was lying at her feet.

I loaded my shit in the truck, cursing myself for not getting a rental under one of my aliases. I was closing the door when she walked into the garage followed by Hunter.

"Hunter, stay."

She looked over her shoulder as Hunter walked back into the house with his head down. "Why can't he come?" She crossed her arms protectively around herself. "What if we don't come back?"

"He has a dog door." I'd trained him to unlock it and use it if he needed to. He could get out, but he couldn't get back in. "If I don't come home, he'll go to the neighbor's house." I knew she said *we*, but she never said she didn't want an out.

She looked out the open garage door at the surrounding woods. "You don't have neighbors." She didn't mention coming back.

"Seven miles to the north." Hunter had made the trip a few times. The old man who lived on the next property north of mine always fed him and brought him back.

"And the neighbor will what? Keep him?"

"If he has to." We had a deal. If Hunter showed up at the neighbor's and I didn't contact him within three days, Hunter was his. "Get in." I opened the door for her.

She stepped up on the running board and gracefully got in.

Refraining from touching her, I closed her door then got behind the wheel.

She didn't speak until we were miles from my house on the county road. "You know Viktor can find any properties you have."

Not this one. "My condo is under a holding company." I'd bought it from a guy I'd met downrange. Ex-Danish Military Special Forces, Neil Christensen was the only fucker I knew who was deadlier than me. He'd taken an early retirement and come to the States to raise a nephew after his brother had died. Neil didn't do anything half-assed. He'd gone into commercial construction and now his company was the number-one builder of luxury high-rises all over Florida. I'd kept the condo in his company's name. If I died, he could have it.

"Where are you meeting Viktor?"

"I'm not." I watched the rearview mirrors and road ahead for any signs of a tail.

She turned toward the window. "Do I get to know anything?"

I hated that I couldn't see her face, because her tone wasn't telling me shit. I debated not telling her about Luna but she'd figure it out sooner or later. "Luna's taking the meet. I'm the trigger."

She didn't comment.

I forced the issue. "Anything you want to tell me? Now's the time."

"I don't care what happens to Viktor."

She should. "He tried to eliminate you."

"And he's blackmailing you. You know he'll kill you the second he gets a chance."

"He won't get a chance."

She didn't reply.

Fifteen minutes later, she still hadn't said a word. I made two extra loops and pulled into the underground parking of the condo once I was sure we weren't being followed.

I cut the engine and scanned the lot then grabbed my

backpack. "Wait for me to come get you." As I got out of the truck and walked to her side, I cursed myself for never putting in any of my own security cameras for the building.

I opened her door and she silently got out.

One hand on my weapon, the other on her back, I led her to the elevator and punched in the code for the top floor.

She glanced at me. "Penthouse?"

"It was a good investment." The doors opened on the top floor hallway, and I entered another code to get into the condo. Pushing the door open, I gestured for her to enter first.

"It's dark."

"I keep the hurricane shutters closed when I'm not here." I flipped a few switches and the recessed lighting in the entryway lit up the space.

She walked toward the floor-to-ceiling windows. "I'll open them."

"Leave them." Impact-resistant windows weren't bulletproof.

She paused halfway to the windows and crossed her arms, but it wasn't in defiance. She looked scared as fuck. "I wanted to see the view."

Turning on the phones I found on the counter from Luna, and checking the batteries, I spared her a glance as I walked to one of the side windows and pressed the switch to open that shutter. "One window. No more," I warned.

She nodded and quietly moved to the window as I checked the phones for preprogrammed numbers to make sure Luna had put the numbers in for each phone.

I handed her one. "Here. If you need to call me, the number is in the contacts." I pocketed the other phone.

She took the cell. "Where is your friend meeting him?"

I tipped my chin toward the window I'd just raised the shutters on. "Indigo."

Tension radiating off her, she looked out at the view.

It took an act of God not to touch her or say a damn word.

"That's right next door," she said quietly.

Not technically. "It's across the street." It was a fucking stroke of luck I owned a condo here. Or it wasn't and Fedorov was one step ahead of me and already had someone on the roof. Either way, I was about to find out. "I need to go. Lock the door after me. Call me if anything comes up." I put the earpiece com in one ear and my Bluetooth in the other.

She didn't acknowledge me. She just stood at the window.

I reached for the switch to close the shutter. "You don't need to watch."

Her hand briefly covered mine and determination filtered into her voice. "Leave it."

If she wanted to watch, I wouldn't deny her. "Lock the door after me." I could've locked her in, but I was giving her a sense of control. "Don't let anyone in." I set my second handgun on the counter. "Shoot first, call the cops second."

"You said he wouldn't know about this place."

He wouldn't. But the second I set up on the roof, I'd be visible. If Fedorov was smart, he'd have his own man nearby with a similar vantage point, and it wouldn't take much to send a team to sweep the building. "He shouldn't." I checked my watch. "I have to go."

"Where?"

"I won't be far." The less she knew, the less she could be questioned about if this went south. I hoisted my backpack.

She nodded once but she didn't make eye contact. "Be careful."

I didn't put stock in words. I studied people's expressions, actions, tells, tone, and body language. But she hadn't said the words with any inflection, nor did she give a tell. Both of which was a tell in itself, except I didn't want to fucking acknowledge it.

"See you soon." I didn't kiss her, or hold her or even touch her. I walked out the fucking door because I wasn't her hero. I was half her problem.

Fifteen minutes later, I was looking through the scope with the sun beating down on my back.

I scanned the perimeter for the fiftieth time. "Anything?"

"Not yet," Luna answered through the com. "And it's hot as fuck up here. Where's the breeze?"

"Taking a day off and giving me an advantage." I checked the distance and the lack of wind again then made a slight adjustment on the rifle.

"Anyone ever tell you you're more talkative when you're looking through a scope?"

"No, because they'd be ly—"

"Oh shit," Luna whispered. "South entrance."

I trained the scope to the south.

"Who the fuck is that?" Luna asked.

Goddamn it. Fedorov walked across the patio with four guards and a blonde. "Don't know." But I could guess. White-blonde hair, middle aged.

"We got a problem, amigo." Luna kept his head down. "He's right up on her."

I saw. Fuck, I saw. "Play it out." There was no way from my vantage point to get a shot in on him.

"You're not gonna get a clean shot, amigo."

"I know." *God-fucking-damn it.* "Turn away. Buy me a few seconds."

"He's seen me. His whole fucking entourage is heading right at me." Luna swore in Spanish. "You got two, maybe three seconds, bro. Take the fucking shot if you've got it."

As if Fedorov knew where I'd be, as if he knew the exact fucking projection angle, the blonde was mirroring his every step, blocking him from my line of fire. If I shot at him, I'd be shooting through her.

My cell vibrated. I hit the Bluetooth.

"Oh my God," Irina said in a panic. "That's my mother!"

Fuck, fuck, fuck. "I see."

"What the fuck is going on, amigo?" Luna hissed.

"That bastard is going to take her!" Irina shrieked.

I heard her footsteps.

"Stand down, Irina," I warned.

"*Stand down?*" Hysteria filtered into her voice. "I'm not some military soldier. You stand down! She's wearing my dress! He's going to…" The connection cut in and out. "…wait around… to get… stand in…" The phone went dead.

Goddamn it. "Irina is on the move. Possible breach," I warned Luna.

"Copy," Luna whispered.

"Who are you?" Fedorov's voice filtered through Luna's com.

Luna picked up his glass of water and took a sip. "*No habla ingles.*"

Fuck, I didn't have a shot. "I don't have a clear sight line. Get out of there, Luna."

"Bullshit," another voice spoke. "That's André Luna, boss."

The guard closest to Luna settled his hand on his gun.

Motherfucker. "Watch the guard on the left, Luna."

Luna held his hands up. "*No comprende, amigos.*"

The same guard spoke again. "He's a marine, boss. He knows Marek."

"Really." Fedorov chuckled. "How about I make you a deal, marine?"

The blonde woman looked side to side.

Fedorov leaned toward Luna but not enough for me to take the shot. "You tell Marek to give me my wife and I won't fucking kill you."

The blonde took a step backward, and one of the guards was on her in a second. His gun jammed into her side as he pushed her back into position as Fedorov's human shield. Then he leaned toward another guard and said something I couldn't hear. They both glanced in my direction.

I held my aim.

Luna slowly pushed his chair back and stood. His hands still raised, he smiled and told me in Spanish to take the shot. "*Trata de acetar, hermano.*"

I aimed at the guard who had the gun on the blonde's back.

Fedorov scoffed. "Do you really want to play this no-English game with me?"

I breathed out and readied to pull the trigger.

"Viktor!" Irina ran across the patio.

Six heads turned toward her and three of the guards drew their weapons.

"*Dios mio,*" Luna muttered, drawing his 9mm and aiming it at Fedorov's head.

Irina froze as every other customer on the patio either hit the ground or fled.

Rage consumed me. "Do not let them take her, Luna," I barked.

Luna dropped the pretense and switched to English. "What are you going to do, Fedorov? Your men shoot her, I shoot you."

"No one's going to shoot anyone," Fedorov calmly replied, his gaze intent on Irina. "Well, pet, quite a spectacle you've caused."

"You stupid girl," her mother bit out. "Viktor gave you everything and this is how you repay him?"

"Shut up, Mother." Irina's hands went to her hips. "Let her go, Viktor, or he'll shoot you."

Viktor laughed. "Really, pet. Do you think I am so stupid that I would allow that to happen? Do you really think he has a clean shot? Would I show up unprepared to such a standoff?"

Goddamn it. I scanned the other roof lines.

"Talk to me," Luna whispered.

"I'm looking. I don't see anyone." I trained the scope back on them and a red dot appeared on Luna's chest. *Fuck.* "You're targeted."

Luna glanced down at his chest.

"Ah, there we go, Mr. Luna. It's seems you have lost this round." He grabbed Irina by the back of the neck like a disobedient dog. "Come, pet. I think it's time we go home and you show me how sorry you are."

"Fedorov," Luna called.

Fedorov paused and spared Luna a glance. "Really, Mr. Luna. You are out of choices." The red dot moved to Luna's forehead. "If you shoot me, you die. Is my life worth yours?"

I pulled my cell out and dialed her.

Fedorov spun Irina to face Luna. "Tell your new friends, if they want to live, they'll forget about you." Fedorov gripped a handful of her hair. "Go ahead. I'm sure your new marine fuck toy can hear you through this one's earpiece."

The phone still ringing, I cataloged.

I shoot Fedorov. His sniper shoots Luna, Irina and her mother. He could pluck off the three shots as fast as I could take out the guards. They'd all be dead.

Irina threw the cell phone I'd given her on the table. "Take me home, Viktor."

TWENTY-FOUR

Irina

It wasn't his hand gripping my hair or the cold detachment in his voice. I wasn't frightened of his tone. I wasn't afraid of the body he spent hours working on in his home gym to keep himself as muscular as his guards. I wasn't even terrified of what he was going to do to me.

It was his cologne.

Thick and suffocating and permeating, it spread all over me like a poisonous fog and erased every last memory of Dane's scent.

"Chica," André Luna warned, his gun aimed at Viktor's head. "You don't have to go with him."

The red dot on his forehead said I did.

"Of course she go with him," my mother snapped with her Russian accent. "He is her husband." She shoved Viktor's shoulder. "Go."

Viktor's hand curled around the lock of hair he held hostage and he lowered his face to mine. "Should we show your marine what a real man does with his wife?"

Bile rose and I effected my disinterested expression. "Whatever."

He lowered his voice and dipped a finger into the

waistband of my leggings. "Did you forget what happens when you wear pants in public with me?"

I wanted to spit in his face. "My marine fuck toy picked them out after he screwed me with a dick that works."

Viktor backhanded me.

"*Fedorov*," André barked. "You hit her again, you're dead."

Blood pooled in my mouth.

Viktor laughed. "You move a single inch before I walk out of here and you are dead." His hand still in my hair, he dragged me toward the restaurant as he spat out orders to his guards in Russian.

"Stupid girl," my mother hissed.

I didn't bother speaking to her. She had no idea how disposable she really was to a man like Viktor.

"You should listen to your mother," Viktor mused, dragging me through a now empty restaurant. "Did I not give you what you need?"

A few waitstaff huddled in a corner as Viktor led us past them and down a hall. My mother on my heels, the guards on hers with their weapons still drawn, we made our way to a service elevator.

I didn't bother answering Viktor, and he didn't push it until we were all in the elevator.

"I asked you a question, pet."

One of the guards eyed me and smirked.

Fucking asshole. "Is this the part where I tell you how great you are?"

Viktor shoved his leg between my thighs. "This is the part where you remember not to speak like a stupid American."

GRIND

I couldn't stop myself, I baited him. "I am American."

He slammed me back against the elevator wall as he grasped one of my nipples through my blouse. "You are what?"

I glared at his washed-out blue eyes and rugged features that I used to think were handsome. "*American.*"

He twisted my nipple, hard.

I bit back a cry.

He smirked. "We will fix that later, pet. That's a promise." He turned to my mother but addressed me. "Irina, did you know your mother has decided to move in with us?"

Disgust made my stomach bottom out. As much as I hated my mother, she was my family. My only family. But she was too stupid to realize she was Viktor's next target. I'd realized it the second I saw him show up at the rooftop restaurant with her wearing one of my dresses. I should've seen this coming years ago, but I was in denial.

I glanced at my mother, but she was too busy smiling up at Viktor like he was a fucking movie star. "You two deserve each other."

Viktor pinched her cheek. "She is the mother I never had."

My mother blushed and called him her boy in Russian, despite the fact she was only two years older than him.

The elevator doors opened and Viktor pulled me to his chest like a human shield before walking us out after the bodyguards. "I am wondering, pet." The hand not in my hair snaked under my blouse and shoved into my pants. "What will I find when I touch my pussy?" He licked my ear. "Will it be wet? Will I find she waited for me?"

My nostrils flared and I willed myself not to cry. Fighting to bury every thought of Dane, I reminded myself why I'd done this. Viktor was my problem. I never should've gone to

177

Alex or let him take me to Dane's. And now his friend André was involved and he'd pulled a gun on Viktor. Viktor wasn't going to forgive that.

Attitude my only defense, I channeled it. "You won't find anything." Viktor hated my disinterest. He thought the world revolved around him. "Except a well-fucked pussy by a man who knows how to make a woman come with his dick."

"Oh, pet." Viktor chuckled. "How you like to ask for it."

"If asking for it means telling you how much I hate you, then I'm asking for it." I didn't care anymore what he did to me. This was the only way I knew how to get Dane and his friend out of this.

Viktor's guards led us to the garage and one of them opened the door to a brand-new SUV.

Viktor leaned down to my ear. "You just might make me hard yet." He shoved me into the back seat beside my mother and slammed the door.

One guard got behind the wheel, another got in on the opposite side of my mother and Viktor got in the front passenger seat. The two other guards got in an identical SUV parked next to us.

"How much did the new vehicles cost, Viktor?"

With a smirk on his face, Viktor turned in his seat as we drove out of the parking garage. "Oh, pet, are you worried about my finances? Did you honestly think you were going to get your money after—"

He never got the rest of the sentence out.

Screeching brakes, crunching metal and flying glass all happened so fast, I barely saw it. But Viktor's body slamming back against the seat from the impact of the airbag was gloriously in slow motion.

My body twisted, metal pressed into my side and a hand grabbed the front of my blouse and yanked.

My chest hit my thighs, Viktor landed on top of me and automatic fire started popping over the hissing sound of an engine after a violent impact.

Russian filled my head.

Screaming, yelling, barked orders, panicked voices—none of it outweighed the roar of automatic fire raining down on the SUV like the fires of hell.

I smiled.

TWENTY-FIVE

Dane

"**T**YLER, COLLINS! MOVE, MOVE, MOVE!" LUNA barked into the com. "Front entrance, garage, cover!"

I grabbed the backpack with the extra ammo and I was on my feet.

"I need eyes, Marek," Luna demanded.

Fuck. I paused for half a second and looked through my scope. Luna stood on the patio, arms out wide in surrender. The red dot was still on his forehead. "Still in sights," I warned.

"Goddamn it," Luna snapped. "Get them the fuck off me. Take this fucker *out*."

I followed the projectile and scanned the other buildings, but same as a few minutes ago, I was against the light. The mirrored windows of the building opposite the restaurant was reflecting the afternoon sun right back at me and I couldn't see shit. "I have no visual."

"Find the motherfucking visual." Luna slowly turned in a circle. "I'm no good to you dead, and now I'm pissed the fuck off."

My jaw set, I ground out a response. "You're costing me time I don't have." Fedorov was going to fucking bleed for this.

"You ever seen me pissed the fuck off, brother?" Luna countered.

I blindly aimed at the building, starting halfway up. I couldn't see him, but I knew he could see me. Taking time I didn't fucking have, I started to scan up. "Move two feet left." I needed him in my sights as I scanned.

Luna stepped left. "When I get pissed the fuck off, people die. I'm gonna fuck that Russian up."

Not before I did. "Halt." Luna in my field, I adjusted my aim in a slow, upwards arc. "Hold." The laser stayed on his head. "I'm canvassing. If I give the word, cover right, use the south exit." I put my hand on the scope.

"What's the word?"

Raising my aim, I kept the scope trained on Luna. Three floors up, I hit pay dirt. The laser disappeared off Luna and I gave the command. "*Now.*" I picked off two shots.

"Motherfucker!" Luna dove right and hit the exit.

The distant sound of shattering glass traveled across the street and I was on the move.

Luna breathed heavy in to the com. "Tyler, Collins, you've got Fedorov, four guards and two women coming at you. All exits need eyes."

I didn't wait for the elevator. I took the stairs and jumped every other half flight. Rage like I'd never known ripped through my veins, and I hit the ground level and burst onto the street with my weapon drawn.

Two seconds later, Luna flew out of the side exit of the building. "Marek, conceal!" he barked through the com.

Fuck that. "Where the hell are they?" I yelled.

Luna signaled for me to go left as he went right. "Tyler, report," he snapped into the com.

"Exiting east garage, I have visual. Two white SUVs. Target and women in the rear vehicle. Engage?"

I started running.

Luna, that motherfucker, not only had his men on coms, they were in position. I was too fucking enraged at Fedorov to call Luna on it.

"Collins, call Miami PD for backup. Tyler, hold position and detain. Do not let that asshole get on the street. We're coming around now. Marek and I are on foot."

I heard the crash before I saw it.

My rifle in both hands, I sprinted around the corner as automatic fire started raining down around me.

A white SUV T-boned by a black Luna and associates vehicle was halfway up the exit ramp of the garage. The driver door of the Luna and Associates vehicle was open as Tyler crouched behind the bulletproof armor and returned fire at the men in the front seat of the T-boned SUV.

A second white SUV was street level but was blocked in by a second Luna and Associates vehicle as the driver of Luna's SUV shattered the windshield with automatic fire.

"Cease fire, cease fire!" Luna yelled.

I didn't fucking hesitate. I walked straight at Tyler as he eased off the trigger and slammed the butt of my stock into the side of his head.

He dropped like a fucking stone and I spun, weapon aimed. "Fedorov," I growled. "*Get out.*"

A guard sitting in the seat behind the dead driver extended a shaking arm around the bloody mess of the driver. His body riddled with seeping bullet wounds, he aimed his weapon at me.

The telltale click of an empty chamber sounded in the sudden silence.

My nostrils flared, my jaw clenched, I put one round between his eyes then trained my gun on the passenger door and forced myself to wait. If she was fucking shot by Tyler, I was going to kill him then and there.

The back door of the SUV creaked open and her feet, then her knees hit the ground. Her back arched as the top half of her body stayed in the vehicle. I couldn't see her face but her chest rose and fell in rapid succession.

My heart pounding, I held my aim. "Fedorov," I warned.

With her hair in his fist and his gun shoved against her temple, the fucking coward stepped out of the vehicle and yanked Irina to her feet, pulling her against his chest.

Fedorov looked me up and down then smiled. "You can shoot me. But then I will shoot her."

"Shoot him," Irina demanded.

At the sound of her voice, I fucking took a breath, but this wasn't over. Not even close. My gaze locked on Fedorov, I didn't spare her a single glance. "You injured?"

"No," she bit out. "What are you waiting for?"

"He's not going to shoot, pet. Calm down." Fedorov pressed the gun harder into her temple. "But he is going to give me the vehicle of the marine he hit in the face. Then he's going to back away like a good little soldier."

He wasn't going anywhere with her.

The fucking asshole kept talking. "Do you know why, pet?"

Irina didn't hesitate to answer. "Because he's going to shoot you once you're in the vehicle so he doesn't have to drag your stupid body across the ground."

Luna moved into my peripheral vision. "Not a clean shot." His whispered warning came through the com. "Keep him talking. I'm circling behind him."

"You always did have a flair for the dramatic, pet." Fedorov chuckled. "Maybe I did take you too young."

"Let her go," I demanded.

"So you can kill me like you killed my men?" Fedorov outright laughed. "Not today, soldier." He pulled on Irina's hair. "Come on, pet. Watch your marine do nothing as I walk away with you." He moved toward the SUV.

I raised my aim.

Luna's voice came through the com. "Don't risk it."

Sirens sounded in the distance.

Fedorov backed into the driver seat, dragging her with him.

I exhaled.

"*Stand down,*" Luna ordered.

His grip on her tight, Fedorov climbed over the center console, careful to keep her between him and my aim. "You remember how to drive, don't you, pet?"

My eyes on Fedorov, I still saw the change in her.

The anger contorting her face bled into disinterest, and like a fucking switch was flipped, her expression shut down. Jamming the gearshift into reverse, she locked her glare on me and threw two words out. "*Fuck you.*"

She stepped on the gas. The SUV's tires screeched and she spun the wheel like a fucking pro.

TWENTY-SIX

Irina

H E DIDN'T TAKE THE SHOT.
He didn't take the shot.
Gripping my hair, his gun shoved into my temple, Viktor grinned at Dane.

I threw the SUV into drive and gunned the engine.

TWENTY-SEVEN

Dane

"Help me." Her mother's accented voice came from the back seat as the sirens drew closer.

I lowered my weapon.

Luna put his hand on my shoulder. "You didn't have the shot. The risk was too great. We'll get her back."

I glanced at Tyler on the ground then glared at him. "That's how you fucking train your men? To shoot at hostages?" I was so fucking pissed, I couldn't see straight.

"Boss?"

I spun and glared at the asshole who must've been Collins. "Did you fucking know who was in the vehicles before you started firing?"

The fucking pussy went white. "Tyler said the women were in the second vehicle. They fired first, sir."

"And you didn't confirm—"

"Marek," Luna barked.

Enraged, ready to lay him out, I turned.

"I'll handle them," Luna snapped, all business. "Get out of here before the cops arrive. Call Neil and Talon, they're both in town. Recon and get a plan together while I take care of this. Don't go after her half-cocked and alone. You'll need backup on this."

I was so goddamn angry, I couldn't speak. I stepped around him and glared at the blonde in the back seat of the SUV who had the same colorless eyes as her daughter. "If anything happens to your daughter, I'm holding you personally responsible."

Sitting with her hand over a bullet wound in her arm, she glared back. "Get me a doctor!"

She could fucking bleed to death for all I cared. "You're lucky you're still breathing." I kicked the door shut.

Luna handed me Irina's cell phone. "Call Neil."

I worked alone, always. Because when you didn't, this was the type of shit that happened. I snatched the phone.

"It would've gone down the same way no matter what," Luna said, as if reading my thoughts. "We were outnumbered."

I was always outnumbered, and I'd never failed before. "That wasn't the problem." I was outsmarted because I didn't plan and I didn't fucking think because I was too goddamn busy getting my dick wet.

Luna glanced up the street as the first cop car rounded the corner. "Go."

I didn't hesitate. I disassembled my rifle as I cut through the garage and exited out the back. Jogging to my truck, I shoved the rifle in my backpack. Two minutes later, I was pulling out of parking garage and dialing, because now I didn't have a goddamn choice. I wanted to drive to Fedorov's and shoot my way through every goddamn one of his guards, but I wasn't stupid. He'd kill her in a heartbeat. My only option was to go in with a coordinated attack.

Neil answered in Danish on the second ring. "Ja."

"It's Dane. I have a situation."

He switched to English, but he had a heavy accent. "You and your escort friend."

I paused. "Which one?"

"Brandt picked a fight with a quarterback."

I didn't have time to dick around. I cut to the chase. "I picked one with Viktor Fedorov."

Silence.

"You there?"

"Ja."

"I'm going after him." I waited to see if he commented. He didn't. "I'm extracting his wife."

"I am assuming this is not a paid assignment."

Neil was one of the few people who knew what I did. "Personal."

"You do not get personal."

No fucking shit. "I do now."

He paused. "Location?"

The slight pause told me he was in. "His residence on Key Biscayne."

"There is only one road in. You will not have the advantage."

"There was an altercation at Indigo. He's now short four guards. It's enough of an advantage." And road access wasn't the only option. "Is your boat still docked in Largo?" He had a house on the water there and a thirty-five-foot Cobalt cruiser.

"Ja."

"I want to go in by boat after nightfall. There are tunnels to access the property and bypass the guarded gate."

"The existence of the tunnels is rumor. The contractor who supposedly built them is dead."

Figures Fedorov would kill his contractor. "I have confirmation of their existence and the location of the end of one of the tunnels outside the main gate."

"The main gate is only one obstacle. He will have men inside. The tunnels could have cameras."

"His wife got out through them without being detected." I fucking hated calling her his wife. "I'm going to assume they're still accessible."

"Ignorance is brought about by assumption," Neil countered.

Fucker was always quoting proverbs. "I'll be armed."

He stated the obvious. "You are not calling because you want to go alone."

"I'm asking for backup." And I felt like a fucking pussy for doing it. I didn't call for favors, ever, and Neil Christensen wasn't a man you wanted to owe.

"And the Cobalt," he reminded me.

"Affirmative. Talon's my next call. Luna's on board once he's done dealing with Miami PD and Fedorov's four dead guards."

"Sunset is at seven-fourteen. I will be at the marina at Luna's condo with the Cobalt in four hours."

I exhaled. "Copy."

Neil hung up, and I dialed Talon Talerco. Talon was a Navy-trained hospital corpsman who'd served with André's unit as their medic. When the Humvee that Vega, Brandt and I had been in got hit with an IED, Talon was the first medic on the scene. He'd saved Brandt's life.

Talon answered on the first ring. "Had a feelin' I'd be hearin' from you." His southern accent was as strong as his attitude.

"Because?"

"Did a favor for Vegas last night." Talon nicknamed everyone, Vega included. "Figured y'all run as a pack. What's up, Ink?"

Talon had seen the tattoo on my back when he'd triaged me after our Humvee was hit. That's when he'd started calling me Ink. "Luna says you're in town."

"I could be," he hedged. "Why?"

"I need backup."

"Thought you worked alone these days."

"Not asking for help with a client." I didn't specify what kind of client. He knew what Vega, Brandt and I did.

"I'm not talkin' 'bout chargin' the ladies." He chuckled. "Although, can't say I'm not curious about y'all's clientele. I'm talkin' 'bout your other job, Ink. The one you pretend I don't know about. Nice work on the Cuban traffickers last month though."

My jaw ticked. I'd taken out the top level of a human trafficking ring out of Havana. The asshole was sending women and children over on makeshift rafts that were drowning faster than the Coast Guard could pick them up.

I didn't know how the fuck Talon knew about it, but I ignored him. Irina was my priority. "I'm going after Viktor Fedorov."

"That's ambitious. Must be some payout. His competition pissed off?"

I ground my teeth. "It's personal."

Talon paused. "How personal?"

"I'm extracting his wife." And killing him.

"Damn, Ink." Talon exhaled low. "I knew you were fuckin' crazy, but come on. That's just askin' for fallout."

"I'm not leaving witnesses."

"I should've fuckin' known." Talon chuckled. "When's this all happenin'?"

"Four hours. Neil's bringing the Cobalt. We're meeting at Luna's condo then going in from the water."

"You got a plan to get in after that?"

"Yeah." Kill everyone I see except her.

"All right, I'm in. I'll shoot some shit up tonight."

"Thanks." I started to hang up.

"Hey, Ink?"

"What?"

"She hot?"

"Fuck you." I hung up to his laughter.

The rest of the drive back to my house, I fucking festered. Replaying every goddamn second, I thought of a hundred different ways I could've handled it, but it all came down to one mistake. I should've left her at Luna's. Whatever the fuck Fedorov was doing to her now was my fault.

I turned into my driveway and the cell Luna gave me rang. I answered without speaking.

"Where are you?" Luna asked.

It was quiet in the background on his end. "Home. I don't hear cops."

"I'm back at the office."

"How'd you walk?"

"Friends on the force. The cops were glad to have Fedorov's men out of their hair. I told them I had to take care of Tyler and get my stolen vehicle back. I promised to give a statement later."

I didn't say shit. I was still irate at Tyler.

Luna read between the lines. "You didn't have to hit

him. Tyler knew what he was doing. He saw the driver and the guard behind him. He watched Fedorov jump in the back seat after impact. He wasn't aiming at the women."

I didn't give a fuck what he thought he was doing. "I'm not going to waste my time having a conversation about ricochet and collateral damage." Tyler was lucky I'd only hit him.

"Fair enough. You get a hold of Christensen and Talerco?"

"Yeah. Neil's bringing the Cobalt to your dock at your condo at seven. Talon will meet us at the same time." I heard Luna start typing.

"How are we getting past his front guardhouse?"

"We're not. We're going in through underground tunnels he has all over the property. Irina gave me the location of one."

"How do you know it's not a setup?"

I refrained from telling him to go fuck himself. "It's not."

"All right, all right. I'm running backgrounds on the guards we took out right now to see if I can find any known associates. Maybe we can get an idea of how many we're dealing with. Did she ever say anything to you about his workforce?"

"No." Another mistake. I should've fucking asked her.

"I'll run a scan on your security when I'm done. Did you have any more problems after last night?"

"Not that I know of."

"I asked a friend on Miami PD about the guard you torched. They don't expect to get an ID and the vehicle was stolen. They don't have any leads."

Fedorov hadn't made good on that threat yet, but he

would. "Copy. I'm pulling into my garage now. I'm gearing up, then doing recon. Meet you at your condo in an hour."

Luna stopped typing. "What kind of recon?"

"Drive by."

"*Mierda.* Are you trying to get killed?"

"I'm going to see what kind of surveillance cameras he has." And let the fucker know I'm coming.

"*Dios mio*, what the hell do you expect to find? He'll have more surveillance than Dade county lockup. He's a paranoid Russian mafia gunrunner. Don't risk it. We'll recon after dark once we get there."

No, we won't. Come sundown, I'm going in and getting her. "I'll see you in an hour."

"Come on, bro. What are you going to do?"

Drive up to his guardhouse and fucking announce myself. Targets never took you seriously when you knocked on their front door. "Don't worry about it. I'll handle it."

"*Shit.*" Luna sighed, exasperated. "Give me twenty and I'll come with you."

Not happening. "I'll see you at your condo." I hung up.

I checked my security feeds on my mobile app then got out of the truck and scanned the perimeter of my yard before I headed inside. Hunter circled around me then whined at the door and barked once. I opened the door, but he didn't go out. He just glanced in the garage then looked accusingly at me.

"She's not here. I'm alone."

He lay down at the door.

Christ. I went to the bedroom and opened my gun safe. Exchanging the rifle for my retrofitted AR15, I loaded up on extra magazines and ammo. Then I dumped food in Hunter's bowl. I was back in the truck in five minutes, and a half hour after that, I was taking the bridge onto Key Biscayne.

I didn't notice the view or the afternoon sun or the boats on the water. I didn't pay attention to the swarm of gardeners cleaning up lawn debris on multimillion-dollar estates. I didn't catalog shit.

I broke every speed limit and tried to convince myself going in now without backup was a bad fucking idea. My control hanging by a thread, I turned down Fedorov's street and pulled right the fuck up to his front gate.

With a rifle on a shoulder harness resting crossways against his chest, an armed guard stepped out of the small guardhouse.

I lowered my window.

"Private property. Turn around." He made a circle in the air with his finger.

His first mistake was stepping up to the vehicle. His second mistake was not keeping both hands on his weapon.

I grabbed the rifle and jerked it and him against the side of the truck as I shoved my 9mm into his temple. "You made a crucial mistake." His third mistake was keeping the safety on.

He swore in Russian. "You're dead."

"Not before you." I quickly scanned the two cameras mounted on the guardhouse and additional cameras mounted on the security wall at every third section. None of them were moving. I spotted the sprinkler pump housing ten yards behind the guardhouse.

"You're on camera," he spat out. "I record everything."

"Good. Make sure Fedorov knows I'm coming for him. Tell him the marine is going to kill him."

The guard yanked against my hold. "You tell him. He will be down here the second he sees you on camera."

"Thinking you had the upper hand with your security cameras and your weapon, you underestimated me. That was your crucial mistake." In one quick, precise movement, I released the rifle, and applied the right amount of pressure at a precise spot on the side of his neck.

He dropped to the ground, unconscious.

I glared up at the security camera for two heartbeats then I threw the truck in reverse and drove to Luna's.

TWENTY-EIGHT

Irina

He didn't burst through the door like the stories of the Militsiya my mother used to tell me about. He didn't splinter the frame with a well-placed kick that made the door fly open. He didn't even make a sound. He was just… suddenly there.

Viktor's arm swung back. Another blow from his paddle about to make contact with my bruised body, he smiled. "Look, petal, we have company." He eyed Dane then brought the paddle down.

Wood hitting flesh echoed in the eerie silence.

I jerked against the restraints and tears welled.

No.

NO.

Three hours and forty-seven minutes. Four whips, three vibrators, nipple clamps, his acrid sweat dripping onto my body and that goddamn paddle, and I didn't shed a single tear. I didn't so much as let him get a grunt out of me. I took every minute of Viktor's assault, but the second Dane's eyes found mine, tears showed up.

I didn't fucking cry in front of Viktor. Not ever.

The ball gag choking me, I didn't just cry either. A monumental wail of defeat reared up and choked my lungs as I fought not to panic. I no longer cared about Viktor. I hated him. I hated every single perverse thing I'd ever let him do to me. I hated his fucking limp-dick, cologne-smelling disgustingness. I hated everything. Including how he made me come four times. But I never hated him more than in that very second when Dane saw what I really was.

I wasn't a woman.

I wasn't strong.

I wasn't a fighter.

Bought and paid for, I was a weak and pathetic slave, and Dane would never unsee that.

It didn't matter that I'd tried to save my mother and André by going with Viktor. It didn't matter that Viktor threatened to kill Dane if I didn't do as he said. It didn't matter that Viktor said he would give the cops those computer files tracking Peter's whereabouts to Dane's house if I didn't come. It didn't matter, period. I was never going to win against Viktor because I was weak. I was weak when he took me on a date five years ago, and I was even weaker now because I let him do this to me knowing what he was.

And that made me pathetic.

Rage and humiliation gurgled up my sobbing throat, and I kicked at my ankle restraints.

The bed posts shook and Viktor chuckled. "Oh look, soldier, you've upset her." He moved to the side of the bed and gripped a handful of my hair, pulling the strands harder than he ever had. "What's wrong, petal?" He lowered his rancid breath to my ear. "You don't want to come in front of him?" He turned up the speed on the vibrator lodged deep in my pussy then grabbed the wand vibrator. Cranking it, he shoved it against my clit.

My back arched off the bed and my legs shook like a train coming into station.

A rush of wind, and the vibrator hit my thigh before falling to the floor. My startled breath wheezed past the gag, and I was staring at Viktor as his eyes popped out of his head. Dane's huge arm across his throat was choking out all of Viktor's air as Dane pressed his gun into Viktor's temple.

"I'm not a soldier. I'm a marine." Dane snapped Viktor's neck.

Like a rag doll, Viktor crumpled to the ground.

I squeezed my eyes shut and fought to keep from hyperventilating.

So gentle that I would never mistake his touch for Viktor's, Dane undid one nipple clamp, then the other. My humiliation ramping up to a level I never knew existed, I fought against the restraints.

"Sh, hold still," his deep voice soothed.

The vibrating anal plug in my ass stopped, and my mortification leapt so far past intolerable, I wanted to die.

The lubed device was pulled out of me.

But that wasn't even the beginning of my horror.

Huge, gentle hands that had caressed every inch of my body last night held my trembling thighs and turned off the vibrator. As he began to ease the device out of my soaking wet, pulsing pussy, his breath hit my clit.

My traitorous, conditioned body reacted.

Wretched, aching need that I had zero control over reared up and stole the very last ounce of my dignity. Head to toe, cunt to nipples, an unprecedented, life-shattering orgasm ripped from my used-up body.

Dane's sharp intake of breath was a knife to my chest.

Disgraced beyond words, I yanked against my wrist restraints, hoping to break my bones.

"Hold on." No force in his tone, it wasn't a command.

I roared with mortification.

His hands fumbled on the ball gag, and I kicked out as he got the buckle undone. Unlike the giant dildo in my pussy, he left the ball in my mouth and quickly moved to one of my wrists.

I spit the ball out. Streams of saliva dripped down my chin, and I kicked against the ankle restraints in humiliated rage. A keening sob worked my sore jaw as I used my newly freed hand to shoved Dane away from my other wrist restraint.

I felt him move to my ankles as the restraints loosened, and I fought from opening my eyes. I fought with everything I had. But when my second ankle was released, it was as if I had to make my destruction complete.

I opened my eyes and looked at him.

His storm-colored gaze unerringly fixed on me, Dane stared at me with the one thing I feared most.

Irony hit me full force.

In death, Viktor had broken me worse than he ever had while he was breathing.

My life shattered, my horror bleeding into rage, I did the only thing I could.

I kicked Dane in the chest.

He stumbled back, and he looked at me like I never wanted him to look at me.

Gone was the locked-down, war-hardened expression of a warrior. Impotence and pity and distress swirled into a hot mess of everything that he wasn't and he looked at me not like a marine, but like a man who didn't know what to do.

I hated it more than I ever hated Viktor.

Venomous words crawled up my ragged throat and spewed past my aching jaw. "Get away from me!"

His eyes widened, his hands went up, and his expression soaked up a thick layer of worry. "Irina."

"*Don't.*" One hand still cuffed, I scrambled back on the bed. "Don't you *dare*. Don't you fucking touch me!"

"Marek," André Luna quietly interjected.

In my utter desolation, I hadn't noticed the other ex-marine enter the room.

As if to shield me from André, Dane moved his impossibly huge body closer to me.

I lost it. "Get away from me! Get out, get out, GET OUT."

"Stand down," André barked. Grabbing a blanket off the floor, he shoved past Dane and put a knee on the bed. His voice dropped and his eyes cut to mine. "It's okay, chica. I got you. No one's gonna hurt you." He wrapped the blanket around my beaten and bruised body and placed a hand over the one I had clawing at my restrained wrist. "I got this," he softly cooed. "Let me get you free, baby girl. You're okay."

I yanked at my wrist. "Get this off me!"

"Almost there, almost there." André unclasped the restraint. "You're free now, chica. Come on, let's get you out of here." He touched a device in his ear and his voice turned commanding. "Collins, I need an extraction. Garages on the west side. Four minutes."

"Luna," Dane bit out.

Scooping me up, blanket and all, André ignored Dane. "Almost out, hang tight, baby girl."

"*Stop*," Dane warned.

André spared him a glance. "Talerco found seven women hostages. Handle it."

"Where are you taking her?" Dane demanded.

I buried my head in the blanket.

"If she doesn't need medical attention, the apartments above my office." André's voice rumbled from his chest.

"Take her to my penthouse. She can stay there."

I didn't hear a response, and I didn't see either of their faces. All I knew was that André started moving again.

I wanted to disappear forever.

TWENTY-NINE

Dane

Four tours, two hundred and forty-three kills, gunshot wounds, death, dismemberment, stab wounds, burn wounds from IEDs—I'd never seen anything that'd made me hesitate.

Until tonight.

The rage of seeing her restrained and beaten was enough to make me lose my mind, but when she didn't want me to even touch the restraints imprisoning her, I hesitated.

I fucking hesitated.

The one goddamn thing she didn't need at the single most crucial moment in her life was me being a goddamn pussy.

"Ink," Talon barked through the com. "We got a situation downstairs. Need you, stat."

I glanced down at Fedorov's body. I fucking hated myself for not making him suffer.

"Ink!"

"On my way." I stepped over him then walked past the two dead guards in the hall and went downstairs.

Talon stood in the entryway with seven women in various states of undress. Scared out of their fucking minds, they huddled together.

Talon, with a rare scowl on his face, gave me a slight shake of his head. "I found them in one of the tunnels making a run for it."

"Let them go."

Talon looked at me like I was crazy. "They're fuckin' naked and none of them have papers, let alone money."

Goddamn it. "Find some clothes." We were in a fucking mansion with thirteen bedrooms. "Then cut them loose or call the cops." The authorities could fucking handle it for all I cared.

"No police!" One of the woman said with a thick Russian accent.

Neil stepped into the entryway. "They are illegal." He switched to Russian and addressed the woman who'd spoken up.

She nodded once then shook her head. "*No*," she said vehemently before saying something in Russian.

Neil glanced at me. "They don't want to be deported. They want to work. Luna said you have a contact."

My mind on that fucking bedroom upstairs, I stared at him.

"The triplets," he quipped.

Fuck. The billionaire real estate triplets, Jagger, Jacek and Jarek Black. They owned an exclusive sex club. I'd done a job for them once.

"Call them," Neil demanded.

I didn't give a fuck who dealt with the women as long as it wasn't me, but even I could see how fucked up it was to send them to the Black brothers without consent. "That's going from one shit situation to the next. They'll be better off with Immigration."

Neil glanced at the woman he'd spoken to and said something in Russian. She immediately nodded.

Neil turned back to me. "They know why they were recruited. They have no objection to working for the triplets as long as they are compensated."

Who the fuck was I to judge? I pulled out my personal phone and scrolled through the few contacts I kept. I called the brother I'd dealt with the most.

Jagger picked up with music playing in the background. "Not sure if this is a good sign or bad that you're calling."

"I need a favor."

Jagger laughed. "Sure, whoever you want. Come down to the club and pick one the girls."

"Not that kind of favor." I rattled off Fedorov's address. "Get here ASAP."

He sobered. "Key Biscayne?"

"Yeah."

"Give me ten minutes." He hung up.

I nodded at Neil. "Ten minutes. The property cleared?"

"Ja."

"How many?" Intent on finding Irina when we'd breached the property, I hadn't bothered with a body count. I'd put the first guard I'd seen in choke hold and demanded to know where she was. Once he'd told me she was upstairs, I broke his neck then I shot the two armed guards outside the door to Fedorov's bedroom. I didn't even take any satisfaction that Fedorov had taken my earlier warning seriously and posted men outside his bedroom. I was too fucking enraged at myself for letting him take her in the first place.

"There are three restrained in the kitchen," Neil answered.

"Luna and I got two with the women," Talon added. "Another one was gettin' busy in the study." He glanced at one of the girls.

Fuck, we needed to contain this. Without Luna here and his ties to law enforcement, I could only think of one solution. I glanced at Neil. "Fire?"

"No." Neil tipped his chin toward the girls. "Get the women out and we will talk."

I nodded and glanced at my watch. "Affirmative." Luna had walked out with her three minutes ago. It felt like a fucking lifetime.

"Go," Neil commanded. "He has not yet left with her."

I didn't hesitate. I ran through the house to the garage and hit the door just as Luna was carrying her out to one of his SUVs. The sight of her bare feet hanging out from the blanket both gutted and enraged me.

I lashed out at Luna. "I said I didn't want any more of your men on this."

Luna looked over his shoulder as he opened the back passenger door. "Good thing I wasn't stupid enough to listen."

He was right. If he'd listened, we'd all be on Neil's Cobalt, the seven women included, and I knew Irina enough to know she would've hated more of an audience than she'd already had.

I took the cell phone I had from Luna and handed it to him after he put her in the vehicle and shut the door. "Give this to her."

Luna clipped out a nod and took the phone as he got in the front passenger seat.

This was fucking killing me. I should've been the one getting her out of here. I should've been the one holding her, and

I sure as hell should've been the one taking care of her. Not fucking Luna. The hand not on my AR15 fisted and I leveled Luna with a look. "Take care of her."

"Copy that." He shut the door and they took off. As the vehicle rounded the bend, it had to pause for a Maserati coming up the driveway.

Jagger pulled his car up right in front of me, and he and his brother Jacek got out.

Both blond, both the exact same height, both with the same haircut, I could tell them apart only from their shirt colors and dispositions.

Wearing a light-colored shirt, Jagger eyed my weapon and smiled. "You didn't tell me what kind of party this was."

His brother Jacek didn't say shit and he didn't smile.

"Inside." I walked back into the garage and closed the door.

Jagger glanced over his shoulder at the closing door. "What's up with all the secrecy?"

"I've got seven Russian illegals inside who don't want to be deported."

Jacek crossed his arms and spoke up. "Not our problem."

"Seven Russian women," I clarified.

Jagger smiled wide.

Jacek shook his head. "We don't sponsor work visas and we don't hire off the books."

Jagger clapped Jacek on the back. "Yes, we do. Ignore him. They hot?"

I didn't fucking know, I'd barely looked at them. I nodded once.

Jagger grinned wide. "Let's meet them. They speak English?"

No clue. "Yeah."

"Jagger," Jacek clipped. "We can't afford the heat on this."

Jagger laughed. "We can afford anything we want, brother." He walked into the house.

Jacek looked at me. "This is Viktor Fedorov's house and there's a body at the guard shack where there should be a guard."

"It was his house," I corrected. "Now he's dead."

Jacek cut to the chase. "Is this going to come back on us?"

He wasn't an idiot. I didn't lie. "Only if one of the women says something."

He eyed me for a second. "This makes us even."

Fucker had balls. This wasn't close to equitable in my book. Seven women didn't compare to a deadbeat father with two decades of dirt on his sons and a team of lawyers I'd had to handle, but I gave him the win. "Copy that."

"Do I want to know what happened to Fedorov?" he asked.

I gave Jacek credit. He'd never served, but he was shrewd as fuck and he didn't take shit from anyone. The brothers' entire empire was built on Jacek's decisions. "He mistreated his wife."

A rare smile spread across his face. "Let me guess. She's a young, hot Russian and she's now yours?"

"Need to know."

"Of course. *Need to know.*" He walked into the house.

I made to follow and my cell vibrated. I glanced at the display and swiped across the screen, then I waited for Luna to speak.

"She's at your place and she's refusing medical attention. I didn't get a good look at her, but there wasn't any blood on the blanket. Your call."

"Leave her." I didn't thank him. I was still too fucking pissed at him for overstepping.

Luna sighed, but he didn't comment.

"Speak," I demanded.

"She's not talking."

I wouldn't either. "She doesn't have to."

"*Jesucristo*, she's going to have to talk eventually, and she needs clothes, at a minimum. Grab something from Fedorov's and I'll have Collins run it over."

She wasn't going to wear a fucking thing from this house. "I'll get her clothes. Leave her alone."

"I already fucking left, *pendejo*. Chill the fuck out. I'm waiting for the elevator."

Luna rarely lost his shit. "What happened?"

"Nothing happened. I took her exactly where you wanted me to take her, which was not where she wanted to be. You need to get your shit together. You pull me out in a fucking hurricane for a damn pick up, get me caught in the crosshairs of some asshole's scope, you take out one of my men, then I'm explaining four dead bodyguards to the cops only to turn around and have another half dozen of them down along with a dead Russian arms dealer. How the fuck am I supposed to explain that? *I'm pissed the fuck off.*"

Neil stepped into the garage. "Put Luna on speaker."

I didn't know how he knew who the hell I was talking to, but I'd ceased questioning his shit years ago. I put the phone on speaker. "Neil's here."

"What the fuck are we doing to contain this?" Luna snapped. "We've got one hell of a cleanup."

"I will call ATF," Neil interjected.

Luna swore. "That prick agent Ben Olsen you know?"

Neil didn't nod, he didn't even blink. He stood perfectly still. "We give this to him."

"How the hell do we know he'll leave us out of it?" Luna argued.

"I will tell him to," Neil stated.

I wouldn't fuck with Neil if he told me to do something, but I had to at least ask if he had leverage over the agent. "What do you have on him?"

"He owes me a favor."

"That doesn't tell us shit," Luna quipped. "Everyone owes you favors."

"You are out of options," Neil warned. "I will call ATF."

"*Mierda.* All right, all right, but wait until I get back there and do a sweep of Fedorov's computers before you call. He has shit on Marek, and I want to wipe his security cameras."

"Fine," Neil answered.

Luna exhaled. "What's up with the women? Do I need to bring more transport?"

I looked at Neil.

Neil answered. "The triplets are taking them."

"Are they gonna talk?"

"I spoke with them. They will not say anything," Neil confirmed.

"How'd you manage that?" Luna asked. "None of them spoke English."

"I speak Russian."

"*Christ,*" Luna muttered. "Of course you do."

"We are wasting time. Get back here, wipe the computers and we will handle the rest." Neil inclined his head once at the phone.

I hung up. "What's up?"

"Is your female going to talk?"

"She's not mine." Not at the moment.

"Is Fedorov's wife going to talk?"

I ground my teeth. "No."

He ignored my denial of her being mine. "You will have repercussions once you go public with her."

"I'll handle it." I'd kept myself alive this long. I wasn't a fucking idiot.

"It will appear that you orchestrated this."

"Nothing's going to come back on me. If Luna does his job and wipes the computers and if your ATF agent does his, my name will stay out of it."

"That is a lot of ifs."

"Your point?"

"You have handled your business alone up to this point. No man is an island."

That's why I fucking wanted her. Any damn way I could have her. "I don't plan on staying in the business. I'll be fine."

Neil stared at me like he could see every fucking lie I was telling myself. "The female does not deserve a warrior who brings the battle home with him."

I threw it back on him. "One day, you're going to be that proverbial warrior."

"We are not discussing me."

"I wasn't aware that we were having a discussion at all." He was lecturing.

"We are not."

Fucking great. "Anything else?"

He opened the garage door. "Have Luna's man drive you to the female. Tend to her. We will handle the rest." He looked over my shoulder.

Sure enough, a Luna and Associates black SUV was pulling up the driveway.

If I was a bigger man, I would've fucking thanked him and told him I owed him. But I didn't. A weight the size of every mistake I'd made with Irina sat on my chest, and I couldn't fucking focus.

I walked to meet the SUV as Luna got out. "I need a ride."

Luna nodded and glanced at the driver. "Collins, take him wherever he needs to go then check in."

"Roger that."

I hated not driving, but I got in the passenger seat. Luna inclined his head once and shut the door.

"Where to?" Collins put the vehicle in gear.

I glanced at the clock on the dashboard. Nine fifteen. Fuck. "I need to get some clothes." I set my AR15 on the floor behind my seat, dumped my extra magazines, then shrugged out of my vest.

He gave me a sideways glance. "For the girl?"

"Yeah."

"Target's still open."

I unstrapped my thigh holster and shoved my 9mm in my back waistband. "Fine." I untucked my T-shirt to cover my weapon.

We drove for ten minutes before he spoke. "Tyler did two tours. He knew what he was doing earlier."

Could've fucking fooled me. "Yeah?" I didn't wait for a response. "Then why were your targets under control within a few shots while he kept unloading on his?"

"Both of mine were in the front seat. The windshield was easy to breach. Tyler's second target was behind a body. The projectile wasn't in his favor."

"And that made it okay to fire into a vehicle with two innocents?"

"Not how I would've handled it, but he wasn't firing at the women."

"One was shot," I reminded him. Not that I gave two fucks about her mother.

Collins didn't comment as he pulled into the parking lot of the store.

"Drop me off." I took a few bills out of my wallet and handed them to him. "Get her some food then meet me back here."

He pocketed the money. "You want anything?"

I thought for a second. Would she eat with me? Fuck, would she even let me into the condo? I shook my head. "No. Give me ten minutes."

"Got it." He pulled up front.

I walked into the fucking store.

THIRTY

Irina

MY BODY BRUISED AND BEATEN, MY CORE throbbing, the smell of heavy, sick cologne all over me, I didn't speak as André carried me into the elevator.

"Almost there, chica, almost there."

The floors ticked up to the top.

The elevator pinged and the doors slid open.

"Come on, let's get you settled."

I didn't know why he was bothering. I wasn't going to be settled. I was in a dead man's blanket, going to another man's condo while my mother was in a hospital somewhere with a gunshot wound.

Viktor didn't die of a gunshot wound.

André punched in the code and let us into Dane's penthouse. The faint smell of Dane that had lingered earlier this afternoon after he'd left was gone.

"Couch, bed or do you need the restroom?" André asked.

I didn't answer. I stared at the one window not covered by shutters.

André followed my glance. "You want the shutters open?"

I might've nodded.

His muscles bunched as he set me down on the couch, then he made quick work of opening all the shutters.

Moonlight danced across the waves and the lights of adjacent condos lit up the night as if life was picture perfect. If I concentrated, I could smell salt and sand and soft breezes.

I stared at the view.

A six-foot ex-marine made his way back to the couch, put his hands on his hips and looked down at me. "Talk to me, chica."

I knew he was looking for something from me, but I was out of somethings.

"You need a doctor?"

I shook my head.

"What can I get you?"

I sunk further into the couch and pulled the blanket around me. The ghost scent of the ocean at night fell away. I was back to a dead man's cologne mixed with desperation and sweat.

André sank to a squat. "You know what my madre always says?"

There was kindness in his eyes, but there was also something else. Something a lot like Dane. I didn't give him an answer because I had no idea what his mother always said.

"She says God gives us tomorrows."

I didn't want a tomorrow. I wanted a next year.

"You know what I say, chica?"

I pulled my legs up.

He didn't wait for a response. "I say it's up to us how we use those tomorrows."

Nothing was up to me. Nothing had been up to me

for five long years. That's why I'd left, but now here I was in another man's clutches.

André continued as if we were having a two-sided conversation. "I don't know what's gonna happen come sunup and I can't predict the future, but I know this—your story doesn't end here. This is just temporary. You're gonna get a tomorrow, you hear me?"

If someone had told me twenty-four hours ago that I was going to be getting a pep talk from an ex-marine who quoted his mother after I let my husband beat me with a paddle, then watched the stranger I'd had unprotected sex with kill my husband, I would've accused them of being insane.

But here I was, lucky to be alive, waiting for a promised tomorrow.

André put a hand on my shoulder. "I know you hear me, chica. I'm not gonna force you to talk, but I need to know if you're gonna be okay for a bit by yourself so I can go handle a few things. Give me something, baby girl."

I nodded.

His hand squeezed then let go. "*Gracias*. Me or Marek will be back in a bit." He pulled a phone out and messed with it a moment, then placed it on my lap. "You got mine and Marek's numbers in there. You need anything before one of us checks on you, call. Understand?"

I turned away from him. More than the bruises on my body, it hurt to think about Dane.

He stood. "All right, I hear you, chica. Try to get some rest. Tomorrow's coming, I promise." He walked out.

I waited until I heard the door shut then I slowly got up. The phone fell to the floor and I stared at it a moment. Then I stepped over it. Walking wasn't as painful as I thought. In fact, it didn't hurt at all like my ego hurt. Not even close. Sore, I made my way to the door and threw the dead bolt. Then I dropped Viktor's bedspread. Refusing to look down at my naked body, I made my way back to the couch and picked up the blanket lying on the back. I wrapped it around myself then sat back down.

I stared out at the ocean.

Viktor's blanket on the floor by the front door, Dane's around my body, I'd traded one blanket for another.

One man for another.

Except I didn't have the second man and the first one was dead.

I should feel something about that. But I didn't. Not gratitude, not guilt, nothing. It was as if I'd gone numb.

I was still staring at the nighttime ocean when a quiet knock sounded on the front door. My heart leapt and I pulled the blanket that didn't smell a thing like Dane tighter around me. You had to enter a code into the elevator to even get up to the penthouse, so I knew it could only be one of two people, but I was sure it wasn't André.

I didn't get up. I didn't have to. A second later the dead bolt was unlocking and I could feel him.

I didn't turn. I didn't shift. I didn't take my eyes off the ocean, because I didn't want to see him. I couldn't see the look on his face when he saw me.

I smelled him a second before the soft rustle of plastic bags landing on the coffee table broke the silence in the penthouse.

The couch dipped.

"Irina."

His deep, quiet voice rumbled from his chest and spread

across my skin like comfort. My heart ached, and I longed to reach for him, but I stayed perfectly still.

Gentle fingers brushed my hair aside and swept it behind one ear.

"I brought you some clothes and food."

I wanted to cry. Gone was the rage that'd had me kicking him away from me. In its place was sorrow so profound, I didn't understand it. I felt bonded to a man I'd known less than twenty-four hours and losing that bond was gutting me worse than anything Viktor had ever done to me.

I forced the truth past my dry mouth. "You will never unsee tonight."

He didn't hesitate. "I don't need to."

Yes, he did. He needed to never see me as I was with Viktor. That woman could never be with a warrior like him. The temptation to just lean into him and feel his warmth was so great, I had to inch away from him.

His voice dropped so low, it barely disturbed the air. "I'm sorry I failed you."

I looked up.

Anguished storm-colored eyes stared at me with the same intensity I'd grown addicted to. "I was selfish," he confessed. "You never should've been a witness to the meet. I should've taken you to Luna's where you would've been safe."

"He would have killed your friend and given the cops the information on Peter's tracking device." I saw the red dot from a laser scope on André's forehead. I knew what it meant.

"I would've handled it."

It was what he didn't say that alarmed me. He would've handled a dead friend and Viktor destroying his life, but he wasn't handling what he saw Viktor do to me. I turned back toward the ocean. "What's done is done."

"Is it?"

I didn't know if he meant what Viktor had done or if he meant us, but it didn't matter. It was the same answer. "Yes."

He grasped my chin and turned me back to face him. "There is nothing I blame you for."

Shame burned my cheeks. "I'll leave tomorrow and you can have your condo back."

He didn't move, or even blink, but I saw the shift. Part of him shut down. "Stay here. However long you want."

I pulled out of his grasp. I would beg my mother to take me in before I'd stay here. "I just need my suitcase from your house." Because I was never going back to Viktor's. I didn't want any of the clothes I'd left behind that he'd bought me.

"There'll be federal agents crawling around the Key Biscayne property." The softness in his voice when he'd said my name was gone. "It's not safe to go back there."

His tone made my guard go up. I turned and looked at him. "Not safe for me, or not safe for you?"

"You," he ground out.

The connection I'd felt to him last night took a major blow. I could've told him I was never going back there, even if I'd inherited the whole damn estate, which I knew I wouldn't. Viktor never missed an opportunity to tell me I would get nothing if he died. I could've told Dane all of this. But the fact that he thought I wanted to go back there told me I had no connection to him. If he couldn't see that I'd only gone back to save his friend and my mother, then I had nothing to say to him.

I turned away from him. "You can go now."

"Because you're angry with me or because I saw what he did to you?"

I hated how he picked up on the truths I wanted to hide. Subtle, obvious, it didn't matter. He was either incredibly perceptive or I was a hell of a lot worse at hiding my emotions than I thought I was. "Does it matter?"

"Look at me," he demanded.

Swirls of awareness crawled across my skin, and the hair on the back of my neck stood at attention. Nothing about my reaction to his command felt sexual, because the mere thought made my stomach turn. But there was a power in his voice, and in his presence, that made me want to crawl onto his lap and forget who I was.

I wanted to feel his arms around me, to hear his heartbeat, to have his scent erase every memory of Viktor. It would be heaven. But to have his voice be the first and last thing I heard every single day? That would be a dream.

Except that dream was ruined.

"Just go," I whispered.

THIRTY-ONE

Dane

THE NEED TO CLAIM HER WAS SO FUCKING INTENSE, I fought from pushing her back on the couch and sinking inside her. Knowing what she'd been through, knowing what her body looked like under that blanket, I hated myself for even thinking it. In the same damn breath, I was fucking certain she needed it. We both did. We needed to remember what we felt like together.

This bullshit wall she was putting up was going to come down. One way or another, I'd find a way around it. That's what I fucking did. I found solutions. I fixed problems, and I was going to fucking fix this. Strategically.

She wouldn't look at me? Fine. Then I'd fucking go to her.

I kicked the coffee table back and got on my knees. Before she could draw in a shocked breath, her face was in my hands.

I showed no mercy. "You know what I'm not going to do?" I didn't wait for an answer. "I'm not going to walk. You want space tonight? Fine. Take it. But I'll still be here tomorrow and the goddamn days after that." If she wanted to kick me out tonight, I'd sleep in the fucking hall, but I wasn't leaving her alone. "You want a different place to stay? I'll find you a different place. But I'm not going to let you hide from me." I touched my lips to her forehead because I couldn't not touch her, then I stood and picked her up. "Come on."

Alarm spread across her face. "What are you doing?"

"Putting you in a hot bath." She fucking smelled like him. I wasn't having it another goddamn second.

"I don't want a bath."

Petulant and almost full of attitude, her tone washed over me like a fucking drug and relief spread through my veins. "It'll make you feel better."

Expecting her to argue or tell me I didn't know what would make her feel better, I was ready with half a dozen comebacks. But she didn't say a word as I walked her into the master bathroom.

I set her on her feet and turned the water on full blast in the jetted tub. She didn't walk out, but she wouldn't look at me.

Fuck this.

I did what I'd wanted to do since I'd laid eyes on her again. I put my arms around her and I fucking held her. Her body stiffened, but as the bathroom filled with steam, she relaxed in my embrace.

I didn't say anything. I didn't have to. I knew she took comfort in my arms as much as I took comfort in holding her. If I had to find my way back to her inch by inch, then that's what I'd fucking do.

I watched the water level rise and waited until the last second before reluctantly letting go of her to shut the water off. "In you go." I grasped a corner of the blanket.

She jerked away. "*No.*"

This time, I didn't make a crucial mistake. I didn't hesitate. I took her chin and I bent my knees to get closer to her eye level because I knew exactly what this was about. "I saw your body yesterday and I've seen your body today." I held her gaze like I should've done earlier. "Nothing's changed. You were beautiful then and you're beautiful now." I started to push the blanket off her shoulders.

"Don't do this," she pleaded.

My heart rate kicked up. "The only thing I'm going to do is watch my woman get in the bath." I slowly dragged the blanket off her.

She closed her eyes and I stole a glance at her body.

Jesus. Fucking. Christ.

Every last molecule in my body went into rage mode. Her wrists and ankles were red with restraint marks, her nipples were swollen, and darkening welts crisscrossed her inner thighs.

Using every goddamn tactic I'd ever learned in the military, I fought to keep my voice even. "I'm lifting you up. You tell me if it's too hot."

She didn't open her eyes or move a muscle.

Cradling her back, I put my arm behind her thighs, and as gently as possible, I lifted her. "Feet first, sweetheart." I lowered her into the water.

She inhaled sharply.

Fuck. "Too hot?"

She frantically shook her head.

Inch by inch, without letting her go, I lowered her into the tub. The rigid stiffness in her posture eased and her head fell back on my arm.

My fucking heart started to beat again. "Lie back, love, that's it."

"Don't call me that," she whispered.

I kissed her temple as the hot water soaked my shirt. Seeing her body, I couldn't even smile at her attempt to sway me from calling her what I wanted to fucking call her.

She glanced at me then quickly looked away. "You're getting wet."

I didn't give a fuck. "I want you comfortable." And I wanted any damn thing she was willing to give me right now. A wet T-shirt was a small fucking price to pay.

"You were right." She exhaled. "The hot water feels good."

"Sometimes I know what I'm talking about." I would've given anything to be in that tub with her. Hell, I would've given anything to kiss her.

"And other times?"

"I fucking fake it."

She didn't even crack a smile. "How is your side?"

The question, her concern, it gutted me. "I'm fine." My voice rough, I stroked her cheek.

She turned away from my touch. "I need to wash my hair."

"Give me a sec." I gently extracted my arm from behind her head and got up to grab the shampoo out of the shower. When I turned, she was staring at her wrists.

"I didn't know he had restraints," she quietly admitted. "The kind with buckles."

I should've been fucking thankful he hadn't used rope, but all I wanted to do was kill him all over again with slow, torturous brutality.

Tempering my rage, I knelt next to the tub. "You don't have to worry about that ever again." Or fucking think about it. I cupped the back of her head. "Lean back."

"I can wash my own hair."

"I could've put in my own staples." I gently leaned her

head back to wet her hair. "But sometimes we let other people do things for us."

"You can do things I can't do."

I wet her hair. "Ditto." She looked a thousand times more fragile with her hair slicked back.

"I know what you're trying to do, but the reality isn't equitable."

I squeezed shampoo into my hand. "It's not about being equitable. Reality is a balance of power. For every action, there's a reaction. I wouldn't have lasted five minutes with that asshole, let alone five years, but you kept that balance."

"There was never any balance. I was eighteen and I wanted to get away from my mother. He offered me money I was too lazy to come by honestly."

"He offered, you accepted. Action, reaction." I didn't see giving up five years as lazy.

"Not everything is black and white."

No, but the important things were. "We are." I worked my hands through her hair.

She looked away. "This was never going to work."

"It was always going to work." I washed away the scent of that asshole from her.

"I'm not a reaction to your action."

The corner of my mouth tipped up at her using my analogy on me. "No, sweetheart, you're not. You walked into my life and when I saw you, *I* reacted." I tipped her head back. It was always about me reacting to her, never the other way around. My reaction to her was the trigger. "Close your eyes."

Without hesitation, her eyes shut.

Her quiet submission was the bullet. She and I, we were so fucking black and white, nothing in my life made more sense.

Not even when I was an eighteen-year-old enlisting with a wedding band on my finger. I rinsed her hair then sat her up.

She changed the subject. "How do clients find you?"

Did. Past tense. "Referrals." Mostly. The US government on occasion.

"Are they going to keep finding you?"

"No." I cupped handfuls of water and rinsed her shoulders.

"What about Viktor's guards?"

"Of the ones that are still alive? Doubtful. Were any of them legal?" The fuckers had all spoken Russian.

"Probably not."

"They'll be deported. Without Viktor's money, it'll be hard for them to find their way back to the States."

She pulled her knees to her chest. "And if they do?"

I didn't hesitate. "I'll handle it."

"Like you handled Peter?"

"If I have to."

She dropped her chin to her knees. "I'm tired."

"Hang on, I'll get you a towel." I grabbed one off the rack and held it out. "You need help getting up?"

"I'm not an invalid." With the grace of her usual movements, she got up, but I saw the slight twist in her face when she straightened her legs and stood to her full height.

My eyes trained on hers, I wrapped the towel around her. "Clothes, then food."

"I'm not hungry."

She was so fucking beautiful and fragile, it was almost impossible not to take her in my arms. "You're still going to eat."

"You're not my boss."

"No, I'm not." I grabbed another towel for her hair. "I'm the man who cares about you." I ran the towel over her wet locks and draped it over her shoulders. "There's probably a comb in one of the drawers." I didn't spend much time here. "I'll grab you something to put on."

She stood silent as I walked out of the bathroom.

When I returned, she still hadn't moved. I held out a T-shirt from the few things I kept in the penthouse, and the bag of clothes from the store. "You should be able to find something comfortable."

Her hand reached out from under the towel and she took them. "You bought me clothes from Target."

No intonation in her voice, I studied her face. "Interim. Until you get new clothes."

"Why didn't you just bring my suitcase from the house?"

"I didn't take the time to drive there and back." And the real reason. "Nor did I want you wearing anything of his."

She held the clothes tighter to her chest, but she didn't comment.

"You can shop when you feel up to it. I keep an extra car here. The keys are in a kitchen drawer. You have money in your account."

Staring at her feet, she nodded, but otherwise she didn't move.

"You need help?"

"Do you know what happened to my mother?"

"She went to the hospital." I assumed. "She'll be fine." But she'd never be a decent fucking human being.

She nodded again.

"I'll be in the living room. Get dressed, then come have something to eat."

It killed me to leave her standing there, but I didn't want

to undo any progress I'd made, so I grabbed a dry T-shirt for myself then walked to the kitchen. I was getting water and some silverware when she quietly walked to the couch in only my T-shirt and sat. She looked so damn defeated, it simultaneously made me want to kill and protect.

I handed her the silverware and a bottle of water. "Here."

She took it. "Thanks."

I pulled the coffee table back by the couch and opened the take-out containers. "I have no idea what this is." The first container had beans, rice and meat. "Looks like Cuban." The second container was salad.

"You didn't get this?"

"No, one of Luna's men did." I set the first container on her lap.

"The one you hit?"

I momentarily froze. Then my training kicked in. I cataloged. There was only one way she would know about that. "Fedorov told you." I sat down next to her.

She set her water down then moved the fork around the food. "He mentioned it."

"What else did he mention?"

"That you were a killer and you would hit me like you hit your own men."

My jaw ticked. "Interesting tactic."

"He is… was, manipulative."

I didn't address that. "Eat."

"I'm not hungry."

"You're too thin." I could tell she used to have curves.

"You liked me fine last night."

"You were too thin last night as well." I put my feet up on the coffee table and my arm on the back of the couch behind her.

"I don't eat when I'm stressed." She hesitantly put a bite of rice to her mouth and eyed me. "If you are going to watch me eat, you can leave."

I refrained from smiling. I reached over and snagged a hunk of meat then ate it.

"That's disgusting." Her tone was scolding, but she took another bite.

"The meat or using my fingers?"

"Both."

"You don't eat meat?"

"Not if I can help it."

"You ate eggs," I pointed out.

"That wasn't meat."

"Still comes from an animal."

"I didn't say I was vegan."

"Vegetarian?"

She sighed and put her fork down. "I know what you're doing."

I picked the fork up. "What's that?" I took another bite of the pork.

"Distracting me, getting me to talk, to eat…." She looked up at me. "Not tell you to leave."

I set the fork down and winked. "You don't want to tell me to leave, sweetheart."

She picked it up and took another bite.

I gave her a smile. "Nice diversion tactic."

Heat hit her cheeks and she looked down at the food. "You're leaving after I eat."

"No can do. You can lock yourself in a bedroom if you need to, but I'm at least staying on the couch." Fuck the hallway outside.

"You can't leave Hunter alone all night."

Wouldn't be the first time. "He's been fed. He can get out if he needs to."

"That's cruel."

"Then come with me to get him." She could use the distraction.

"I'm not dressed."

"You have clothes here you can wear." I took the fork from her hand, speared a chunk of the meat, ate it, then forked some rice and held it up.

She stared at me.

"Eat."

"I can feed myself."

"You weren't doing it fast enough." I had an idea.

She took the bite.

I refrained from smiling at the win. "You need protein." I forked up some of the beans. "Do you eat dairy?"

"Yes." She ate the next bite.

I liked feeding her. "Fish?"

"Yes."

I could work with that. "What's your favorite food?"

"Coffee." She took the fork back.

"Not a food group."

"It is when you put enough cream in it. What's your favorite food?"

I thought about it. I usually ate for energy, and when I was on a job, I ate what I could, when I could. "Steak."

"Typical man."

"You expected something different?" I teased.

She dropped her attention to the take-out container and pushed the fork through the rice. "I expect nothing."

I sobered. "You should." A man who didn't beat her, for one.

"Life must be very easy for you. You have training, discipline, wealth."

"I didn't always." I was raised by a single mom, just like her.

"But now you do."

"Highlighting our difference doesn't change a thing about the here and now. We're both sitting on the same couch, eating the same food, sharing the same space."

"Your couch, your food, your space," she corrected.

"And you're in it. Know why?"

"Because you're the fixer."

"Because I want you here." I grasped her chin. "I want to be where you are."

"For how long? Until my bruises fade? Until the newness wears off?"

I wasn't going to lie to her. "There are no certainties in life."

"Exactly."

It was too soon, but I didn't fucking care. I laid it out. "But there is commitment."

Her body stiffened and she sucked in a breath as she tried to hide her reaction. She put the food on the coffee table and got up. "I'm going to bed."

I sat perfectly still on the couch. "Which part scares you? That I said it, that I meant it, or that you want it?" I wasn't afraid of commitment, and I knew she wasn't a woman who did casual.

"Go get your dog." She walked into the master bedroom and shut the door.

THIRTY-TWO

Irina

Hot breath wafted across my face and I heard panting.

I opened my eyes.

Lying on the pillow like a human, a German shepherd with morning breath was inches from my nose.

"I was asleep," I grumbled.

He nudged my hand.

"What?" Damn dog.

He nudged me again.

"Fine." I scratched his head like I'd seen Dane do. "How did you get in here?"

"He cried at the door last night until I let him in." Dane's deep voice carried across the room.

I looked up and my heart jumped at the sight of him standing in the doorway. "He slept with me?"

Dane nodded once. "All night." His stare intent, he stepped into the bedroom. "How are you feeling?"

I stretched my legs. My pride was worse than my body. "Fine. What time is it?" I couldn't believe I'd slept through a canine getting into bed with me, let alone the sunlight streaming into the room.

"Just past ten. Breakfast's ready."

I didn't want him seeing me last night, and I certainly didn't want him rescuing me, because I felt like I deserved everything I got from Viktor. After five years of being reminded you were nothing but a business transaction, you started to feel like one. I fell asleep last night thinking over everything that had happened. I'd thought I was saving my mother. I'd thought I was saving Dane and his friend. But all I was doing was perpetuating the cycle I'd put myself in with Viktor. I wasn't ever going to save Dane or André. They could save themselves. And my mother was beyond saving. She was never going to change. I hadn't realized that last night, and I hadn't wanted Dane to see me how I was, but with each maddening moment he wouldn't give me space, I wanted him around even more.

Stuck in thoughts, I didn't notice he'd come over to the bed until he sat down.

I glanced out at the sparkling turquoise ocean. "Nice view."

"Agree." His gaze fixed on me, he didn't even look toward the windows.

I slid out of the other side of the bed and Hunter got up with me. I glanced down at him then at Dane. "What's wrong with him?"

"He wants to go with you."

"Why?" I wasn't even nice to the mutt.

"He's worried about you."

What a load of crap. "You can't tell that." The dog sat down at my feet.

"Hunter," Dane called.

The dog looked over his shoulder at his master.

"Are you worried about Irina?" he asked.

Hunter barked once then looked back at me and his tail thumped.

The corner of Dane's mouth tipped up.

My heart skipped a beat. "That doesn't prove anything." Dane was devastating when he smiled.

He leaned back on one elbow and shrugged. "Ask him another question."

"He doesn't know what I'm saying." He was a dog. A dog that Dane had lovingly trained, and that stupidly only made me more attracted to him.

"He understands a lot more than you think."

I didn't know what dogs knew, but I was willing to play his game because every interaction with Dane was like discovering another piece of the mystery that was uniquely him. "Hunter, are you hungry?"

He barked once and his tail thumped against the floor twice.

If I liked hairy, shedding animals, I would've admitted he was cute. "Hunter, why are you following me?"

He nudged my hand, leaving a cold wet mark on the back of my fingers.

I wiped my hand on my shirt.

Dane laughed.

I scowled. "This isn't funny."

A smile on his face, Dane agreed. "No, it isn't. He's a damn traitor."

Hunter made a sound in his throat similar to a person saying *aw-aww* with an inflection in the middle.

"That's right," Dane taunted the dog. "I called you a traitor. What are you going to do about it?"

Hunter barked once and trotted over to Dane. His tail wagging, he got right up in Dane's face.

"Nope." Dane shook his head. "You had your chance."

Hunter nudged Dane's hand then put a paw on his leg.

Dane didn't give the beast an inch. "Nice try."

Hunter jumped up on the bed and put both of his front paws on Dane's chest.

"You're going to have to do better than that." You could clearly see the love he had for the animal.

Hunter cried and tucked his muzzle against Dane's neck.

Dane didn't budge. "I paid your vet bill when you ate my damn socks."

One of Hunter's paws moved to Dane's shoulder.

"I also let you chase every rabbit on the property."

Hunter's giant tongue came out and licked the side of Dane's face.

Dane chuckled. "Fine, I forgive you." He lay back on the bed and the canine stood over him and lick-bathed every inch of his face.

It was the cutest, most disgusting thing I'd ever seen. "You need a shower now more than me."

Dane sat up and dislodged the hundred-pound beast as if he weighed nothing. "Is that an invitation?" He lifted his T-shirt and wiped his face, exposing a strip of his rock-hard abs.

My heart leapt to my throat and swirls of awareness I never thought I'd feel again fluttered around in my stomach. "No."

The corner of his mouth curved up again. "You hesitated."

I channeled all the attitude I could muster. "You wish." I walked into the bathroom and shut the door.

My heart pounding, I leaned on the counter. Two deep breaths later, I turned on the shower and stripped.

The hot spray hit my body hard, but I didn't have nearly the amount of soreness I had last night. My thighs looked worse, black and purple and yellowing at the edges, but they didn't hurt as I soaped myself.

I tentatively washed my breasts even though the pulsing ache in my nipples had disappeared. They were still red, but the hurt was thankfully gone. Washing my hair with Dane's shampoo, smelling his scent all around me, it made desire pool between my legs.

Inhaling, I dragged a finger through my folds. Wet that had nothing to do with the shower coated my finger, and my core throbbed with need. Despite Viktor's vibrators, I wasn't sore. At all. I'd been conditioned. A single touch and I was achy with need.

Ignoring the pulsing between my legs, because I'd also been conditioned to deny myself, I got out of the shower. I towel-dried my hair and didn't bother combing out the slight waves. I also didn't bother with makeup. Half of me thought it made me less attractive to Dane not to be made up, but the other half had me hoping it didn't.

I walked into the bedroom and my heart skipped a beat when I saw my suitcase. Knowing he'd gotten it for me when he'd retrieved Hunter made me feel both grateful for his consideration and sad that I wouldn't being staying here. I dressed in another one of his T-shirts I found in a drawer, and my own leggings. Sucking in a deep breath, I walked toward the kitchen.

Sitting at the kitchen table in front of two plates of pancakes, Dane immediately looked up. His gaze locked on mine, he tossed his phone on the table and stood.

My heart started to race.

In three strides, he closed the distance between us, and without a word, he pulled me into his arms. The scent that was uniquely him filled my head and sank into my heart.

Encircling me in his strong embrace, he simply held me.

My thoughts in overdrive, my fears and hopes and dreams all mingled into a fast reel of all my moments with him. Seeing him walk into his house for the first time. Hearing his voice as he held me in the dark. His hands as he handled a gun. Stapling his wound. His retreat when I told him to stop. His gentle touch. His mouth on me. His fingers pushing his seed back inside my body. His face when he looked at me shackled. His determination when he'd kneeled in front of me. All of it swirled together and made this moment possible, but none of it felt like this, like rightness and hope.

I wanted the moment to last forever.

"That is a proper good morning, beautiful," he murmured, kissing the top of my head.

At the sound of his voice rumbling from his chest, tears sprung. It was so quick and unexpected, I didn't stand a chance of stifling it. A sob broke free and too many emotions mixed with overwhelming gratitude and tears dripped down my cheeks.

Horrified, I tried to pull away.

His arms tightened. "No, sweetheart, not this time. I'm not letting you go. It's okay. You're okay. You're safe."

My tears stained his shirt as I desperately tried to regain control.

"I'm not going to let anything happen to you ever again." His hand brushed over my hair. "I'll never hurt you, sweetheart."

Everything he did hurt. It hurt because he knew what I

needed before I did. It hurt because I wanted him so much. It hurt because a man who loves his dog like he did would love children, and that's all I kept seeing—him as a father. I didn't see him as the man who'd killed Viktor with his bare hands, or shot Peter. I saw him as the man who'd saved me from myself, and that made me cry harder.

"It's okay, love. Let it out." He stroked my back. "I'm right here."

Oh God. "I am *not* crying," I sobbed.

"I know. And I didn't freeze like a fucking pussy when you kicked me in the chest."

I didn't want to laugh. I didn't even want to smile, but a hiccupped half cry, half laugh escaped.

He pulled back just enough to look down at me, and his lips turned up. "You think that's funny?"

His attempt at a joke staunched the worst of the tears, and I sucked in a deep breath. "I didn't aim for your stitches."

"Lucky me." His thumbs brushed at my tears and his expression turned serious. "You okay?"

No. But for the first time in five years, I started to feel like I would be. "Yeah." The tears, his arms, they were more cathartic than any drug.

Hunter nudged my leg and cried. We both looked down at him.

"Pretty sure he thinks he's keeping you." Dane scratched behind his ears.

I swiped at my face and inhaled. "He's just been deprived of female company for so long, he doesn't know how to act."

Rich and intoxicating, Dane laughed. "Probably. Come on, you need to eat." He led us to the table, but before we could sit, a knock sounded at the front door.

THIRTY-THREE

Dane

My hand automatically went to my gun in my back waistband. I spared her a glance. "Wait for me in the bedroom." Goddamn it, I needed to redo the security here. I hated not having a fucking visual on the hall or lobby.

Hunter's hackles went up and he let out a low growl.

Irina looked nervously toward the door. "Who is it?"

"Probably Luna." Except he would've called first. He knew better than to show up unannounced. "Get in the bedroom. There's a 9mm in the nightstand."

The little color she'd had in her cheeks when she'd come out of the shower disappeared. "Am I going to need it?"

Only if I was fucking dead, but I wasn't going to let that happen. "No."

The knock sounded again.

"Go." I tipped my chin toward the bedroom. "I'll handle this. Hunter, go with Irina." I waited till she was secure. Then I went to the front door and glanced out the peephole.

Fucking hell. I opened the door. "What do you want, Jacek?"

A grin cut through his grim expression.

I realized my mistake. "Jagger," I corrected.

"You're losing your touch, Marek. You should've had it on the first try."

"You never look serious."

His hand rubbed his chin and he looked serious again. "I don't?"

"You know you don't. What do you want?"

He glanced around my place then his gaze landed on my kitchen table. "Breakfast for two? I never pegged you as the type." He laughed. "Me personally? I like to—"

"Cut to the chase, Black." I didn't have time for his bullshit.

"I lost one of your girls last night," he said casually.

Shit. "They aren't my girls."

"Well, she's gone now, and incidentally, I heard one of the guards escaped ATF custody."

Fuck me. "When?"

"I don't know. You should ask your security expert friend that, or Neil. He seemed chummy with the ATF guy. Which is funny because I thought he was former military, not a Fed." Jagger nodded toward the ocean. "You like my view?"

"It's not your fucking view." I grabbed my cell out of my pocket and scrolled to Luna's number.

"It was my view before it was yours. Who do you think backed Christensen Construction when Neil bid on the old dump that was here before he tore it down and rebuilt?"

Christ. I'd made this asshole richer by buying this place?

"Smart investment going for the penthouse." Jagger slapped my shoulder then dropped to my chair at the table. "Looks good. You made buttermilk pancakes?"

If he touched them, I'd consider shooting him. "Get to the point."

Jagger laughed. "Don't tell me you set a place at the table for your dog?"

"Fuck you." I dialed Luna.

Luna picked up immediately. "I'm coming up. I just pulled into your garage."

"Who else did you give my elevator code to?" I snapped.

"No one." He sounded surprised. "Who's there?"

"Black."

"Which one?"

"Does it fucking matter?"

"Probably not." A car door slammed shut. "Be up in a sec." Luna hung up.

Jagger smiled. "In case you were wondering, I know the elevator code because I owned the building before Neil paid me off."

Luna walked in without knocking. "You've got shit for security, Black."

Jagger smirked. "I've got great security, where I need it." He leaned back in my chair and put his hands behind his head.

"You needed it last night," Luna quipped.

"Hey, I'm not in the business of keeping women against their will. I don't have to. They want to leave, they leave." Jagger shrugged. "But if they want to work, they know they won't find a better gig anywhere."

"You agreed to take them," Luna countered. "Part of the deal was keeping them out of sight until shit settled down."

"Yeah, about that. How were you going to keep it quiet about offing Fedorov then killing his bodyguards and taking his women?" Jagger glanced at me. "Coming in from the intracoastal on Christensen's Cobalt wasn't exactly stealth." He looked back at Luna. "I thought you were supposed to be good at what you do."

I only refrained from kicking him out because I needed information out of him. "We had no intention of not being seen." Once we were inside.

Jagger smirked. "Like what? Bust down the front door and let them see you coming? My dick's bigger than yours sort of thing?"

Luna's hands went to his hips. "Which girl did you lose last night and when?"

"How should I know? It wasn't like they told me their names."

"Description," I bit out.

"Blonde and hot." Jagger glanced toward my closed bedroom door. "Kinda like Fedorov's wife."

Refraining from killing Jagger on the spot, I looked pointedly at Luna.

Luna clipped out a nod then addressed Jagger. "You taunt him again, you're on your own. He's out of patience and so am I. When did you notice she was missing?"

"Around ten last night. Before I opened the club, I stopped to check on them. I'd put them up in a couple apartments above the club, but they'd all migrated to one unit. Well, all except one. When I asked where number seven was, they just looked at me."

"They don't speak English."

Jagger laughed. "Oh, they speak English, when they want to."

Luna frowned. "They're legal?"

Jagger smirked. "I didn't say that."

I was done with this conversation. "Tell us what you know or get the fuck out."

"It's not what I know. It's what I don't know," Jagger countered.

"Which is?" Luna asked impatiently.

"Where the missing bodyguard is or how he got through my security."

"Who says he got into your place?"

"One of the women told me last night. Well, more like this morning, anyway, irrelevant. Number five said the bodyguard came for number seven."

Luna looked incredulous. "You fucking numbered them?"

Jagger shrugged. "I'm not like your cocky surfer friend, Talon. I couldn't come up with seven nicknames on the spot."

There was something more besides the security leak that he wasn't telling us or he wouldn't be here. "What's the other problem?"

Jagger crossed his arms. "Fedorov's deal was guns, not women, and those seven blondes? They're not off the street. They were handpicked and someone paid a small fortune to get them here. I suppose it could've been Fedorov, but it also could've been someone else."

I put it together before he finished speaking. "You don't want that someone to come looking for them."

Jagger nodded. "I don't need that kind of attention at my club. I'm not equipped to handle it."

Luna swore in Spanish. "I'll take them. I'll put them up at Luna and Associates until I can get them sent home, wherever the hell that is."

"I didn't say I didn't want them," Jagger clarified. "I just don't want anyone else coming after them. Or me for that matter." He looked at me. "That's where you come in."

"No." I didn't fucking hesitate. "Not my specialty."

"It's exactly your specialty. You fix things. You coerce

and use scare tactics and force when needed. I know what you're capable of. Make the girls mine. That's all I'm asking."

"No." No fucking way.

"I'll double your normal fee," Jagger offered. "Just find out where they came from and make sure I don't have a problem."

Luna looked between us.

"I said no."

Irina stepped out of the bedroom with Hunter at her side. "You should do it."

My gaze cut to hers. Then I took in every inch of her. "I'm not in procurement," I ground out.

"They were already procured," Luna interjected.

"They need a chance," Irina said quietly.

I heard what she wasn't saying. The women needed a chance like she'd been given a chance, but she was my priority now and the answer was still no. I rephrased. "I'm booked." My focus was her now. Period.

Irina stepped up to my side and laced her fingers through mine. "I'm asking." She squeezed my hand. "Will you please help them?"

I cataloged.

Blonde hair, blue eyes and the face of an angel.

Luna's five o'clock shadow.

The muted colors of Jagger's clothes.

Hunter's defection as he stayed at Irina's side.

The cold breakfast. The angle of the sunlight. The scent of sweat and woman on Jagger. The scent of gunpowder on Luna. My T-shirt covering her body. The concealed desperation behind Jagger's request.

But none of it stood out like her hand in mine.

It was a victory I was unwilling to overlook.

I squeezed her hand back. "I'll give it thirty-six hours."

Relief washed across her face. "Thank—"

"On one condition," I warned. "You stay with Luna in the secure apartments at Luna and Associates." I glanced at Luna. "Double protection, twenty-four seven, extra perimeter and patrols." Fedorov was dead, but I wasn't taking any chances this time.

Luna nodded. "Copy."

I looked at Jagger. "Triple the regular fee, Luna's expenses, seven individual accounts funded at two-hundred K each, and you will never use my elevator again." I didn't need the fucking fee, and I could've set the women up with accounts myself, but his fucking comment about Hunter pissed me the hell off.

Jagger smiled for real. "You drive a hard bargain, but done." He held his hand out.

I didn't shake it. "If the women want out, they're out."

Jagger sobered and lowered his hand. "That was never an issue."

"Then confirm it."

He held his hands up in fake surrender. "They're free to walk at any time and take their money. I'm assuming that's who the seven accounts are for?"

Smarmy fuck. "You assumed correct."

"Then we have a deal." Jagger stood and smiled at Irina. "Miss…?"

"Tsarko," she answered.

"Miss Tsarko, Jagger Black. It's a pleasure to make your acquaintance. Thank you for your alliance and persuasion. I'm sure the women will appreciate it." The fucking prick held his hand out to her.

"You're welcome." She shook his hand and I saw red.

THIRTY-FOUR

Irina

"LEAVE," Dane barked at Jagger.

Jagger's smile didn't falter. "On my way." He nodded at Dane then André. "Gentlemen."

André tipped his chin.

Dane turned to face me. "That was unnecessary."

With the hard set to his jaw, and the impenetrable mask on his face, I couldn't tell if he was angry or worried or both. "They need help."

"Not my concern."

His body heat radiating off him, his masculine scent all around me—his presence was so commanding, he could've been touching me and I wouldn't have felt it any less.

I swallowed past the sudden dryness in my mouth. "I asked you to make it your concern."

His hand gripped the side of my face and his voice came out rough. "Do not ask me to do that again."

I could have hidden my emotions behind a mask of disinterest. I could've snapped back with a disrespectful retort or said I would do what I wanted, when I wanted, but I didn't. That woman was gone. She died when Viktor died, and I needed to bury her. I was grateful to this man standing in front of me for saving my life. I wanted his attention, and I wanted to be worthy of it. I didn't want to mess that up by being flippant or dishonest, so I gave him what he was giving me. Respect.

"I promise." I wrapped my hand around his thick wrist. "I won't."

His curt nod and his intense stare were stronger than any words of response.

"Marek," André interrupted us.

Dane didn't take his gaze off mine. "Wait for us in the hall. I need a few minutes."

"Copy."

I heard a door shut and Dane's lips were on mine. Soft and gentle, but oh so demanding, he slid his tongue in and stroked through my mouth as if he were starved for me. My toes curled, and need pooled low in my belly. Every second of last night was forgotten with one single kiss.

I wasn't Viktor Fedorov's wife. I never was.

I was the woman desperately straining on tiptoes to kiss back the man who was showing me with his hands grasping my face and his knee between my thighs and his erection straining against my belly, that I was his. Utterly and completely *his*.

But before I could hitch a leg around his waist and show him he was mine, he pulled back.

His lips against my mouth, his breath feathering across my skin, he gently caught the outside of my thigh and pushed my leg down. "No."

Shame tinted my cheeks and I looked away. "I'm sorry." I had misread his intent.

"Look at me," he demanded, turning my face back to his. "I am not rejecting you."

"I understand." He was being careful, but it still felt like rejection.

"No, you don't."

I understood perfectly. "You don't want to touch me... looking like I do."

"No, goddamn it. I want to touch every inch of you." His hands gripped me tighter. "But I am not making love to you until you heal." He kissed my forehead. "I don't want to hurt you. Understand?"

A warmth in my chest so intense it hurt, warred with my shame and I gave him the only truth I really understood. "I want you to touch me. I want your marks on my skin, not his," I disgracefully admitted. "I want you to make me yours." My whispered admission took what little I had left of my pride and laid it at his feet.

Anger contorted his features like I'd never seen, and he gripped my chin so firmly it startled me. "I will *never* do that to you."

I knew he would never touch me like Viktor had. That wasn't what I meant. But I didn't know how to give a voice to the need deep in my soul that had nothing to do with what Viktor had done to me and everything to do with wanting this man in front of me to claim me.

I wanted my thighs to have Dane's fingerprint bruises. I wanted my lips swollen from his punishing kisses. I wanted my pussy to ache like fire from being stretched and well used by his huge cock. And I wanted his seed dripping down my leg with every step I took because I wanted his marks everywhere on me.

I pulled at his hand holding my face. "I know."

He didn't budge. "Then explain."

"I can't." I couldn't tell him that I wanted him to love me like he'd never loved another. I couldn't tell him that I needed that to feel secure.

"Not hurting you doesn't mean I don't have feelings for you."

This conversation, him leaving, my own disgrace, it made me want to crawl into a hole. "I know."

"Then tell me why you want me to mark you," he demanded.

"Tell me why it matters," I snapped.

He searched my face as if looking for cracks. "You need to say the words."

I broke. "Do you think this is easy? Do you think I wanted to say what I did? Do you think I want you to walk out that door and help other women like you helped me? I don't. I don't want you to be anyone's hero except mine, and I don't want you to be gone for one single second because I want you here with me. I want you to show me I'm *yours*." Tears dripped down my cheeks, and I forced the rest out in an ashamed whisper. "I want to matter to you more than anything in this stupid world because that's what you are to me."

Huge, muscular arms full of strength and forgiveness and life and everything that meant anything to me pulled me into his embrace. "Irina—"

"I don't want you to go," I interrupted. "I don't want to be that selfish. But I am. I'm broken and selfish, and I don't care anymore about being whole. I just want to be yours."

He held me tighter.

I choked on a sob. "And I hate crying. I don't want to do it in front of you anymore, so go." I took a step back. "Just go."

He didn't.

He followed my step and caught my face. Then he stared into my soul with his storm-intense gaze and he gave me his words. "You are mine, Irina Tsarko. And I am yours."

I wanted to believe it, God I wanted to believe it, but self-doubt crowded my head. "You deserve more." He deserved a woman who didn't cry or let another man use her.

"You're perfect." Tender and sweet, he kissed me once then released me. "Get your things."

An invisible tether broke the second he let go of me, and I wanted to rush back into his arms. I knew when I'd heard them talking that he had to help the women. When Viktor had taken me upstairs yesterday, I hadn't even known there were other women at the estate. It made me sick to think about them being captive. They needed the kind of help Dane and his friend André could give them.

But I needed something from Dane before he left. "Promise me you won't get shot. Or stabbed."

A half smile tipped the corner of his mouth. "I promise I'll come back to you."

He didn't give me what I asked for, but he gave me something more. I didn't hesitate. I closed the distance between us and wrapped my arms around his neck. Burying my head against his chest, I did something I should've done when he'd rescued me. "Thank you," I whispered.

His huge hand caught the back of my head as his lips touched my hair. "You're no longer broken, love. You're free."

THIRTY-FIVE

Dane

She needed to understand that no matter what happened to me, she was free of him. She could move on with her life, with or without me. I wasn't under any illusion that the past three years of my life would stay buried if I walked away from it. I knew the risks going in, and I knew the risks getting out. I had no right to drag her into this life. She wasn't the selfish one. I was. I'd handle the escaped guard and find the missing woman. But then I was coming back for her and I wasn't going to fucking let go.

I dropped my arm, but this time I stepped back so she couldn't reach for me again. "Get your suitcase."

Alarm spread across her face. "You said you were coming back."

"I am." One way or another.

Her expression relaxed but suspicion filtered into her tone. "Then why can't I leave it here? You said thirty-six hours."

I smiled even though I shouldn't have.

Tension eased out of her shoulders. "What?"

"I like this version better."

Heat hit her cheeks and she morphed into the woman

who put staples in me. "That's not an explanation." A hand went to the slight swell of her hips.

Remembering exactly how her skin felt there, my dick stirred. "The version of you that's not trying to run from me."

She blushed hard and inhaled. "I had a good reason to run from you."

I could've interpreted that a couple different ways. "You still do."

"Are you going to answer my question?"

Luna was in the hall, I had a guard to find before he found us, but in that moment, I didn't give a fuck. I dragged my gaze the length of her. I wasn't thinking about what that piece of shit did to her. I was thinking about the woman who fell apart under me, and I wanted to know what I was dealing with.

"Come here," I quietly demanded.

Her demeanor changed in a nanosecond. Attitude gone, face flushed, she took a step toward me. "Why?"

I gave a hand signal to Hunter to stay, but I held her gaze. "Closer."

She bit her bottom lip and took another step.

I dropped to my knees. Her sweet cunt inches in front of me, I could smell her desire. "Closer," I roughly commanded.

She took the final step. "What are you doing?"

Her soft, submissive voice made my pulse race and my dick throb. "I'm looking at what's mine." My mouth watered to taste her. "Lift your shirt."

Her small, delicate hands fingered the hem of my T-shirt. Her chest rose with an inhale then she lifted the material above her bare breasts.

I wrapped my hands around her waist and gently touched my lips to her flat stomach. My soap mixed with the scent of her skin, and I wanted to fucking devour her. Holding back, I took in every inch of her flesh she hadn't let me see last night. Her pale skin flawless, her pebbled nipples much less red than last night, she held perfectly still.

I brushed a thumb over her small breast and she sucked in a breath. "Does this hurt?"

"No," she whispered.

I kissed one nipple then the other as I slipped my fingers into her waistband. Slow and careful, I peeled her leggings over her hips and halfway down her thighs.

The black and blue paddle marks that covered the inside of her thighs looked worse than last night. My nostrils flared and I wanted to murder Fedorov all over again.

"Wait." Alarm bled into her tone. "Stop." She pulled her shirt down.

I fucking knew bruising looked worse before it looked better. "No." I dragged the material down to her knees. "How much does this hurt?"

She reached for her pants. "I'm fine."

I caught her wrist. "Answer my question."

Her pulse in her neck jumped and her voice went quiet as fuck. "Don't do this."

"Don't what? Look at you?" Touch her? Question her? Get irate? Too fucking late. For all of it.

"It will fade," she barely whispered.

Jesus fuck. I looked up at her panicked face. "Is that what you're worried about? How you look to me right now?"

She hesitated then nodded once.

Two breaths and I reined in a temper I never fucking had before a few days ago. "You're beautiful. Every goddamn inch. Don't ever doubt that."

She looked away. "Not like this."

I stood and took her face. "Do you know what's beautiful?" So fucking beautiful, it hurt to look at? "A woman who sacrifices herself for me." She'd never said, but I wasn't fucking stupid. I knew what Fedorov had used against her. Me and her mother. It was the only leverage he'd had. She'd already walked.

"No." She pulled out of my grasp and dropped her head. "I'm not heroic. I didn't—"

"I know exactly what you did. It was fucking dangerous and you shouldn't have done it, but it was brave as hell." I tipped her chin. "You will never do that again, though. Understand?"

She bit her bottom lip, but she nodded.

"You need to trust me."

"I do," she whispered.

I laid it out. "I need to trust you."

She stilled. "Okay."

"That means you tell me when you're hurting."

"I'm sore," she quickly admitted.

"Where?" I wanted details.

"The inside of my thighs, just a little, when I walk." She laid a hand over her breast. "Here is still a little tender."

I kissed her once. "You were right. You will heal." I ran my thumb across her lips. "But bruises don't make you unattractive. No makeup, dressed in cheap clothes, wearing marks you got protecting me, you've never been more beautiful."

She sucked in a breath. "I don't want to lose you."

The six words hit me harder than her kick to my chest. "You're not going to." I gently caressed between her legs because she didn't say she was sore there. "We're not done," I warned. "We haven't even begun." I sank my tongue into her mouth as I circled her clit.

She moaned as her arms wrapped around my neck.

Already addicted to her, I used every ounce of restraint I had and only kissed her once. Pulling back fucking sucked, but dropping to my knees and kissing her sweet cunt was torture. I wanted inside her so fucking bad. I wanted to erase every goddamn thing he'd ever done to her, but I wasn't an asshole. Not to her.

I kissed her wet pussy and made her a promise. "The second you're not sore, I'm going to make you come so damn hard, you'll see stars." The soft moan of need and desire that escaped her lips filled my dead fucking heart as I pulled her pants up and stood.

She leaned into me and grasped my arms, as if she needed me for balance. "I want to see stars now."

I smiled. "I know, sweetheart, but you're going to wait for me."

She closed her eyes and inhaled. "Then I'm leaving my suitcase here."

I leaned down to her ear. "You do whatever you want with your clothes." I nipped her ear. "Because you're not going to need them when I get home."

Her nails dug into my arms. "I changed my mind." She exhaled. "I think I hate you."

I chuckled. "There's not a single thing I hate about you." I breathed in her intoxicating scent then kissed her neck. "I gotta go. But I want you to do something for me."

"What?"

"Ice those bruises then take a hot bath."

She looked up at me. "Okay, but I meant what I said about not getting hurt."

"I know." I didn't want her worrying, but that didn't mean I didn't love the hell out of her caring about me. I took her hand and opened the front door.

Luna looked up from his phone. "We ready?"

"All set." I gave him a warning look. "Take care of her."

He tipped his chin. "Consider it done."

I turned to Irina. "Take Hunter with you." I kissed her once then whispered in her ear, "And wait for me, love."

THIRTY-SIX

Irina

My stomach knotted as he walked to the stairwell and left without a backward glance.

"How you doing?"

I turned to André. "I'm fine. Thank you for last night." I should have been embarrassed, about a lot of things, but André wasn't a man who made you uncomfortable. He made you feel respected.

He smiled and his whole face changed. "Anytime, chica. You need to get anything?" He nodded toward the apartment.

"Let me just clean up the dishes." I didn't want to leave food out for thirty-six hours.

"Marek has a housekeeper. She'll handle it. We should go."

At the mention of a housekeeper, irrational jealousy flared.

André chuckled. "You gotta work on that poker face, chica."

"I didn't say anything." Hunter nudged my side.

"You didn't have to. His housekeeper is my housekeeper, and she's old enough to be our mother." He winked as he scratched Hunter's head. "You don't need to worry. Grab your bag."

Relief washed over me. "Just give me a second." I went back inside with Hunter at my heels. Now that Dane was gone, the place seemed too big and too empty, and his scent everywhere made me not want to leave.

I grabbed some underwear from my suitcase and briefly thought about the clothes in there. I was ashamed to admit that I didn't want to wear chain store clothes compared to the designer dresses Viktor had bought for me. I would've been comfortable in the clothes Dane had given me, but they didn't make me feel like a woman. I was vain enough to admit I wanted to look better than I did now when Dane came home.

I tucked my toiletries case into the purse Dane had brought from his house, slipped on flats, and Hunter and I walked back into the living room.

André saw me and put his phone back in his pocket. "Marek says you need to eat."

"I just need some coffee." I didn't want to ask for food because I was going to use up my favors another way. "I was hoping you could help me with two stops."

"No problem on coffee. What stops?"

I'd noticed when I first met André that he had an edge to him that was hidden just under surface, but he also had a gift of making you feel at ease. "I would like a few minutes to see my mother."

His face went blank. "The second?"

I named a department store in Coral Gables. "Just twenty minutes." That would be long enough to grab a few things, and I could get more when my time was my own.

André was already shaking his head. "No woman comes out of a store in twenty minutes, chica."

"I do."

His hands went to his hips and he dropped his head. "*Mierda*," he quietly swore in Spanish. "Marek's gonna kill me."

"I promise, I'll be quick."

He looked at me without lifting his head. "I'm not talking about the clothes, woman."

I didn't want to see my mother. I was furious with her. But she was my mother and she was hurt. "Is she still in the hospital?"

"Yeah, but she'll be released sometime today." He rubbed a hand over his chin. "Look, here's the deal. Until we get this situation handled with the guard, I'm not comfortable letting you get close to anyone who was in Fedorov's camp. No offense, but I don't care if she is your mother. Her alliance was clear. But we can swing by the office, grab backup, and I'll give you ten minutes in the store." He glanced at his watch. "If we go right now."

I could work with that. "Can I call her?" She didn't have a cell phone, she didn't believe in them, but André knew which hospital she was in.

He nodded once. "From the car. Let's go."

A few minutes later, all three of us were on the road and André had already taken four work calls.

I waited until he hung up the last call to speak. "I'm sorry to interrupt your work."

He gave me an ironic smile. "Chica, this is my work." He turned the Bluetooth on in the car then dialed a number.

"Regional Hospital, how may I direct your call?"

"Room four-oh-six," André replied.

There was a pause and I tensed in my seat as I waited for the call to be connected.

Three rings then my mother answered. "Who is this?"

She sounded weak and faraway and tired, but I knew better. "Mama. How are you?"

"Stupid girl," she spat out. "None of this would've happened if you would've kept your legs shut. Where is my Viktor? I don't want to talk to you. I want him to pick me up."

Until that very moment, I hadn't realized the impact she'd had on my life. Every bad decision, every choice not to leave Viktor the first, or second, or even one hundredth time he'd mistreated me, abused me, paddled me, tied me up, and degraded me, it all clicked into place.

I'd let Viktor abuse me because that's what I knew. My mother had always been controlling and spiteful, but when I'd hit puberty, she'd become competitive. She never missed an opportunity to tell me she was prettier or smarter, or my clothes looked better on her. And when Viktor saw the two of us having lunch at a South Beach restaurant and came to our table to introduce himself, she never let me forget that he'd said hello to her first. She'd told me more than a dozen times I was lucky she hadn't been dining alone that day or Viktor would've been hers.

My mother had never treated me with respect. She didn't care about me. I was just someone to take life out on, and that's exactly what I'd let myself be to Viktor.

No more. I was done being the victim and the doormat. Twenty-three years of bullshit lifted and utter calm settled in.

"Viktor's dead. Goodbye, Mother. Have a nice life."

André ended the call then grasped my shoulder. "Amen, chica, amen."

For the very first time in my life, I felt free.

THIRTY-SEVEN

Dane

THE FIRST TEXT CAME IN AS THE SUN SET.
    Her: *Hi*
    My pulse jumped like I was in high school.
Me: *Hello Beautiful. How are you?*
Her: *I'm ok. You?*
Cramped in my fucking truck and missing her.
Me: *Still in one piece*
Her: *That's not funny*
Me: *Sorry, love. I'm fine*
She didn't respond.
Me: *Still can't call you that?*
Her: *What do I get to call you?*
Any damn thing she wanted.
Me: *Your one and only*
Her: *I like Dane*
I smiled.
Me: *Good*
Her: *Your friend André told me God gives us tomorrows but I had my tomorrow today*
My smile dropped.
Me: *Why are you talking to Luna?*

Her: *Do you want to know about my tomorrow or are you too jealous to listen?*

Jesus. I chuckled and ran a hand over my face.

Me: *Too jealous*

Then I added an afterthought.

Me: *If he touches you, he's dead*

Her: *I learned my lesson. There's only one man I want touching me*

I sobered.

Me: *Good*

Her: *I also learned something else*

The lights went off in the living room. I sat up straighter and fired off a response.

Me: *What's that?*

Her: *I'm better off without my mother*

Motherfucker. *If Luna took her to the hospital while I still didn't have this wrapped up, I was going to fucking pound him. A light turned on in the bedroom of the apartment.*

Me: *Did you see her?*

Her: *No, I called her. Well, André called her for me*

I exhaled.

Me: *What happened?*

Her: *It doesn't matter. She doesn't care about me*

A bathroom light turned on in the apartment.

Me: *Agree*

Her: *I get that now*

Me: *Good*

Her mother was a fucking joke. The sooner she was gone out of her life, the better. I picked up my binoculars and scanned the parking lot of the neighboring strip mall. Two cars were suspect. I trained the binoculars back to the bedroom window of the apartment and my cell vibrated with a new text.

Her: *Your answers have gotten shorter.*
Me: *Still here, love. Working.*
A minute passed.
Her: *Why do you call me that?*
Fuck. It was too soon.
Me: *I'll tell you when I see you*
Her: *When is that?*
I smiled.
Me: *Soon*
Her: *Promise?*
The lights in the bathroom then the bedroom turned off.
Me: *Always. I have to go. Wait for me.*
Her: *Always*

Just the thought of her waiting for me made my dick hard.

I trained the binoculars on the front door of the apartment. Ten seconds later, the guard's ex-girlfriend came out, then she took off in her car to her nightshift job. Luna had dug the info up on her, and I was playing out a hunch.

I waited three minutes.

One of the cars I'd spotted pulled out of the strip mall parking lot and rolled up to the apartment complex. Fedorov's guard and a blonde got out, then they went into his ex's apartment. Fucking prick didn't even have enough sense not to park in front.

I dialed Luna.

He answered immediately. "You find them?"

"Yeah." The living room light went on. "At the ex's. Give me twenty then tell Neil to call his ATF contact and give him the address."

"The Feds aren't on the ex's place?"

I scanned the lots again, but I'd been the only one here for hours. "No."

"Fucking amateurs. I'll let Christensen know."

"You get anywhere on the information I asked you for?"

"Yeah. Fedorov never married her and his estate goes to his adult kids. As far as the ATF is concerned, she was never there. Your name never came up in the raid or questioning. I wiped all his security feeds and all the files he had on the trackers for his guards. Probably why ATF couldn't find this one. Anyway, you're clean on this one."

"Thanks."

"Anytime. So, you retiring from your solo career?"

"Which one?"

He laughed. "Both."

"Yes."

"Smart move." He turned serious. "You ready to come work for me?"

"No. But if you need me, I'm around." I owed him.

"Good to know, brother, good to know."

I glanced at my watch. "One more favor."

"Shoot."

"Take her back to my condo. I'm going to wrap this up tonight." I didn't want to dick around with this bullshit anymore. The Feds could clean this up, and Jagger could deal with the woman.

"Copy that."

"I want one of your men in the hall until I get home though."

Luna snorted. "I only got one free right now and his face looks like a fucking train hit it thanks to you."

"He deserved it."

"I'm not disagreeing with you, but I would've handled it differently. You need to be more judicious when dealing with my men."

"He's lucky he's still alive."

"Come on, man, work with me on this."

I didn't respond.

He cursed in Spanish. "Fine, you crazy fuck. But if you want her watched after I drop her off, it's Tyler or no one."

Christ. "Is he going to shoot at her?" I was only half kidding.

"I'll tell him specifically not to aim or fire in her direction," Luna deadpanned.

"You sound like a corporate prick."

"I am a corporate prick."

He didn't used to be. He was the best damn sniper I'd ever seen. "Your talents are being wasted." He could make bank hiring out.

"My *talents* are being used in a legal, law-abiding manner."

I couldn't help it, I laughed. "Right."

"*Damn, amigo.* Did you just laugh? Did I actually hear the great Dane Marek laugh?"

"It happens on occasion."

"First I'm hearing of it. I was beginning to wonder if you or your nine lives were even human. You're like the fucking Energizer bunny. You keep getting shot but you just keep going."

"I'm retired now. No more gunshot wounds."

"Let's fucking hope not."

No kidding. "I gotta go."

"Keep it real, brother."

"Later." I hung up and called Jagger.

He picked up with music playing in the background. "Twice in one week. Damn, I'm a lucky son of a bitch. You find my girl?"

"She's shacked up with the guard." I rattled off the address and the apartment number. "Come get her."

He paused. "Does she want me to come get her?"

"No fucking clue."

"Shit, Marek, did you ask?"

"That's up to you." The light went off in the apartment. "You got ten minutes to get here."

"I'm on my way." He hung up.

I double checked my magazine and my ammo and screwed on my silencer. Then I got out of the truck. Taking the stairs two at a time, my weapon drawn, I kicked the door in.

The fucking guard couldn't move off the couch fast enough. His pants down, his dick buried in the blonde, his bare ass barely had time to look up before my gun was jammed against his head.

"What the fuck?" He reached for his weapon on the coffee table as the woman screamed.

I shoved the muzzle of my gun harder into his temple. "Do me a favor. Make a grab for it."

His hands went up. "Who the fuck are you?"

The blonde kept screaming. "Shut her up or the cops will be here faster than ATF."

He shoved a hand over her mouth and growled at her, "Calm down." He barely moved his head to glance at me. "I'm getting the fuck up and putting my cock away. You need to shoot, shoot."

I eased back six inches and let him pull his pants up. "Far enough. Sit." I stepped back a foot.

He turned, sat his ass down and gave me a once-over as the blonde cowered next to him. "You're the one who took his wife."

My glare not leaving his, I tipped my chin at the blonde. "Tell her to get dressed."

"Put your clothes on," the asshole barked the order at the blonde.

She slowly pulled a dress over her head. A dress she hadn't had when I'd seen her last.

The guard sized me up. "What do you want? A piece of Fedorov's business?"

I cataloged the contents within arm's reach of either of them as I counted off the minutes. I didn't respond.

The guard kept talking. "I know where he kept his inventory. There's no one to go for it except you and me. We can both walk away rich. We'll cash in. Half and half."

I ignored him.

At nine minutes thirty seconds, Jagger walked through the door. "Looks like a party."

Fucking prick. "Ask her."

The guard looked between us with confusion.

"Hey, babe. Long time no see." Jagger nodded at her dress. "Looks good on you. Glad you like the dress I picked out."

"What the fuck?" Anger contorted the guard's face. "Don't talk to her."

Jagger ignored him. "So, one-time offer, babe. You can come with me or you can take your chances with him. No strings." He laughed. "Well, except one. You forget about this asshole and how we met and basically everything leading up to this offer." Jagger nodded at the guard. "Or don't. And see where he takes you."

The blonde glanced between all of us then slowly slid away from the guard and stood.

The guard moved to get up, and I shoved my gun back against his temple. "She made her decision."

Jagger held his hand out to the blonde like the fucking gentleman he wasn't. "Shall we?"

The guard switched to Russian and started yelling at her, but she was already walking out the door.

Jagger slapped me on the shoulder as he left. "Always a pleasure, man."

The guard lunged. For me, for Jagger, I didn't fucking know and I didn't care. I shot him in the foot.

He dropped and grabbed the gushing wound. "What the fuck! *What the fucking fuck!*" He rolled to his side.

I brought my booted foot down on his neck and aimed at his head. "You want to live through the next minute, tell me where the women came from."

"*Fuck you.*"

I clocked him on the side of the jaw with the butt of my gun. The strike was enough to cause maximum pain but still keep him conscious.

I shoved the muzzle back against his temple. "Last chance." Physical violence was tolerable in theory, but shoot an untrained man then pistol whip him, and he'll fucking sing.

The asshole couldn't talk fast enough. "Fedorov bought them. He was branching out. He paid to get them over here. He was going to sell them!"

"To who?" I demanded.

"I dunno! No one yet. He was letting us have a turn at them before he put them on the market. Then the hurricane hit." Holding his foot, he writhed in pain. "That's all I know. I swear. I need a fucking doctor!"

I didn't give a fuck what he needed. "What's the address of the warehouse?"

"Take me to the hospital and I'll tell you."

I took my foot off his neck then slammed it down over his hands as he held his bleeding foot.

He wailed like a fucking pussy.

I jammed my silencer against his dick. "Address," I demanded.

He rattled it off then spat on my foot. "You fucking asshole!"

I shifted the muzzle two inches and shot the floor between his legs. "Last question."

"What the fuck!" He jerked like a goddamn coward.

I jammed the barrel against his temple and moved my foot back to his neck. "You want a second chance with the Feds or do you want to leave here in a body bag?" I didn't give a fuck which.

"What the fuck do you think I'm going to choose? I already escaped the Feds once. I can do it again."

I applied pressure to his trachea with my foot. "You escape, I hunt you down and you die. You talk to the Feds, you die. You tell them about me, my men, or the warehouse, you die. You tell them a goddamn thing except your name and the color of the pussy that just walked out on you, you fucking die."

His bloodied hands clawed at my boot as he gasped for breath.

"Blink if we have an understanding."

He started blinking, repeatedly.

I yanked zip cuffs out of my back pocket and kicked him to his stomach. Seven seconds later, his hands and ankles were cuffed and I was walking out the door as I dialed Luna.

THIRTY-EIGHT

Irina

HUNTER WAS SITTING AT MY FEET AND I WAS TAKING the tags off my new clothes when a knock sounded at the door. With the dog on my heels, I walked through the modern apartment André had put me in and looked out the peephole.

I opened the door. "Mr. Luna."

André smiled. "I'm mister now?" He scratched Hunter's head.

All men were mister now, except one. "Yes, but I might be persuaded to make an exception because you took me shopping."

He chuckled. "Gotta hand it to you, chica. Twenty minutes, one and done. Impressive."

I was motivated. "Thank you again."

He waved me off. "Marek sent me to take you home."

My heart leapt and my pulse raced. It'd only been twelve hours. "So soon?"

"He doesn't mess around." André eyed me as if to tell me something I didn't already know.

"No he doesn't. Let me get my things." I was so excited to see Dane, I threw my clothes back in the shopping bag without folding them, and grabbed my purse. "I'm ready."

André led me and Hunter to the elevator and we took it to the garage where another man in a Luna and Associates shirt was waiting next to one of André's black SUVs. The left side of his face was swollen and black and blue.

André made the introductions. "Tyler, this is Miss Tsarko. Irina, this is Tyler. He's going to be outside your penthouse until Marek gets home." He didn't mention Tyler's face.

Looking less than happy, Tyler eyed the dog then nodded at me. "Ma'am."

My heart sunk. "Dane isn't at his penthouse?"

André opened the back door and Hunter jumped in. "Not yet. Soon, chica." He helped me inside then got in the front passenger seat as Tyler got behind the wheel. "You know where you're going?"

"Affirmative," was all Tyler said.

Luna's phone rang as Tyler pulled out of the underground parking. "I'm running your errand…. Copy. Address?" Luna nodded. "Hold on." He handed the phone to me. "It's for you, chica."

Butterflies swirled in my stomach and heat hit my cheeks as I took the phone. "Hello?"

"Hi, beautiful."

Deep and rough and so very sexy, his voice filled my head and my heart. "Hi." I wished I wasn't in a car with two other men.

"You waiting for me?"

The question made my skin tingle with awareness as an ache built between my legs. "Yes."

"Did you do as I asked?"

My voice went even quieter. "Yes." The ice and the bath.

"You feel any better?"

"I'm fine." A little soreness wasn't going to stop me. I wanted his hands on me the second he came back.

"How's Hunter?"

"Persistent." He'd followed me everywhere today except when André took me into the store.

Dane chuckled then turned serious. "I miss you."

I closed my eyes for a brief moment. "Same." God, I missed him.

He dropped his voice to pure seduction. "I want my mouth on yours."

I sucked in a breath. "Same."

"Your responses are getting shorter," he teased.

"You know why."

"Mixed company. I get it." His tone went all business. "Did you eat today?"

"Yes." André had religiously fed me three square meals and Hunter once, as if he would get in trouble from Dane if he didn't.

"Good. I'm going to be a few more hours. Go to bed and I'll let you know when I get home."

The whole conversation from an outsider's perspective would've seemed so normal. And it was, but it was also surreal and it made my stomach flutter and my skin tingle and it planted a seed of hope in my heart that I'd never had.

I glanced at André and Tyler, but they were quietly talking. "I like that," I admitted.

"Like what, sweetheart?"

Every time he called me sweetheart or love, I felt myself falling harder. "The last word."

His voice softened. "Ditto. See you soon." He hung up.

I handed the phone back to André.

He raised an eyebrow at me. "You good?"

"Fine, thank you."

He nodded and a few minutes later we were in the underground garage of Dane's penthouse and André was helping me get out of the car. Hunter hopped out next and kept to my side as we all walked to the elevator.

"Hold up. Keep an eye on her a sec, Tyler." André patted his leg twice. "Hunter, come."

Hunter followed André out of the garage. I was a terrible dog watcher. That was three times today André had remembered to take Hunter out.

They returned a minute later and I pet the top of Hunter's head as he came to my side. "He's well trained." He didn't even need a leash.

André chuckled. "Would you disobey Marek?"

Heat flamed my cheeks. "No."

"Smart move," Tyler grumbled.

"Watch it," André snapped.

I looked between them and instinct kicked in. "Did Dane do that to your face?"

Neither of them said a word as we got into the elevator.

The doors slid shut and I demanded an answer. "What happened?"

Resigned, André exhaled. "He was shooting at you. Marek got pissed." He glanced at Tyler. "Rightfully so."

Tyler shook his head at André. "I knew what I was doing, boss. I saw her. I wasn't shooting *at* her. I was returning fire at the driver and the guard behind him."

"You hit her mother," André countered.

"She was waving her arms around like an idiot!" Tyler yelled.

André smirked. "You don't want collateral damage, don't shoot at another man's woman. You're lucky that's all he did to you." He tipped his chin toward me. "Might want to apologize."

Tyler looked at me with absolute sincerity. "I apologize and I'm very sorry about your mother. It won't happen again."

"Apology accepted." He didn't need to know how I felt about her, and the irony wasn't lost on me that we both had bruises from disobeying Dane.

The elevator doors slid open and Andre let me and Hunter into Dane's penthouse. "Tyler will be out in the hall until Marek returns. If you need anything, let him know."

I hugged André. I didn't know why I did it. I wasn't a hugger, but it was instinctual and he'd been kind to me and I wanted to thank him. "Thank you."

His arms, big and strong like Dane's, wrapped around me and he hugged me back, but there was nothing similar about the way he and Dane felt. "Anytime, chica, anytime." He released me and squeezed my shoulder. "Glad you got your tomorrow. Take care of yourself." He winked and walked out.

Tyler handed him the keys, and I watched André get in the elevator.

"Do you need anything, ma'am?"

I glanced at Tyler. His back to the wall by the door, he stood with his legs slightly apart and his hands clasped in front of him. A gun sat in a holster attached to his belt.

"Do you want a chair?" Standing for hours wouldn't be comfortable. Viktor's bodyguards had never stood for hours.

Tyler smiled and I could see he would be handsome if his face wasn't a mess. "I'm fine, ma'am."

I nodded. "How are you going to get back to the office when Dane comes home?"

"I'll call base for a pickup, ma'am."

I knew why Tyler didn't have his own vehicle. The one I'd driven away from the shootout had so many holes in the hood, it was smoking by the time I'd gotten back to Viktor's. Surprisingly, the windshield had been intact, but the car itself was totaled. "I'm sorry you're short a couple vehicles."

"No worries, ma'am. All part of the job."

I nodded, but I still felt bad. "Okay. Good night, Tyler."

"Good night, ma'am."

I locked the door and ten minutes later, I was in bed with a canine lying across my legs.

THIRTY-NINE

Dane

Neil walked into the warehouse as Luna and I loaded the last crate.

He glanced at the two rented SUVs I'd put fake plates on. "How many?"

"Hundred and twenty crates," Luna answered.

It taken us all night to load the vehicles and make runs to Luna and Associates.

"What are you doing with them?" Neil asked.

I shook my head. Luna and I had argued all night about it. I told him I'd fence them and he'd have more than enough money to replace his shot-up vehicles. He wanted to fucking turn them over to the Feds. "Ask Mr. Clear Conscience."

Neil looked at Luna. "You want to turn them in." It wasn't a question.

Luna threw his arms up. "You say that shit like I'm in the wrong."

"You are," Neil quipped.

I hid a smile.

Luna pointed at me. "Not fucking funny." He looked accusingly at Neil. "You got a better idea?"

"Yes," was all Neil said.

Luna waited like he'd get a further explanation from Neil. He didn't.

"Then it's settled. Christensen takes them." I shut the back door to the SUV.

Neil eyed Luna. "How much do you want?"

Luna swore in Spanish. "You both are fucking crazy. I don't want a damn dime from this shit." He got behind the wheel and slammed the door.

Neil glanced at me and raised one eyebrow.

"He needs three new vehicles." Two to replace the totaled ones, and a spare.

Neil nodded once. "How is the female?"

"She's fine."

"Tell him I will get the crates tomorrow night."

"Will do."

Luna rolled down his window. "You coming, Marek?"

I glanced at Neil. "You didn't tell me you did business with the triplets."

"You did not ask."

"Tell me I didn't make those fucks richer."

In a rare display of emotion, the side of Neil's mouth twitched up. "Their return on investment was below market value."

I slapped him on the shoulder. "Good man." I got in the second rented SUV. "You have a buyer in mind for all these?"

"I did not say I was selling them."

I smiled and shook my head. "Right." Because a commercial contractor needed one hundred and twenty crates of semi-automatic rifles and hand guns. "Good luck."

"I do not need luck."

No, he probably didn't. "Later."

Neil left and I rolled out after Luna. One stop after dropping this last load, then I'd be home to my woman.

I fucking smiled.

FORTY

Irina

The bed dipped and I smelled his soap and musk.

I turned, but I didn't even get a chance to say hello.

His lips covered mine as his rough, warm hands cupped my face. His tongue sank into my mouth, and it was as if a switch had been flipped.

Desire, sharp and painful, exploded like a fire inside me. My arms went around his neck and I couldn't get close enough. Arched, clawing, I groaned into his mouth and ran my hands over his shower-wet, closely cropped hair.

"That's my fix," he growled, rolling me to my back and thrusting his hips against mine.

I cried out with need and spread my legs wider. Frantic desperation raced through my veins and slammed into my core. My pussy pulsing and clenching with aching emptiness, I dragged my nails down his back and aimed for his boxers.

Something plastic caught under my fingertip.

His mouth moved to my neck as he rocked his dick against my wet pussy.

I stilled. "What is this?" I touched the thin plastic covering his lower back.

He bit under my ear and I shivered.

"Dane?"

His hand moved to his boxers and he pushed them down only far enough to fist his cock. Rubbing the head of his dick across my pussy, his dark storm-colored gaze landed on me.

My mouth opened and a desperate gasp filled the silence.

He licked my bottom lip and hoarsely whispered, "Tattoo." Then his tongue sank into my mouth as his cock sunk into my pussy.

Oh. *My God.*

He thrust deep.

A full body tremor started at the base of my spine and radiated down my legs. My trembling hands grasped his biceps for purchase, but it was too late. I was already falling.

"Fuck yes, that's it, sweetheart. Come."

Oh my God.

My legs shook. My heart pounded and wave after wave of unbelievable pleasure shocked my body.

I saw stars.

Big, beautiful, overwhelming stars.

"Dane," I blindly cried.

Sunk to the hilt, his hips grinding into my clit, he took every last fear I had and destroyed it. His cock, his tongue, his whole body claiming me, marking me, changing me, he commanded my very being.

His mouth on my ear, his hands in my hair, he whispered, "You are mine." He thrust hard and stilled. "And I am yours."

A groan ripped from his chest.

And I knew.

His hot seed pumped into my body.

I was his. *All his.*

With his chest heaving, he latched on to my neck and swirled his tongue. Moving to my collarbone, kissing, biting, he covered my nipple and gently, so gently, he sucked.

A fresh wave of desire bit into my womb and my back arched.

Swirling dark green, brown, and gray eyes looked up at me.

Every emotion in my heart, all the words I wanted to roll off my tongue, they stuck in my throat as I stared at the most beautiful man in the world.

He reverently kissed the pale skin over my heart. "I am inside you." He pulsed deep inside me and whispered, "This is my home now."

A tear slid down my cheek. "I'm not sad."

With a shallow thrust he ignited a new fire inside me. "I know." He kissed my cheek then brought his forehead to mine. "I'm going to take you again."

I wanted him to. Again and again. Until I couldn't feel my legs and all I smelled was him and his release all over my body. "Please," I begged.

His shallow thrusting turned into a slow grind, then he pulled almost all the way out. "Wrap your arms around me, love."

I wrapped my legs around his hips and grasped his face. "You promised," I reminded him. "Tell me."

The tip of his cock hovering against my entrance, his forearms braced on either side of me, a slow, devastating smile spread across his face. "You ready for me?"

"Yes." God yes.

He drove into me.

"*Ahhh*." Pleasure-pain shot through my pussy.

He started pounding into me. "You want to know why I call you love?"

My fingers dug into his shoulders. "Yes, yes, yes." Every thrust stroked my G-spot and hit my cervix, then he ground against my clit.

"Because I love your cunt wrapped around my cock."

I loved his dirty mouth.

He stroked through our cum. "I love feeling my seed inside you."

My stomach fluttered at the very thought.

He kissed one nipple then the other. "I love every goddamn ounce of attitude and submission you give me."

I grabbed the back of his head and pulled up.

He brought his lips to mine. "I love holding you as much as I love fucking you."

I kissed him.

Gentle and loving, he stilled and kissed me back. Then he looked down at me. "You're the only woman I want."

He was the only man I wanted. But caught up in his words, his beautiful words, I didn't give him mine, not yet. I kissed the hard angle of his jaw.

He touched his lips to my forehead and slowly thrust. "You never even blinked when I told you who I was."

Oh God. I loved who he was.

"And you feel so fucking right." He sank deep inside me.

I rocked my hips into his.

"I call you love…" He went perfectly still. "Because I love you, Irina Tsarko."

It was too soon. It was crazy. It was risky. It was messy and imperfect.

But it wasn't wrong. *He* wasn't wrong. Nothing in my

life had ever felt more perfect. He gave me hope. He gave me strength. He gave me himself.

And I loved him.

I'd loved him the second he took a risk and trusted me with everything about him. I'd loved him when he saved me. I'd loved him when he said I was broken, and I'd loved him when he taught me how to open my heart.

"I love you, Dane Marek."

His lips crashed over mine, and he did more than just make love to me. He gave me everything I'd ever wanted. He gave me a future.

EPILOGUE

Dane

I WOKE TO SUNLIGHT HEATING THE BEDROOM AND THE delicate touch of her fingers tracing the ink on my back. Inhaling, I smiled, but I didn't roll over. I fucking loved her hands on me. "Good morning, beautiful."

"You haven't seen me yet this morning. You don't know if I'm beautiful."

I fucking knew. "Did you shave your head while I was asleep?" Not even that would detract from her beauty. She was the perfect recipe of strength, grace, attitude and submission.

"No, but that isn't funny. Every woman wants to know she will be loved when she gets old and loses her hair."

I rolled and caught her gorgeous face. "I was right. You're beautiful."

She peered up at me. "You say that now."

"I'll say it every day." She'd started to fill out in the weeks I'd been feeding her and fucking her. That's all we did. Eat and fuck and walk Hunter. And talk. About every damn thing and sometimes nothing. She laughed more. She touched me more, and her bruises had healed. I'd never been happier. I fingered a lock of her soft hair. "I'll also tell you I love you."

She stared at me a moment then glanced at my back. "Anything else you want to tell me?"

I was wondering when she was going to notice it. The night Luna and I had loaded the crates, I'd stopped at my tattoo artist's place before going home to add more feathers to my back. Then I'd had him inscribe one of them. She'd noticed the feathers that morning but not the small inscription.

I kissed her once. "I said it two weeks ago." I loved the way she smelled in the morning with my scent on her skin. "I knew then what I know now." My gaze locked on hers, I rolled to my stomach so she could see the ink. Then I quoted the inscription. "She is mine and I am hers." I cupped her cheek. "I love you."

She wrapped her hand around my wrist. "What if you were wrong?"

"I wasn't. I'm still not." Short of her leaving, which she could have done that night but didn't, there wasn't anything that was going to change my mind about her. I'd given her money and freedom. She could've left. But she never went further than her own head. After everything she'd seen me do, everything we'd been through, she'd stayed. She'd stayed and she'd let me take her, over and over. I was never more sure of a damn thing in my life. She and I were real. "You waited for me."

"That night?"

"Yes." And every other night.

"You had one of André's bodyguards outside the door. Where was I going to go?"

"Anywhere you wanted. He would've taken you." Luna too. I'd instructed them not to detain her if she'd wanted to go. "You had money."

Heat tinted her cheeks. "You didn't need to put five-hundred thousand dollars in my bank account."

"Yes I did." I wasn't like that fucking asshole who'd thrown away five years of her life. She'd worked for that money, she'd sacrificed for it and she'd deserved it. I had it to give, and as far as I was concerned, it didn't matter where it came from. That money was her price for freedom, and I could give her that. I knew if she was ever going to be mine, it needed to be her choice. "The money gave you a choice."

"I didn't know I had it."

"Maybe not at first." But she'd bought clothes. She'd used her bank card. She knew there were funds available. "But it was there if you needed it."

"What if I need it now?"

I inhaled. The question wasn't one hundred percent unexpected. She liked to push boundaries. She questioned me at every damn turn and challenged me in ways no one ever had. I loved every fucking second of it. But occasionally, like now, I had to strategize. "It's yours. There're two vehicles in the garage. Take one." I stared at her a moment. "You have a choice…. You always have a choice."

She dropped her gaze to my back and her finger traced the feather. "The ink on your back says differently."

"No, it says I already made my choice."

A sweet fucking smile spread across her lips as she wrapped her hands around my arm and snuggled into me. "I like it here."

Fucking brat. I laughed. "I know you do."

She ran a hand over my closely cropped hair then dragged her fingernails down my neck. "Then why say those things?"

I leaned over and kissed her. "Because you needed to hear

it. You have a choice, love. Always." I wasn't going to keep a woman who didn't want to be kept. I'd already tried that and it didn't fucking work.

She was quiet a moment then she looked away. "I'm not here because you gave me money."

I tucked her hair behind her ear. The tops of her ears got red when her cheeks got red. "I know." She'd wanted that money from Fedorov because she saw it as her only way to a new life, but money didn't drive her. She hadn't asked for shit in the two weeks she'd been with me. I'd offered to take her shopping for clothes, shoes, jewelry, whatever the hell she'd wanted, but short of a bikini for the beach, she'd declined.

She got quiet for a moment.

I traced an invisible line from her shoulder to her hip. "You want to ask something."

"How do you know?"

She had tells. A hundred of them. I'd been cataloging. "Body language, facial expression, stillness—I pay attention."

"Are you going to tell Alex about us?"

My hand on her hip, I dragged my thumb back and forth along the soft skin of her thigh. I phrased my response carefully. "I don't make it a habit of spending any time with Vega." Unless I went to the boxing gym he and Brandt went to, I never saw him. But I hadn't been there in weeks, and I only ever went when I needed to pound the shit out of some dumb fuck. I used to use it to release aggression when I was too wound up to fuck a client, but I didn't need that release anymore.

"That's not an answer."

I didn't fucking think about Vega and his past with her. Ever. If I did, I got pissed the fuck off. "You want the truth?"

"Yes."

"He doesn't deserve to know." I studied her a moment. "Why are you asking?"

"He's your friend."

I didn't have friends. I had brothers from the Marines, and I'd had clients. That was it. Vega wasn't my fucking friend. "I keep to myself."

She shifted her hips, putting her cunt closer to my touch. "André calls you."

"He wanted something."

"What?"

"My time."

She stiffened. "Are you going back?"

I knew what she was asking. She'd asked it before. "I told you I'm out."

"But you also said you would help André if he needed it."

"I did. Why are we talking about this?" I had an idea why. I splayed my hand out flat on her stomach. She wasn't carrying my child. She'd gotten her period last week. Her not being pregnant was the one thing we hadn't talked about.

"You should call your friends. You'll get sick of me if it's just you and me all the time."

"No, I won't." I caressed the smooth skin of her stomach. "If you're worried about it, give me a child." I winked.

"That's not funny."

I smiled. "You're right, it's not." I grabbed the back of her neck and brought her mouth to mine. "I want you pregnant." I kissed her. My tongue demanding, my firm hold, I showed her what my words couldn't. I pulled back just enough to stroke her cheek and see her eyes. "I'm ready."

"What if I'm not?"

I didn't hesitate. "Then I'll wait."

"For how long?" Her gaze dropped and her fingers fidgeted.

She was nervous. "What do you need from me?"

She looked up. "I don't know what I want," she blurted.

Not showing a reaction, I kept my tone even. "Do you want children?"

"Yes, yes, of course." Her demeanor eased from tensed restraint to mild irritation. "That's not what I meant."

I exhaled in relief. I fucking wanted a kid. "Then tell me."

Her hand fluttered through the air. "I know I'm being ungrateful. You've given me whatever I've wanted, but that's not the same as knowing what I want." She frowned. "I've never had to choose a career, or make a living, or do anything beyond… look pretty." She drew in a breath. "What if I'm not ready to be a mother and I have a child and I wind up resentful like my mother?"

It fucking clicked. That's what I was missing. She didn't want to be like the fucked-up woman who brought her into this world. "The simple fact that you are concerned about it means history will not repeat itself." I stroked the very edge of her sweet cunt. "And you wouldn't be doing it alone."

"Ever?" She lifted her hips to meet my touch. "No matter what?"

I couldn't guarantee shit. I couldn't guarantee my past would stay quiet like it'd been for two weeks, but that wasn't what she was asking. Those risks she'd seemed to already accept.

"I'm not going anywhere, sweetheart." I pushed her to her back and rolled on top of her. "I'll always take care of what's mine."

She spread her legs wide and lust deepened her voice. "What else are you going to take care of?"

"Your sweet little cunt." Fisting myself, I dragged the head of my cock through her wet heat.

She grabbed my ass and moaned. "Don't tease me."

"Woman, you've been teasing me since you walked into my life." I rubbed my dick in a tight circle over her clit.

"I have not." Her eyes fluttered shut and she arched her back.

Fuck, I loved seeing her like this. Under me, her lips parted, her nipples hard and her pussy wet and throbbing, she was so fucking beautiful, I wanted it all.

I leaned to her ear and whispered, "Give me children." I didn't want to just fucking claim her, I wanted her to be the mother of my children. I wanted her to raise them with the same grace and quiet resolve that she herself possessed.

Her eyes popped open. "Now it's children?"

I smiled and cupped her face. I'd been waiting for this moment. "Summer nights and porch swings and little feet running through a house with a screen door." I gave her exact words right back to her. "Let's make that happen, beautiful."

Tears welled in her eyes. "Dane."

"Marry me."

Shock carried across her features and the tears fell, but a smile spread across her face that was so fucking beautiful, it constricted my heart.

"Yes." She gripped my wrists. "Yes, Dane Marek, I will marry you."

I sank inside her and made her mine.

THANK YOU!

Thank you so much for reading GRIND! If you were interested in leaving a review on any retail site, I would be so appreciative. Reviews mean the world to authors, and they are helpful beyond compare!

Have you read the other books in the Alpha Escort Series?
THRUST—Alex's story
ROUGH—Jared's story

Have you read the Uncompromising Series?
TALON
NEIL
ANDRÉ
BENNETT
CALLAN

And check out the new Alpha Bodyguard Series!
SCANDALOUS – Tank's Story
MERCILESS – Collins's Story
RECKLESS – Tyler's Story
RUTHLESS – Sawyer's Story
FEARLESS – Ty's Story
CALLOUS – Preston's Story
RELENTLESS – Thomas's story

Turn the page for a preview of SCANDALOUS, the first book in the exciting Alpha Bodyguard Series about the men who work for André Luna at Luna and Associates!

SCANDALOUS

Bodyguard.

Babysitter.

Chauffeur.

Not what the hell I thought I'd be doing with my life.

Especially not for a spoiled Hollywood actress on location in Miami Beach. But triple pay and carrying a gun had its advantages. I'd shove away paparazzi and screaming fans for a lot less. The Marines trained me to be Force Recon—intimidation and crowd control was child's play compared to four tours. This assignment should've been easy money.

But the doe-eyed starlet with the perfect ass dragged me down her rabbit hole. Living for the spotlight, she leaked the perfect scandal. I warned her making headlines wasn't in my job description, but she kept smiling for the cameras.

Now she was going to find out just how scandalous a bodyguard could be.

*SCANDALOUS is the first standalone book in the Alpha Bodyguard Series.

The Alpha Bodyguard Series
SCANDALOUS—Tank's story
MERCILESS—Collin's story
RECKLESS—Tyler's story
RUTHLESS—Sawyer's story

ACKNOWLEDGMENTS

Even though writing is a solitary endeavor, I never create a book alone. I have such an incredible team behind me. I couldn't do what I do without them. Virginia and Olivia are the best editors I could ask for. They whip my alpha heroes into shape and make them shine. Clarise designs all these sexy, amazing covers and I am so lucky to have her. Stacy takes all the words and formats them into this work of art you are reading right now. And last, but so not least, is a super special someone who I have come to adore as much as I rely on for all of her insight and witty comments and awesome sense of humor, but mostly for her friendship—Kristen Johnson, my beta reader superstar. Kristen has beta read this entire series and without her, my alpha heroes just wouldn't be the same.

I don't know if you noticed my dedication for this book, but it's true, Mr. Bartel hasn't read one of my super alpha, scandalously sexy, books yet, LOL! So he doesn't know that he saved Dane from using the word "glisten," or that he's (unintentionally) given me some of the best alpha hero one-liners and comebacks ever. But just in case he reads this, thank you, honey, you ROCK!

And to all my readers who took a chance on me—I love you so hard! XOXO -Sybil

ABOUT THE AUTHOR

Sybil Bartel grew up in northern California with her head in a book and her feet in the sand. Trading one coast for another, she now resides in Southern Florida. When Sybil isn't writing or fighting to contain the banana plantation in her backyard, you can find her spending time with her handsomely tattooed husband, her brilliantly practical son and a mischievous miniature boxer...

But Seriously?

Here are ten things you probably really want to know about Sybil.

She grew up a faculty brat. She can swear like a sailor. She loves men in uniform. She hates being told what to do. She can do your taxes (but don't ask). The Bird Market in Hong Kong scares her. Her favorite word has four letters. She has a thing for muscle cars. But never reply on her for driving directions, ever. And she has a new book boyfriend every week.

To find out more about Sybil Bartel or her books, please visit her at:
Website: www.sybilbartel.com
Facebook page: www.facebook.com/sybilbartelauthor
Book Boyfriend Heroes:
www.facebook.com/groups/1065006266850790/
Twitter: twitter.com/SybilBartel
BookBub: www.bookbub.com/authors/sybil-bartel
Newsletter: http://eepurl.com/bRSE2T

Printed in Great Britain
by Amazon